ANCHOR

A Novel by

By

Robert Aston Jones

This book is dedicated to Linda, my wife of 46 years. I am grateful to her for slogging through the early drafts of this and many other manuscripts, making suggestions as to what works and what doesn't work, and encouraging me to pursue my dream of becoming a published author.

ANCHOR

PART ONE

CHAPTER 1

Thirty-two-year-old Blake Turner turned his head to the right and stared at his reflection...and his reflection stared straight back at him from a massive plate-glass window, one of the hundreds of mirror-like windows that seemed to cover every square inch of the John Wexler Business Tower. At five feet and seven inches tall, Blake was shorter than most of the pedestrians walking alongside him. That fact, combined with his bright blue eyes and sandy blond hair, set him...and his reflection...apart from the rest of the crowd.

As Blake neared the Wexler Tower's revolving door, he realized he had rudely stepped in front of two women, both of whom he judged to be in their mid fifties. He slowed down, stepped aside, and politely waited until the women walked past him. He then acknowledged their "Thank You" with a softly-spoken "You're Welcome," waited until the women entered one of the door's chambers, and, with perfectly timed steps, entered the empty chamber that opened up behind them.

Blake followed the women through the crowded lobby. A moment later, walking side-by-side, the three approached three elevators situated in the center of a marble-covered wall. Out of habit, Blake raised his right hand and extended his thumb toward the "up" button. However, just before his thumb reached the button, he realized the "up" arrow was illuminated—which told him someone had already pressed the button—so he dropped his hand to his side and stepped away from the panel.

The two women suddenly spun around and walked away from Blake. At first, he thought they wanted to avoid riding the elevator with him, but quickly realized they had been summoned by one of their co-workers. He assumed—and assumed correctly—the women were about to share the latest gossip. Blake stared at the women a moment, then returned his attention to the elevators.

And the young woman who had stepped up beside him.

The two exchanged a quick glance with each other, but otherwise showed little acknowledgment of the other's presence. They just stood there, waiting for a green light to come on above one of the paired, stainless steel doors. Finally, after a full minute, one of the lights illuminated and two soft "ding" sounds came from somewhere inside the wall. A couple of seconds later, the doors slid open.

Blake waited calmly while the young woman—a shapely and stunningly-attractive brunette in her mid-to-late-twenties—stepped inside. For a brief moment, he considered passing up this elevator and waiting until the next one arrived. However, a quick glance at the large clock mounted on the wall above the middle elevator told him that waiting for the next one, even if only for a few seconds, would make him late for work, and being late for work was something Blake Turner could proudly say he had never allowed himself to be. He reluctantly followed the young woman into the elevator.

The woman flashed a shy smile in Blake's direction, pressed the button for her floor, and stepped away from the control panel.

Blake waited until she moved out of his way, then stepped over to the panel, pressed the button for his own floor, and wasted no time in moving to the wall at the far end of the box-like car. He couldn't help smiling when he realized both he and the young woman had placed themselves as far apart from each other as they could possibly get.

Blake's eyes again met the young woman's eyes. And then, for three or four seconds, the two simply stared at each other. Blake finally flashed the woman a quick, self-conscious smile, gave her a barely perceptible nod of his head, and looked away. It was not that he had found something more interesting than the woman to look at; he simply felt compelled to look at something other than her.

And then, Blake second-guessed himself.

Perhaps, even though it will make me late, I should get off this elevator and wait for the next one.

Blake would have to act quickly if he hoped to step through the doors before they closed.

Yes. That's what I'll do. I'll get off this elevator and wait for the next one. There is no reason—no reason whatsoever—for me to place myself in such an awkward situation as this. Why should I punish myself when I can easily avoid it? So what if I'm a minute or two late? No one will know but me.

Blake pushed away from the wall, shifted his weight to his left leg, lifted his right foot, and took one step toward the open doorway. But that's as far as he got. He had waited too long. The doors had already begun sliding shut, and he knew, from a recent bone-crushing experience, he did *not* want to get pinned between this particular pair of doors while they were in the process of closing.

Blake looked down at the floor, pursed his lips, and shook his head.

Why, he asked himself, *why-oh-why did I allow myself to get caught in the same elevator...not just any elevator, but this elevator...and not with just any woman, but with this woman?*

Blake stole a quick glance at the young brunette...

And stopped breathing.

She is staring straight at me!

Blake again diverted his eyes from the young woman, looked down at the floor, and pretended to study an imaginary scuff mark on one of his shoes.

How could I have been so foolish as to allow myself to get on an elevator with no other passenger in it except this young woman? Not just any elevator, but this elevator. And not just any woman, but this woman?

Blake stole another glance at the young brunette.

She's still staring at me!

And the young woman continued staring at Blake...

And he at her...

Until the massive steel doors demanded their full attention. The doors would have already met in the middle had not a large, heavy-set man—who, Blake guessed, was at least twice his age and three times his size—thrust his grossly-overweight bulk inside the elevator.

In reality, the man had managed to thrust his bulk only halfway inside the elevator. The heavy doors had closed upon his shoulders and, like a pair of shiny, stainless-steel jaws, refused to let him retreat *from* the elevator or advance *into* it. The elevator's safety device, which should have sounded a loud, piercing alarm to alert everyone within hearing distance that an obstacle had blocked its doors, remained absolutely silent while the man...who remained equally silent...continued his struggle to overcome the doors' powerful closing mechanism.

The doors seemed to possess a mind of their own. They seemed alive. Not merely alive, but fully intent on crushing the man—who was now cursing and groaning under his breath as he continued his effort to escape the doors' powerful, vise-like jaws.

Blake was tempted to laugh—after all, the scene *was* comical—but he never showed the slightest hint of a smile. Instead, recalling his own recent*...and very painful*...experience with these same doors, he winced in empathy.

The overweight man finally managed to squeeze his bulk through the narrowing slot. The moment he did, the doors slid the last few inches and slammed shut with a sharp, metallic clang. Throughout all this time, other than the man's constant mutterings and groanings, no one made a sound.

The elevator finally got underway, dinged softly as it passed the second floor, and dinged twice to announce it had arrived at, and was stopping at, the third floor. The instant the massive steel jaws slid open, the large man, still rubbing his bruised shoulder and rib cage...and still mumbling curses under his breath...stormed out of the elevator. A few seconds later, the doors reversed themselves and slid smoothly...*and with deceptive hunger*...until they clanged shut.

Blake made a mental note to call the maintenance department, exactly as he had done a few days earlier when those same doors had tried to eat him. However, after thinking it over a few seconds, he thought:

No, I will not call Maintenance. I called them before and the secretary apparently forgot my call the moment she hung up the phone. So, this time, I'll document the fact I notified them by sending an email directly to the Manager of Maintenance, along with a complimentary copy to my boss. Perhaps, that way, my message will reach the right person...he'll have no choice but to take ownership of the problem...and he'll make sure something is done about it.

But was it really necessary to send an email to the Manager of Maintenance? Why, Blake asked himself, should he go to the trouble of reporting the problem to anyone? After all, he had already reported it once, and felt certain the doors' most recent victim would also report it.

In fact, I'm willing to bet that man is headed straight for his phone at this very moment.

Blake's mind snapped back to the present...and the realization that he and the attractive brunette were alone.

Just the two of them.

Blake reluctantly tore his gaze from the ravenous steel jaws and turned his head toward the young woman. This time, however, instead of merely glancing at her eyes as he had done before, he looked *into* her eyes. An instant later, when it occurred to him the young woman had been staring—*and was still staring*—into *his* eyes, he looked away again.

Blake had looked into the woman's eyes for no more than two or three seconds, but those seconds had provided him more than enough time to notice her eyes were filled with a strange mixture of embarrassment, apology, and regret.

There followed an additional two or three seconds of silence.

To Blake, those two or three seconds seemed like two or three minutes. And then, the worst thing that could possibly happen—and the last thing Blake wanted to happen—happened.

The young brunette spoke to him.

"Blake, I am *so* sorry about Saturday night."

Blake kicked himself—figuratively speaking—in the seat of his pants. He had known better than to place himself in such an awkward situation.

Why on earth did I get into the same elevator as this young woman? In another week or two, being alone with Gigi will be something I can do with relative ease. But not today. Not right now.

Blake realized both he and Gigi needed more time to recover from the unbelievably embarrassing events of Saturday night. And then, he again cursed himself.

Why on Earth did I get on the same elevator as Gigi? I'm not ready to be alone with her. Not this soon, anyway. And yet, here she is. And here I am. A captive audience, so to speak.

Blake did not want to *think* about Gigi, let alone *look* at her. And he *certainly* didn't want to *be* with her. However, what he wanted or didn't want no longer mattered. Whether he liked it or not, he *was* with Gigi, which left him no choice but to think about her, to look at her, and, because she had spoken to him, to speak to her.

Blake forced himself to look into Gigi's eyes. He then did something that required an even greater effort: He forced himself to speak to her.

"It wasn't *all* your fault, Gigi."

"Oh! But it was. Every *bit* of it was my fault. Oh, Blake, certainly you don't think I'm that kind of…. I don't know what came over.... I can't believe I...."

Two dings announced the elevator had arrived at, and was stopping at, the fourth floor. Gigi fell silent, the doors opened wide, and two middle-aged men, accompanied by an older woman, stepped inside. From that point on, Blake did all he could to avoid looking at Gigi...and Gigi did all she could to avoid looking at Blake. Each pretended to have developed a sudden and intense interest in the elevator's wood paneling, despite the fact they had both ridden these elevators hundreds, if not thousands, of times.

Blake studied a particularly intricate swirl on one of the wood panels. He then smiled, aware his accountant's mind had begun whirring away in the background.

How many times have I ridden these elevators?

Each morning, Blake rode one of the elevators to the floor on which his office was located. And, each day at noon, he rode one down to lunch. He rode one up again after lunch, and down again to go home. That added up to a minimum of four rides each day.

I ride these elevators five days a week...

And I work fifty weeks a year.

Four rides a day...multiplied by five days.... That comes to twenty rides per week. Fifty weeks per year...multiplied by twenty rides per week.... That makes a hundred rides per year. No, that's not right. I left off a zero. That comes to a thousand rides per year. And, since I have worked in the Wexler Tower for ten years....

Blake smiled a second time.

Imagine! Who would have thought I have ridden these elevators—at a minimum—ten thousand times?

Blake smiled a third time when another realization hit him. Despite the fact he had ridden these elevators more than ten thousand times, not until this time had he noticed...*truly* noticed... the elevators had pricey...*very* pricey...solid wood panels. At least, they *looked* solid.

And then, when another realization hit Blake, he smiled a fourth time. The panel before him was the most beautiful piece of wood he had ever seen. Tight, intricate knots and long, sweeping swirls covered every square inch of it.

And, finally,, Blake smiled a fifth time. Because, until now, he had been so preoccupied with his mental calculations to determine how many times he had ridden these elevators, and had become so absorbed by the beauty of the wood panels, he had not looked at Gigi—had not even *thought* about Gigi—so he had no way of knowing what Gigi had been doing. Had she also been tallying the number of times she had ridden the elevators? Had she also been studying the intricate designs in the wood panels? Or, as he suspected, had she been staring at him?

Blake could be certain of only one thing: Regardless of what Gigi had been thinking, and regardless of what Gigi had been looking at, he was not about to look at her. Because she was not talking. And that was a good thing.

A *very* good thing.

If I avoid looking at Gigi, I might get lucky and get off this elevator before she has a chance to say more than she has already said.

Blake thought about it a moment, and then shook his head.

Who am I kidding? Of course Gigi is looking at me. But at least she's not talking to me.

Except for the soft whir of a small fan mounted somewhere in the ceiling—and the soft, annoying, omnidirectional "ding" that came from who-knows-where each time the elevator passed a floor —the elevator remained absolutely silent.

Blake finally pulled his eyes away from the wood panel and concentrated his attention on the row of numbers centered on the wall directly above the door. The numeral 14 changed to a 15...another soft ding came from nowhere and everywhere...and the numeral 15 changed to a 16. The next ding was quickly followed by a second ding, the elevator slowed to a smooth stop, and the doors—*those ravenously hungry doors*—slid open.

Blake quick-stepped out of the elevator. He was in a hurry, partly to avoid those vise-like jaws, and partly to get away from Gigi. Without so much as a glance over his shoulder, he set off in the direction of his office. And then, after striding half a dozen steps down the hallway, he did something he would later wish he had not done: He stopped walking...twisted his neck and torso around...looked over his shoulder...and stared at the elevator. Gigi, who had remained inside the elevator, was staring straight down the hallway.

Straight at him.

Blake noticed Gigi's face exhibited the same, embarrassed. and regretful expression he had seen on it a minute or two earlier when she had made a clumsy effort to apologize to him. He continued staring at her, and she continued staring at him, each maintaining eye contact with the other until those massive stainless-steel doors—this time harmless and victimless—slid shut with a sharp, metallic clang.

And then...

Blake continued standing there...

And continued staring at the doors...

Long after they clanged shut.

I'm sure Maintenance already knows about it. In fact, I'll bet that man is on the phone right now, at this very moment, reporting it to them. But I'll send them an email anyway, simply because it's the right thing to do.

And Blake Turner always…

Always…

Did the right thing.

Blake untwisted his neck and torso until he faced forward again. Only then did he realize he had stopped walking…and that everyone in the hallway was staring directly at him. He knew each and every one of those people, most of them by their first names. He also knew each and every one of them was asking many questions, questions that included: Why did Blake Turner stop walking? And what…or whom…had Blake Turner been staring at?

Blake smiled and shook his head, as much for his own benefit as for the benefit of his onlookers. He then set off at his normal walking pace.

Thank Goodness! he thought. *Saturday night—and Gigi—are both behind me.*

CHAPTER 2

Blake, known by all of his friends and acquaintances to be a creature of habit, quickly put thoughts of Gigi out of his mind and settled into the comfort of his daily routine. First, he did something he did every morning upon arriving at the office: He paused at the table with the coffee urn, sat his briefcase on the floor beside the table, and lifted a clean ceramic mug off the top of the stack. He then filled the mug with piping hot coffee and prepared it just the way he liked it.

Blake sprinkled a pinch of salt into the cup, a trick he had learned from his father to cut the coffee's bitterness. Like many of his coworkers, he swore this urn made the most bitter coffee in the world. He then poured in two packets of sugar and one packet of creamer...stirred his coffee with a tiny, plastic, straw-like, red-and-white, candy-striped swizzle stick until all evidence of the sweetener and creamer powder dissolved...and tossed the swizzle stick, along with the empty sugar and creamer packets, into the trash basket. Next, he lifted a napkin off the top of the stack, wiped away the stray droplets of coffee and sprinkles of sweetener and creamer—despite the fact he had been very careful and knew for a certainty none of the droplets and sprinkles had been his own—and tossed the napkin into the trash. Finally, after surveying the table from one end to the other to make certain he had completely cleaned up the mess left by his fellow employees, he retrieved his briefcase from underneath the table and continued his walk down the hallway toward his office.

For the next fifteen minutes Blake worked in silence. *Peaceful* silence. *Productive* silence. If he could have his way, he would work in silence all day every day. However, as happened every morning about this time, his quiet solitude came to an abrupt halt the moment thirty-six-year-old Fred Johnson entered the tiny room. Blake looked up, made a quick assessment of Fred's appearance, shook his head, and gave Fred a condescending, yet good-natured, half-smile, half-smirk expression to exhibit his disapproval.

On this morning, as on most mornings, Fred had entered the office fifteen minutes late, wearing a shirt so badly wrinkled it appeared he had slept in it. With Fred's top button left undone, and a mismatched and poorly-tied tie draped around his open collar, Blake found it hard to believe Fred was a happily married man.

But, then again, thought Blake, *when you consider the fact both Fred and his wife are pursuing professional careers while, at the same time, contending with three young, hyperactive children....*

"Good morning, Blake!" exclaimed Fred, pretending nothing was amiss.

As always, Fred was in a jovial mood. Blake nodded once, his way of making an informal bow to acknowledge Fred's enthusiastic greeting. He then returned Fred's greeting with one simple—and decidedly *un*enthusiastic—word.

"Fred."

A greater contrast between two men would be difficult, if not impossible, to find. Upon his entry, Fred had spoken to Blake in a loud, confident, and cheerful voice—as if he considered his tardy behavior perfectly normal and, something even worse, perfectly acceptable. In contrast, Blake had replied to Fred in a much softer voice, a voice Fred realized had been tinged with a hint of disapproval.

Blake and Fred differed in other ways, as well—not the least of which was the fact Blake always made a point to arrive at the office at eight o'clock. Not just eight o'clock, but eight o'clock *sharp*. It was also Blake's habit to place his briefcase very gently, almost ceremoniously, in the space reserved for it on his spotlessly-clean, dust-free, and neatly-organized desktop. Fred, however, in addition to always arriving at a ridiculously-late ten or fifteen minutes past the hour, had a habit of tossing his tattered briefcase on top of a deep pile of dust-covered clutter...so much clutter that not a single inch of his desk could be seen. Blake swore, if forced to testify in a court of law, he would deny he had any knowledge of whether or not Fred actually *had* a desk. He assumed a desk lay there...somewhere...beneath all that clutter, but, like Fred, he had not seen it in years.

Blake glanced back and forth between his and Fred's desks while making no effort to conceal from Fred that he was comparing the two. Blake took great pride in the fact he kept his desk clean. He also took great pride in the fact he lived—whether at work, in his apartment, or in his secluded week-end cabin—adhering to the proverbial mantra of "a place for everything, and everything in its place." Blake finally moved his eyes away from the two desks and took another look at Fred. Only then did he notice Fred's eyes were darting back and forth between the two desktops.

It's been so long since Fred saw his desk he's looking at mine, hoping to see something...anything...to joggle some hidden memory as to what his desk used to look like.

Blake took one more look at Fred's cluttered desktop, and then took another look at Fred's disheveled appearance. Again, if forced to testify, he would swear Fred had gone out of his way, and invested a considerable amount of time and energy, to achieve his disheveled look, a look that went far beyond what one would call "casual." Blake, on the other hand, took great pride in the fact he came to work each morning dressed in a clean, crisply-ironed shirt and, on most days, a neatly-tied tie, each carefully chosen to match his wrinkle-free suit.

"I swear, Fred, you never cease to amaze me."

This time, Fred did not need to rely on imagination to detect the unmistakable tone of disapproval in Blake's voice. He stared at Blake a moment, and then exploded, as if he had been deeply wounded.

"What!?"

Fred stared at Blake a moment longer, and then pretended to pout, as if Blake's comment had truly hurt his feelings. Blake, familiar with the ruse, again displayed his half-smile, half-smirk expression, and then continued his critique.

"Fred, you should stand in front of a mirror and take a long look at yourself. I swear! You look like a wino somebody dragged in from the gutter."

Fred showed the slightest hint of a smile...his smile grew into a wide grin...he lifted his chin...and stuck his nose high into the air.

"Sticks and stones, Blake. Sticks and stones."

Blake silently finished the ancient rhyme inside his head.

Amazingly, and despite their many differences, Blake and Fred were the closest of friends...which was a good thing, because they had shared the claustrophobic closeness of their tiny, eight-by-twelve-foot office for more than ten years. Blake studied Fred a few moments longer, gave him a brief smile, followed the smile with a soft, good-natured chuckle, and, once again, shook his head to show his disapproval. And, with that, Blake considered his and Fred's daily, ritualistic exchange of greetings to be complete. He gave Fred a final nod, then returned his attention to the brightly-lit computer screen that sat in the center of his desk.

His dustless...

And uncluttered...

Desk.

No sooner did Blake channel his mind back into his work than Fred burst through his thoughts to start a new conversation.

"Hey, Blake. You hear about *Hamburg*?"

Blake—half of his brain focused on his work, and the other half grappling with the disastrous Saturday evening he had spent with Gigi—looked up from the Accounts Receivable menu on his computer screen and gave Fred a long, blank stare. Blake's eyes glazed over as he struggled to rearrange his thoughts...the Leslie account clinging to one side of his brain, Gigi refusing to leave the other, and Fred's question about *Hamburg* trying to worm its way between the two. Fred's question finally won the battle, stood front and center in Blake's brain, and demanded Blake's full attention. Blake looked up, refocused his eyes, and stared at Fred.

"Hamburg? What do you mean, 'Have I heard about Hamburg?' Of *course* I've heard about Hamburg. Who hasn't?"

Fred plopped his lanky frame into his plush leather chair, rolled the chair up to his desk, placed his hands on his computer keyboard, and entered his username and password. Fred, a master at multitasking—or, at least, someone who *thought* he was a master at multitasking—resumed the conversation while continuing to stare at his computer screen, uncertain as to whether or not he had properly entered his login information.

"Well, Mr. Smarty Pants, if you've heard about *Ham...*"

Fred, puzzled as to why his login was taking so long, became silent. And then, when his computer finally showed signs of proceeding to the next screen, he turned his head to face Blake and restated his question.

"If you've heard about *Hamburg,* why don't you tell me what *Hamburg* is?"

Blake released a long, exasperated sigh. And then, while staring straight at the wall in front of his desk, he just sat there a few moments, puzzled as to why Fred would interrupt his work to ask such a basic question. Finally, he rolled his eyes, shook his head, released another exasperated sigh, and answered Fred's question with a bored, matter-of-fact voice.

"Last time I checked, Fred, Hamburg was a city in Germany. That, of course, assumes you're referring to *the* Hamburg. If not, I believe there are several smaller Hamburgs here in the United States, and probably a few in other countries, as well."

Fred looked at his computer screen. And then, again thinking his computer had locked up, Fred continued staring at the screen until it showed signs of proceeding to the third stage of his login. He finally sat up straight, swiveled his chair until it directly faced Blake, and, in a good-natured tone of voice—accompanied by a theatrical display of mock exasperation—exclaimed:

"No, no, and *no,* you socially-deprived moron. *Hamburg* is *not* a city in Germany...it is *not* a city in the United States...and it is *not* a city in any other country."

Fred flipped the latches on his briefcase, lifted the top, locked it open, and pulled out the unsorted hodgepodge of notes and papers he had taken home the previous evening. Blake assumed, as he always assumed—and, as always, he assumed correctly— Fred's good intention of working at home had been exactly that: little more than good intention. As usual, family and social matters had taken up so much of Fred's time he had not given a single thought to the affairs of the Wexler and Ferguson Accounting

Agency.

"You doofus," continued Fred. "I'm not talking about Hamburg the *city.* I'm talking about *Hamburg...*the *play.* Well, actually, *Hamburg* is not a play. Not in the truest sense of the word. It's a *musical.* Been showing about a week now. Karen and I went to see it last night and, let me tell you, it's the best musical I've ever seen. Not that I've seen that many plays or musicals—and, of course, I'm not a world-renowned expert on either one—but, *still,* you simply *have* to go see it."

Slowly, and in dramatic fashion, Blake pushed away from his desk, swiveled his chair until it squarely faced Fred's chair, and leaned back. He then folded his arms across his chest, narrowed his eyes, and stared directly into Fred's eyes.

"What on earth has gotten into you, Fred? If I have told you once, I have told you a thousand times: I am not a play guy."

Fred held up his right hand, pointed his index finger toward the ceiling, tilted his chin downward, and cocked his head to one side.

"Correction, Blake."

Fred moved his right hand to his briefcase, nonchalantly removed a pocket-sized notepad, and, while continuing to stare at Blake, flipped the notepad—using the same, side-armed manner in which he threw Frisbees to his children—onto his cluttered desktop. He would later spend a full ten minutes digging through the clutter looking for it.

"*Hamburg* is not a *play,* Blake. It's a *musical.* Remember?"

"Yeah, Fred. Right. We already established the fact I don't like plays. And, as you well know, I *detest* musicals."

Fred furrowed his brow and stared at Blake for several seconds. And then, with the same good-natured disapproval he had displayed toward Blake moments earlier, he pursed his lips and shook his head from side to side. Fred found it hard to believe, despite the fact he had known Blake for a decade, and despite the fact he knew Blake better than he knew anyone on the entire planet —with the possible exception of his wife—he had barely begun to understand the man. When Fred next spoke, it was with heavy, sincere, and heartfelt exasperation. And, this time, there was nothing mock about it.

"You are *hopeless*, Blake. You...are...absolutely...*hopeless*."

Using only his arms, Fred pushed his chair away from his desk. And then, using the tips of his toes, he swiveled his chair until he sat face-to-face with Blake. He stared at Blake a few moments, then placed the palms of his hands on his thighs and leaned forward.

"Blake, one of these days—and you can mark my words on this—one of these days I'm gonna give up on you. I swear, if we hooked an EKG up to your social life we'd see nothing but a flat line. You live the most boring life of anyone I know."

Feeling both confident and justified in his judgment of Blake, Fred frowned and shook his head in an effort to emphasize his disapproval of Blake's pathetically-boring lifestyle. Blake, however, believed Fred had judged him unfairly and proceeded to let him know it.

"Fred, I'll have you know you wouldn't say that if you had been with me on Saturday night. That...that...that *girl* you hooked me up with...."

Blake was so exasperated about his recent misadventure with Gigi he couldn't say another word. He *tried* to say something, but only a few unintelligible sounds escaped his lips. Finally, aware he couldn't start another sentence, let alone finish one, he released an explosive sigh...shook his head...rolled his eyes...and waved his hands in a gesture meant to shoo Fred away.

Fred, a wise and perceptive man, despite his outward displays of nonchalant behavior and slothful appearance, took Blake's gesture to be a strong and definitive indication that his date with Gigi had not gone as planned. Also aware he was partly to blame for Blake's disastrous weekend, he made a sincere effort to smooth things over.

"Well, then. I guess I owe you an apology, Blake. It's just...well...you never go out on dates, and, to me, anyway, Gigi seemed like she would be a lot of fun to be with. You must admit, Blake, she's as cute as they come."

"Gigi *is* cute, Fred. She's as cute as a button...*when she's sober*. But when she's *drunk*...."

Fred winced.

"Again, Blake, I owe you an apology. I had no idea Gigi was a heavy drinker."

"That's just the problem, Fred. Gigi is *not* a heavy drinker. She's not *any* kind of drinker. And neither am I, really. *Neither* of us are drinkers, and, of all things, you gave us a pair of tickets to a champagne social. *For crying out loud, Fred. What were you thinking?* Sure, I've done a little drinking, but not much. I've never had more than one drink on a single occasion...I've *never* had champagne...and, since I had no idea how multiple drinks—especially champagne—would affect me, I was careful to take tiny sips and make each glass last as long as I could. But Gigi? *No way!* She drank the stuff like it was water. The more she drank, the more she wanted. And that's not the worst of it. Before I knew what was happening, she started taking her clothes off, right there in the middle of the banquet hall. Thank goodness I was able to get her out of there and into a taxi before she totally embarrassed both of us."

Fred grinned, cocked his head to one side, and lifted his eyebrows.

"Well?"

"Well, *what*?!"

Fred smiled.

"Well...? Tell me how the rest of the night went. Did you and Gigi...? *You know....*"

"No, Fred. We didn't *you know.* But it wasn't because Gigi didn't want to. As soon as I got her inside the taxi, even before I closed the door, she was all over me. She took her clothes off almost as fast as I put them back on. And then, to make matters worse, she got sick all over me *and* the back seat. On top of all that, somewhere between the restaurant and her place, she passed out. The taxi driver—I'm sure that man will go to Heaven, because God knows he deserves it.... Anyway, the driver helped Gigi's roommate and me get her out of the taxi, inside her apartment, and into her bed. I spent the next two and a half hours helping the driver clean out his taxi. And, finally, as if all that was not enough, I felt morally obligated to reimburse the driver for the fares and tips he would have received during the time we spent getting Gigi situated and his taxi cleaned out. Please, Fred, whatever you do, don't *ever* try to hook me up with anyone again. Especially when the main entertainment—no, the *only* entertainment—is alcohol. *Never.* Is that clear?"

"Okay, okay. I've already apologized, Blake. I've apologized twice. And, for good measure, I'll apologize a third time. Look, I made a mistake. I thought maybe...*just maybe*...I could be a matchmaker. But, now...well...now I know I'm *not* a matchmaker. So, I'm down on one knee—figuratively speaking—begging your forgiveness."

Fred suddenly slid forward off the edge of his seat.

"Oh, what the heck, Blake. Forget the figurative stuff. I'm down on *both* knees, humbly admitting it was wrong for me to think, for a single minute, I could arrange a date for you. I meant well. I had good intentions. *Honest* I did. I mean.... I just thought...."

Fred finally did as Blake had done a few moments earlier. Unable to verbalize his thoughts, he raised both hands high into the air and waved them from side to side, a clear indication he had given up all hope of reforming Blake's social life. He then rose from his kneeling position and sat down in his chair.

"Look, Blake. I've learned my lesson. If you don't want to date anyone, that's fine with me. I promise I will not play matchmaker ever again. Not for you, nor anyone else."

"Swear to me you really mean that, Fred. I mean, at least, when it comes to me, is that a promise? A *sincere* promise?"

"I've never been more sincere about anything, Blake. But, still, you have *got* to get a life. You do the same thing, day in, day out. Don't you think it's time you branch out and do something different?"

Fred's expression suddenly changed from heavy and serious to light and upbeat.

"And I've got just the thing for you, Blake. *Hamburg* is the perfect place to start."

"Look, Fred. We've established several facts. First and foremost—and something I thought I made quite clear—I don't care to go out again with Gigi...or, for that matter, any *other* girl you want to hook me up with. Second, I am not a play guy. And third, I am *definitely* not a musical guy. So, for now at least, just leave me alone and let me enjoy doing the same thing, day in, day out."

Fred stared at Blake a moment, shook his head in disapproval, and swiveled his chair until he squarely faced his desk again. And then, for several long seconds, he just sat there, staring at the blank wall that filled the space in front of him. A few moments later, he gave Blake a brief, sideways glance...turned forward to stare at the wall again...and turned to look at Blake again. Fred finally gave Blake a slow, disapproving shake of his head, looked forward one last time, grabbed his desk with both hands, and pulled himself underneath its lap drawer. He then said:

"Blake, you don't have to go see *Hamburg* if you don't want to...but it will be *your* loss, not mine."

Blake leaned back and watched Fred search for the notepad he had absentmindedly tossed onto his desktop several minutes earlier. Calmly at first, and then becoming more and more frantic, Fred dug down through the clutter in a random fashion, first moving a portion of this pile of paperwork, and then moving a portion of that pile of paperwork, each time burying the notepad deeper and deeper underneath the towering mound of dust-covered papers, magazines, file folders, clipboards, and notebooks.

Even as Fred continued his search, Blake gave a final, disapproving shake of his head, swiveled his chair around until he faced his own desk—his immaculately clean, well-organized, and uncluttered desk—and stole one more glance at Fred, who now displayed genuine signs of panic as he searched for the displaced notepad.

Blake pulled himself forward, slid his knees underneath his lap drawer, and placed his elbows on his desktop. He paused just long enough to take a sip of coffee—which, during the course of his conversation with Fred, had cooled to the point it was barely warmer than room temperature—and returned his attention to the accounts on his computer screen.

CHAPTER 3

The next morning, Blake began his workday with the same routine he began every workday. His clock radio, set to his favorite "easy-listening" station, gently awoke him from a sound sleep at precisely five-thirty AM. Without opening his eyes, he reached out into the darkness, patted his bedside table, found the radio, and fumbled for the snooze button. He then pressed the button, rolled over, and went back to sleep.

Ten minutes later, Blake's radio awakened him a second time. He again reached out into the darkness, found the radio, and pressed the snooze button. A minute later, when he realized he was more awake than asleep, he threw off the covers, swung his legs off the side of the bed, and pulled himself to a sitting position. And then, one more time, he reached out into the darkness, found his bedside lamp, and switched it on.

While waiting for his eyes to adjust to the brightness of the lamp, Blake reached for his radio and set its alarm to the "off" position. He then scratched his scalp with the tips of his fingers, smoothed his hair with the palms of his hands, arched his back, and flexed his arms and shoulders in the classic—though, in his case, not very impressive—he-man pose. Still half asleep, he pushed himself up and off his bed, stumbled from his bedroom, staggered in a not-so-straight line down the short hallway, and entered his apartment's tiny kitchen. *Still* somewhat groggy, he switched on another radio, this one tuned to the same station he had listened to in his bedroom.

A few seconds, later, Blake set about preparing a breakfast of hot coffee, a two-egg cheese omelet, and two pieces of toast lightly spread with butter and jam. And then, despite the fact he continued doing everything as he had always done it, he quickly realized today would be unlike any day he had ever known. He knew this because, from the moment his alarm clock awakened him—before the news, during the news, after the news, and between the songs —the announcer, who was normally a soft-spoken, subdued man, raved constantly about *Hamburg*.

"I cannot say enough about *Hamburg*."

"I simply can *not* say enough about *Hamburg*."

"*Hamburg* is a 'must see'."

"*Hamburg* is a treat for the senses."

"*Hamburg* is the best play I have ever seen."

"*Hamburg* is the best musical I have ever heard."

Blake, who had hoped to glean a few tidbits of news and music squeezed between the announcer's unsolicited plugs for *Hamburg*, continued listening to the radio while eating his breakfast. Finally, while shoving the last bits of egg and toast into his mouth, he got up from the table, decided he had heard all about *Hamburg* he cared to hear, and switched off the radio. He washed his dirty dishes, straightened the covers on his bed, shaved, took a hot shower, put on his clothes, walked to his car, and began his daily, thirty minute drive to work.

Blake drove in silence for almost ten minutes before switching on the radio in his car—the third radio he had listened to since waking up. Listening to the radio in his car usually made the time spent sitting in bumper-to-bumper, stop-and-go traffic pass more quickly. But today, as he quickly discovered, listening to the radio would have the exact opposite effect. Instead of hearing relaxing music on *this* station, or listening to one of his favorite talk shows on *that* station, he found himself constantly switching from station to station in a futile attempt to escape talk of *Hamburg*. Every announcer, every newscaster, and every DJ—*on every station*—talked of nothing but *Hamburg*. So, once again deciding he had heard as much about Hamburg as he cared to hear, he extended his right arm, switched off his radio, and drove the final ten minutes in total silence.

Blake made a right-hand turn off one of New York's busy streets into the cave-like darkness of a parking deck. He then wound his way up to the sixth level, turned into his parking space, and braked to a stop. Even before shifting his transmission into park—with the engine still running, the windows rolled up, and the doors tightly closed—he heard the muffled voices of people talking about *Hamburg*.

Blake switched off his engine and sat there a few moments. He then climbed out of his car, locked the doors, made his way along the rows of parked vehicles, and approached the elevator—the entire time listening to people talk about *Hamburg*. While riding the elevator down to street level, he again listened to lively conversations about *Hamburg*. While walking the two blocks from the parking deck to the Wexler Tower, he listened to *more* conversations about *Hamburg*. The topic of almost every conversation was *Hamburg*. Not politics...not the weather...and not sports.

Hamburg.

Blake, thinking he would find relief upon entering the Wexler Tower, picked up the pace. However, he quickly discovered such a notion was an erroneous assumption....a completely wasted exercise of wishful thinking. Not only did things *not* get any better when he stepped inside the Wexler Tower, they actually got worse.

From the moment Blake stepped out of the revolving door and

into the building...throughout his dash across the crowded lobby...and throughout his ride on the elevator to the sixteenth floor...he heard nothing but talk about *Hamburg*. Everyone around him, whether young or old, male or female, had either *seen Hamburg*, had *read* about *Hamburg*, or had *heard* about *Hamburg* and was eager to discuss *Hamburg*'s pros and cons.

Finally, thankfully...and very mercifully...Blake reached his office. However, on this particular morning, he viewed his office, not as a work space, but as a sanctuary—a quiet place in which he could escape the cacophonous noise that had surrounded him for the past twenty-four hours. He dove inside the room, closed the door behind him, and stared wistfully at his computer screen.

One minute from now—a mere sixty seconds—I'll be deep in my accounts and Hamburg will be the farthest thing from my mind. I won't think about Hamburg—nor will I hear people talk about Hamburg—for eight...blissful...hours.

Blake should have known better. Actually, he *did* know better. After all, he had known Fred Johnson for ten years...which was long enough to know Fred would have something to say to dispel any and all notions about their office serving as a sanctuary.

As it turned out, Fred didn't have *something* to say about *Hamburg,* he had *lots* to say about *Hamburg*. All day, every five minutes—just like clockwork—Fred pushed his chair out from under his desk, turned to face Blake, and made this or that comment about *Hamburg*.

CHAPTER 4

To Blake, it seemed five o'clock would never arrive. The moment it *did* arrive, he fled from his office, rode the elevator down to the main floor, dashed across the lobby—pausing just long enough to grab a paper from the newsstand—and exited the building. He then walked at a brisk pace from the Wexler Tower to the parking deck. Earlier that morning, during his two block walk *from* the parking deck to the Wexler Tower, *Hamburg* had been the other pedestrians' main topic of conversation. But now, some nine hours later, *Hamburg* was their *only* topic of conversation.

Blake walked faster, almost at a jogging pace, driven by the mistaken belief—the belief that, if he climbed into his car, closed the door, turned on the radio, and cranked the volume up twice as loudly as he normally did—he could shut out all the voices. The closer he got to his car, the more excited he became about listening to music and the evening news instead of talk about *Hamburg.*

Blake walked faster and faster.

And talk grew louder and louder.

At *times*, Blake heard only one *Hamburg* conversation. At other times, he heard two. However, most of the time he heard three, or even four, *Hamburg* conversations—*all at the same time.* He wanted to cover his ears—and *would* have covered his ears had the handle of his briefcase not occupied one of his hands.

Blake wanted to run.

Even worse, he wanted to scream.

The moment he got within sight of his car, he pressed the button on his key fob to unlock the door. Seconds later, upon reaching his car, he grabbed the handle with his free hand, swung the door wide open, and did something he had never done...something he had never even *thought* about doing.

He heaved his briefcase across the car.

Blake winced the instant his briefcase slammed into the passenger-side door. He winced a second time when it bounced off the seat and tumbled to the floor. And, finally, he released an audible groan and just stood there, as if in a state of shock, while staring down at his upside-down briefcase.

But Blake stood there only for a brief moment. The second he heard someone say the word *Hamburg*, he dove underneath the steering wheel...pulled the door shut...inserted his key...started the engine...turned on the radio...and cranked up the volume.

Finally!

Just as Blake had hoped, his radio drowned out all the conversations outside his car. He leaned back, closed his eyes, and listened to...

No!

More talk about *Hamburg.*

Blake was in trouble. *Serious* trouble. He listened to his favorite station a moment, decided it should be renamed *The Hamburg Station*, and switched to another station. A moment later, he switched to *another* station. And *another. Every* announcer, on *every* station, talked of nothing but *Hamburg.* Blake quickly tuned in a fifth station. Its announcer also talked about *Hamburg, and nothing but Hamburg.* In rapid succession, Blake tuned his radio to every station it could pick up.

Every announcer...

On every station...

Talked of nothing but *Hamburg.*

Hamburg.

Hamburg.

And more *Hamburg*.

Finally, exasperated, Blake switched off his radio, backed out of his parking space, and drove in silence. Upon reaching his apartment, he parked his car, grabbed his briefcase, hesitated a moment, then picked up the newspaper and climbed out. He pretended to ignore the couple who lived two units down and walked briskly to his own unit. He had nothing against the couple. On any other day he would have stopped and talked to them.

But not today.

Because they were discussing *Hamburg*.

Blake entered his apartment, locked the door, turned his back to it, and leaned his head and shoulders against it.

"Finally!" he breathed. "*Now* I can get some peace and quiet without having to listen to all that talk about *Hamburg*."

For several seconds, Blake just stood there, savoring the silence. He then walked over to the couch and placed his briefcase on one of the cushions. He stared at his briefcase a moment, then gave it a gentle pat, as if to offer it an apology for the way he had mindlessly thrown it across the front seat of his car, crashed it into the door, and watched it tumble, upside down, onto the floor.

Though Blake's briefcase contained nothing breakable, he was not in the habit, as Fred seemed to be, of tossing it around as if it were an inanimate object. Blake knew, of course, his briefcase *was* an inanimate object, but he considered it to be an extension of himself. As a result, he treated it, both consciously and sub-consciously, as if it were alive...as if it had feelings and emotions. He gave his briefcase another gentle pat, then shifted his gaze to his leather recliner.

Blake stared dreamily at the recliner for several seconds. He then walked across the room, eased himself down onto the chair's soft cushion, leaned his head back, and closed his eyes. For the better part of a minute he just sat there, taking deep, relaxing breaths while the day's tension flowed from his body and into the chair. And then, without bothering to lift his head or open his eyes, he reached down with his right hand, wrapped his fingers around the long, wooden handle mounted on the side of the recliner, and pulled upward. In one smooth motion the headrest and backrest tilted back, and the footrest extended forward.

A soft, involuntary "Ahhh" breathed between Blake's lips, the corners of his mouth curled upward, and his body sank deeper and deeper into the recliner's soft padding. He sat there a few moments, then reached up with both hands, loosened his tie, unbuttoned his collar, and breathed another soft, involuntary "Ahhh." Finally, he kicked off his shoes, opened his eyes, and turned his attention to the newspaper he had picked up on his way out of the Wexler Tower.

Just think! In a matter of moments I'll be so immersed in today's news that all thoughts about Hamburg will be purged from my mind.

And so, without further ado, Blake began reading the paper—exactly as he always did—by scanning the headlines on the front page. Just as he had hoped, after reading fewer than a dozen words, he became so lost in the news he completely forgot about *Hamburg.*

"Police Talk Woman Out Of Throwing Baby Off Bridge."

"New York Jets Draft College Junior From Jersey Shore."

"Were They Aliens? Or Teenage Pranksters?"

Blake plodded through the front-page portion of all the articles he considered to be of interest. And, as always, he found himself frustrated by the terse note printed at the bottom of each article's introductory paragraphs.

"See Bridge on A-3"

"See Junior on B-1"

"See Aliens on C-4"

Blake hated the way newspapers and magazines teased their readers by placing the opening paragraphs of an article on one page, only to come to an abrupt halt long before the end of the article. Sometimes an article stopped, not just in the middle of a sentence, but in the middle of a phrase. And, it seemed, the article always...*always*...stopped in the middle of a thought, precisely where the reader would least like the break to occur.

Blake equated the phenomenon to a heavily-loaded freight train, after exerting immense quantities of energy to overcome inertia and accelerate to speed, suddenly slamming on its brakes, screeching to a complete stop, and starting the time- and energy-consuming process all over again. It mostly angered him because of its inherent inefficiency.

But the phenomenon also angered Blake because each article forced him to make a decision. Should he immediately turn to the section and page indicated by the terse statement at the article's break point? No, he reasoned, doing that would consume lots of time and waste lots of energy: first, while he wrestled with the paper to turn to the indicated page; and, second, while he scanned that page, found the appropriate article, and read what remained of it while the "lead in" remained fresh in his mind. Blake figured, if he choose this option, he would *again* have to wrestle with the paper while turning back to the front page, finding the next article, and going through the same laborious process all over again. *And that would only be the beginning.* He would have to go through the same procedure, over and over, time and time again, until he finished reading all the articles on the front page.

A second option would be to read the entirety of the front page, and then the entirety of the second page, the third page, and so on, until he finished reading the entire paper. Blake reasoned this option would also consume a lot of time and waste a lot of energy because, over and over, time and time again, he would find it necessary to turn back to the front page, refresh his mind as to what "Bridge" or "Junior" or "Aliens" had been about in the first place, and then turn back to the remainder of the article so he could read the rest of it.

Blake, always the analytical, calculating accountant, chose the second option. He reasoned, more times than not, he would remember enough of each article's lead-in to avoid turning back to the front page. Besides, he preferred to read each page as he came to it, turning to the indicated page if...*and only if*...the article demanded such intense interest he felt compelled to read it to its conclusion without a moment's delay.

And so, tonight, as Blake did most nights, he read page A-1 in its entirety. He then turned to page A-2, with ten unrelated and unfinished stories floating around inside his mind, each story waiting to be picked up whenever and wherever he happened upon its conclusion.

By the time Blake finished reading page A-1, he felt completely relaxed, both mind and body. However, the instant he read the bold-typed headline—which ran full-width across the top of page A-2—all the day's tension returned...and it returned with a vengeance.

Hamburg
The Hottest Musical to Hit Broadway
Since Phantom of the Opera

In the past, Blake had seldom taken time to read anything beyond the title of Zachary Nelson's column. Normally, Zach's column was buried deep within the entertainment section of the newspaper. Tonight, however, Zach's column had been printed on the second page of the paper's first section, the section reserved for the day's most important news stories. Blake read the title a second time, and then did something he had never, *ever* done: He read the *entirety* of Zach's column. After that, he did something else he had never done: He read the entirety of Zach's column a second time.

The musical play *Hamburg* has taken Broadway by storm. Not because its music is better than that of other musicals; not because it has an intricate plot; and not because it makes deep moral statements about the quagmire into which modern society has plunged itself. *Hamburg* has and does all these things...and many more.

What grabs and holds the audience is the incredible chemistry between the two main characters: one, a tall, rugged, American male; and the other, a diminutive, fragile, German female.

The male role is played by Jack Smith, a six-foot four-inch "string bean" from Texas. You won't find a more "down-home" American than Jack.

And the female role is played by Ava Bechtel, a shapely, five-foot two-inch bombshell from Berlin, Germany. Ava could easily be the poster girl for *Everyman's Perfect Fraulein*.

Both thespians perform their roles with an unbelievable and natural ease, with Jack's syrupy, slow-talking, Texas drawl playing point and counter-point against Ava's harsh, choppy, German accent...

CHAPTER 5

One week later, on a bright sunny morning, Blake's workday began like any other workday. He arrived at the Wexler Tower right on time, prepared his coffee just the way he liked it, walked down the long hallway to his office, and placed his cup, followed by his briefcase, on top of his desk. As usual, he gave each, in its turn—first the cup, and then the briefcase—the same care he would have given a carton of raw eggs.

Fifteen minutes later, Fred stormed through the door and plopped *his* briefcase onto *his* desktop—his *cluttered* desktop—as if it were a bag of potatoes being thrown into the back of a pickup truck. And, as usual, Fred began talking before he finished stepping through the doorway.

"Morning, Blake. Have you gone to see *Hamburg*?"

"*No, Fred!*"

Blake made no effort to conceal his disgust with Fred's constant nagging about whether or not he had gone to see the musical. And then, just to make sure Fred understood how disgusted he was, he drove home his point.

"Listen, Fred, I *still* haven't gone to see *Hamburg*, and, furthermore, I have no *intention* to go see *Hamburg*."

"Really? Karen and I have seen *Hamburg* three times already. Last night, we took our oldest kid with us."

Fred flipped the latches on his briefcase, looked into Blake's eyes, and gave him a mischievous smile.

"And tonight, my friend, I intend for *you* to see it, too."

"For the hundredth time, Fred: I am not interested in plays. And, if it's at all possible, I'm even less interested in *musical* plays."

Fred's smile slowly faded. And then, with his face frozen in a deadpan expression, he stared at Blake for several seconds. Finally, just when Blake was about to say something, Fred spoke again, his dry, monotonic voice the perfect companion to his cold, lifeless expression.

"You need to get a life, Blake."

"I've *got* a life, Fred!"

"Yes, Blake, I'm sure you do. At least, you have a life based upon *your* standards. But I think it's time you step back and take a long, hard look at yourself. Your life is the same ol' same ol', day in, day out."

"*It is not!*"

Fred raised his eyebrows and slowly turned his body until his shoulders squarely faced Blake. He then widened his stance, folded his arms across his chest, and stared down his nose.

"Oh? Let's examine the facts, Blake. How many hours a week do you sit in front of your computer screen? Every morning, without exception, you arrive here at the Wexler Tower long before I come in. And every night, without exception, you remain here long after I leave."

Blake again opened his mouth...and again tried to say something...but Fred cut him off.

"*And,* I am willing to bet, nine times out of ten, when you *do* leave, instead of going out on the town and having some fun, or going home to get some rest, you go to a stuffy library and stare at a stupid book."

Blake opened his mouth to speak—but Fred had already resumed talking.

"*Also,* by your own admission, you often stay in the library until closing time, leaving only when one of the librarians asks you to leave so she can lock the place up."

Blake opened his mouth more quickly this time, and *almost* managed to say something. But Fred, again loaded, cocked, and ready to pull the trigger, cut him off before he could utter a single word.

"*And*, I am willing to bet, when you finally *do* go home, you fall asleep with one of your stupid books clutched in your hands."

One more time, Blake opened his mouth and tried to speak. But Fred, far more experienced at talking than he was, again proved his tongue to be quicker on the draw.

"And *furthermore*, I'll bet the first thing you do every morning, probably before you get out of bed, is pick up the same stupid book you fell asleep with the night before and continue reading right where you left off."

This time, Blake made no effort to speak. Even if he could have gotten a word in edgewise, what would he have said? With almost no exceptions, Fred had described his life to a tee. However, despite the fact he and Fred had been the best of friends for ten years, he refused to let Fred get away with slamming *his* lifestyle without slamming *Fred's* lifestyle in return. He slowly swiveled his chair until his shoulders were square with Fred's. And then, despite the fact he, the smaller man, was sitting in a chair, and Fred, the larger man, was standing on his feet and towering above him, he folded his arms across his chest and made every effort to match Fred's determined expression.

"First of all, Fred, the reason I'm here when you arrive every morning, and the reason I'm *still* here when you leave every evening, is quite simple: I arrive at the office on time each morning, and I remain at the office each evening until I have put in my full eight hours."

Fred nonchalantly shrugged his shoulders, as if to say, *So? What does that prove?* And then, angry with himself for becoming confrontational with his best friend, Fred unfolded his arms, rubbed his palms on his thighs, and slipped his hands inside his front pockets. And finally, hoping the change in posture would make him appear less threatening, Fred spoke with a lighter, softer, and warmer tone of voice.

"Tell me something, Blake. Do you go to the library *every* night of the week?"

Though the two men still faced each other—with Fred standing, his hands in his pockets, and Blake sitting, his arms folded across his chest—the sincere, caring tone in which Fred asked his question melted away the icy, confrontational atmosphere.

"I've never given it much thought, Fred, but, yes, I suppose I do. Well, I don't go *every* night. I didn't go *last* night. I went straight home. But, yes, I suppose I *do* go to the library on most nights. But what if I do? What's wrong with spending my spare time in a library? I like to *read*, Fred. Is reading a crime*?* Is something wrong with it?"

"No, Blake. Reading is not a crime. Nothing is wrong with reading...except for the fact reading is all you ever do."

Without waiting for Blake to respond, Fred shrugged his shoulders, as if it didn't really matter to him *what* Blake did in his spare time. He then changed to a lighter, more cheerful tone.

"But you won't be reading tonight, my friend. You'll be sitting in the theater, warming the seat next to mine while the two of us— you and me—watch *Hamburg*."

Fred withdrew his hands from his pockets and reached into his briefcase. He then pulled out a large, spiral-bound notebook and flipped through its pages until he found two colorful eight-and-a-half-by-eleven-inch printouts.

"Blake, what I have here are two tickets. One for *you*..." Fred leaned over and handed one of the tickets to Blake. "...and one for *me*." Fred placed the second ticket on top of the clutter that concealed the top of his desk. "Unless, of course, you'd like to give Gigi a second chance. If that be the case, you can give *my* ticket to *her*."

Blake, assumed by everyone to be a confirmed bachelor—and that assumption, in his own mind, at least, reinforced by his recent and disastrous experience with Gigi—started to say something. But Fred—who, as usual, was loaded, cocked, and ready to pull the trigger—waved Blake off and resumed speaking before Blake could get his mouth open.

"Sorry, Blake, but I'll be hanged if I'm going to let you argue your way out of this one. Tonight, if I have to chain our ankles together, you are going to see *Hamburg*—and I intend for you to see *Hamburg*, in its entirety, from start to finish."

"Fred, have you not been *listening*?"

"Yes, Blake, I *have* been listening. So! I'll make a deal with you. I promise I will never say another word to you about *Hamburg* —or any other play—if you go with me tonight."

Ten hours later, Blake sank down into a deeply-cushioned, velvet-covered theater seat...scanned the program's synopsis of *Hamburg*...and opened the book he had smuggled into the theater —a book he had smuggled into the theater despite the fact Fred had demanded he leave it behind. Blake then turned to the page he had marked with an index card.

I can't believe I let Fred talk me into coming to a stupid play.

Blake began reading and, within a matter of seconds, became so lost in the text of his book he failed to notice the orchestra had begun playing the overture. He also failed to notice Ava Bechtel when she emerged from the wings and walked to the center of the stage. However, the moment the petite blond opened her mouth to sing her first note, Blake stopped reading mid-sentence, absentmindedly closed his book without marking his place, and stared spell-bound at the young starlet.

There's not an angel in heaven with a voice like that. Nor is there one so beautiful.

In an extreme case of love at first sight, thirty-two year old Blake Turner had been smitten by the twenty-six year old Ava Bechtel.

CHAPTER 6

The next morning, at eight o'clock sharp, Blake gently placed his coffee cup and briefcase in their customary locations atop his desk. He then sat down in his chair, centered his knees beneath the lap drawer, pulled himself forward, and logged onto his computer. He was so excited he gulped down three-fourths of his coffee in the time it took the network's agonizingly-slow login procedure to complete itself. The moment it did, he opened the web browser...searched for the theater's homepage...and scrolled down the screen until he located the phone number for the box office. After downing the last of his coffee in a single gulp, he reached for the phone and, without hesitation, dialed the theater's number. Though disappointed by the fact he got an impersonal, prerecorded message, he listened carefully to every word recited by the robotic, stone-cold voice, made note of the time the ticket office would open —eleven o'clock—and hung up the phone. A quick glance at his watch told him it was only ten minutes past eight...almost three hours before the ticket office would open.

Blake, normally an extremely patient person, was not about to wait three hours before reserving another ticket for *Hamburg.* He immediately typed in the online ticket-ordering address mentioned in the automated message...checked, and then double-checked, to make certain he had typed in the address correctly...and pressed "Enter."

When Fred arrived—fifteen minutes late, as usual—he found Blake staring at his computer screen, seemingly immersed in Balfour Chemical Company's digitized ledger. Something Fred did not notice—and something Blake made certain Fred did not see—

was the online ticket-ordering window that sat behind Balfour's ledger window. Blake made certain his accounting window always sat on top whenever there was even the slightest chance Fred might be watching. Only when he felt confident Fred was *not* watching did he toggle to the online ordering window and wade through the lengthy instructions and indecipherable legalese. Finally, after several frustrating minutes, he figured out how the site worked, reserved a seat for the next showing of *Hamburg*, and discreetly entered his credit card information—all while taking care to prevent Fred from realizing what he was doing.

And so it went for several weeks. Morning after morning, and day after day, Blake logged onto the Broadway ticket-ordering site, reserved a seat for the next showing of *Hamburg,* and made plans to attend. Each night *Hamburg* showed—from the moment Ava emerged from the wings and strode across the stage, throughout her performance, and throughout each and every curtain call—he stared spellbound, as if lost in a trance.

Blake reasoned Ava Bechtel, the young Broadway starlet, was far above and way beyond his league. Logic told him he would be lucky to get within ten feet of her, let alone close enough to speak to her. But that did not matter to Blake Turner, because he had fallen hopelessly, helplessly—and irreversibly—in love with Ava Bechtel.

CHAPTER 7

Each day, from the moment Blake awoke in the morning until he fell asleep at night, he could think of nothing but Ava. And each night, from the moment he fell asleep until his alarm awoke him the next morning, visions of Ava filled his dreams.

After several days of this, Blake became desperate to push Ava out of his mind...desperate to think of something other than her. He finally concluded the only way to get Ava *out* of his mind was to put someone else *into* his mind—and, he finally decided, the only way he could put someone else into his mind was to strike up a romantic affair with one of his office coworkers...provided that coworker's name did not start with the word *Gigi*.

Blake tried for more than a week—he tried *hard*—to imagine himself dating one of the unmarried women in his office building. However, no matter how hard he tried, he failed to cultivate amorous feelings towards any of them. Time and time again he pictured himself taking this woman or that woman out on a date; and, time and time again, whenever he tried to picture himself with this woman or that woman, he saw, not one of their faces, but the lovely face of Ava Bechtel.

In the end, Blake came to one conclusion: No matter how hard Blake-the-dreamer tried, he could care for no one but Ava-the-actress. And yet, Blake-the-realist—and Blake-the-ever-calculating-accountant—knew dreaming of something so unobtainable as the most popular starlet on Broadway was a total and complete waste of his time.

Common sense told Blake he could never be with Ava, and yet he thought about her all day long, every day of the week. During the day, Ava existed only as an imaginary vision inside his mind. Each evening, however, she became the actual flesh-and-blood Ava Bechtel that Blake Turner could see with his eyes and hear with his ears.

Each night, from the time Ava emerged from the theater's wings, walked to the center of the stage, and opened another showing of *Hamburg,* Blake stopped daydreaming about her and, for two and half hours—two and a half *blissful* hours—savored each and every moment of another opportunity to see Ava, not as an ephemeral image conjured up by a vivid imagination, but as the real, live, living-and-breathing Ava Bechtel.

Blake again tried—and again failed—to develop amorous feelings toward some of the unmarried women in the Wexler Tower. He finally admitted defeat, immersed himself in spreadsheets during work hours, and buried himself in books and magazines during off hours.

Perhaps, if I keep my mind occupied with things that have nothing to do with Ava, I'll divert my thoughts away from her...away from women in general...and down a totally different—and infinitely more productive—avenue.

In the end, regardless of what Blake did, his efforts to divert his thoughts from Ava proved fruitless. No matter how many times he tried, and no matter how *hard* he tried, he simply could not break free from the deeply-worn rut of his daily routine.

Each morning, he climbed out of bed...

And began thinking about Ava.

He got ready for work...

While thinking about Ava.

He drove to work...

While thinking about Ava.

He resisted going to *SpeedyOnlineTickets.com...*

While thinking about Ava.

He surrendered to the urge and ordered another ticket...

While thinking about Ava.

He went to the library to get a new book...

While thinking about Ava.

He rode a train to Broadway...

While thinking about Ava.

He waited in line for the theater to open...

While thinking about Ava.

He stepped inside the theater...

While thinking about Ava.

He went to his seat and read his book...

While thinking about Ava.

He sat spell-bound for two-and-a-half hours...

While worshiping Ava.

He rode a train to his car...

While thinking about Ava.

He drove to his apartment...

While thinking about Ava.

He swore he would never again see *Hamburg*...

While thinking about Ava.

He tossed and turned all night long...

While dreaming about Ava.

And he awoke the next morning...

Began another day...

And swore, for the millionth time...

He would stop thinking about Ava.

While thinking about Ava.

And so it went all day. Every day. All day long. Regardless of what Blake did, and regardless of how hard Blake tried, he could not stop thinking about Ava. While at work, he found himself constantly glancing at the little clock in the lower-right-hand corner of his computer screen, as if doing so would make five o'clock—and, three hours after that, the next showing of *Hamburg*—arrive sooner. And, invariably, on the days *Hamburg* showed, when five o'clock finally arrived, he made a quick visit to the library, rode the train to Broadway, stood in line while waiting for the doors to open, entered the theater, walked to his seat, and spent two and a half hours watching *Hamburg*.

And worshiping Ava.

CHAPTER 8

Ever since the first grade, Blake Turner had been passionate about one thing and one thing only: The Written Word. He now found himself passionate about *two* things.

The Written Word.

And Ava Bechtel.

Though not in that order.

When Blake first attended Ava's performances, he arrived at the theater mere moments before the doors opened, calmly located his seat, and waited patiently for Ava to emerge from the wings. However, as the days stretched into weeks, and his passion for Ava continued to grow, he changed his nightly routine.

Only on Mondays, the one night *Hamburg*'s theater remained dark, did Blake's life remain as it had always been. He rose from his desk at precisely five o'clock PM, left the Wexler Tower, enjoyed a sandwich at a local deli, walked to the library, sat down at one of its long, shiny tables, and placed at least one book—and sometimes two or three books—directly in front of him. And there he would sit, lost in the depths of his books, until one of the librarians tapped him on the shoulder to let him know all the other readers had gone home and it was time to lock the doors.

However, on all the other nights...

On the nights *Hamburg*'s lights shined brightly...

On the nights actors and actresses performed on its stage...

Blake did things quite differently.

He still rose from his desk and left the Wexler Tower at precisely five o'clock PM, and he still wolfed down a sandwich at a local deli on his way from the Wexler Tower to the library, but he remained in the library only as long as it took to return one or two of the books he had checked out on a previous visit, and to check out one or two more. He then left the library, boarded a train, and went to the theater. However, unlike in the past when he had timed each night's arrival with the opening of the theater's doors, he now arrived well in advance, concealed himself in the shadows behind the theater, and just stood there, often for what seemed an eternity, while waiting for Ava's taxi to arrive. And when Ava's taxi *did* arrive, he *continued* standing there, as if hypnotized, staring at her as she—accompanied, as always, by Jack Smith—climbed out of her taxi, waved to her fans, walked across the sidewalk, ascended the stairs, and disappeared through the theater's back door. Only when Ava's fans began moving toward the front of the theater did Blake step from the shadows, merge with the crowd, and take his place in one of the long lines waiting to go inside.

And finally, after the show ended each night and Blake felt there would be no more curtain calls, he again merged with the crowd, returned to the back of the theater, and concealed himself in the same shadows in which he had concealed himself earlier. There, once again trembling with anticipation, he waited for one final glimpse of the beautiful Ava Bechtel as she—accompanied, as always, by Jack Smith—emerged from the theater's back door, descended the stairs, waded through the mob of groping and screaming fans, and climbed into a taxi.

A taxi that would take her away from the theater...

Away from the noise and confusion...

And, Blake assumed, to the quiet privacy of her home or apartment.

Despite all these changes in Blake's life, one thing...one *critical* thing...remained absolutely constant. Day in and day out, whether *Hamburg* showed or did not show, Blake never went anywhere—not even to work—without one of his precious books. He never missed an opportunity to read something, even if that opportunity spanned but one or two minutes. No matter where he was, and no matter what he was doing—whether riding the train to or from Broadway...standing in line while waiting to enter the theater...or sitting in his seat while waiting for *Hamburg* to begin, the Intermission to end, or Act Two to begin—the important thing was, regardless of where Blake happened to be, and regardless of what Blake happened to be doing, he never missed an opportunity to read something.

Actually, there was one exception...

One time, and one time only...

When Blake's books and spreadsheets were far from his mind.

The two and a half hours *Hamburg* was underway.

During those moments—those treasured moments in which the lovely Ava Bechtel graced the stage with her presence—Blake Turner morphed into an entirely different person and his ever-present book lay closed and forgotten in his lap, because never, *not even once*, did Blake Turner miss an opportunity to admire the beautiful blond goddess from Berlin. Never, *not even once*, did Blake Turner miss an opportunity to listen to the golden tones that rolled off Ava Bechtel's tongue.

Blake's passion for Ava could find no bounds.

It grew stronger and stronger each and every day.

Until...

On one of the nights *Hamburg* showed...

His passion grew so strong he could no longer stand it.

On that night, instead of leaving his car parked in the deck where it had been sitting all day long, he braved the heavy New

York City traffic, drove to Broadway, and circled the block time and time again until he found an open parking space within sight of the theater's back door. He then parked his car, walked to the back of the theater, and concealed himself in the shadows—exactly as he had done for weeks on end.

And when Ava's taxi arrived, Blake *again* did as he had done for weeks on end. He just stood there, staring at Ava as she—accompanied, as always, by Jack Smith—waded through the crowd, ascended the steps, and disappeared through the theater's back door. And Blake *continued* standing there, and *continued* staring at the back door, for several long seconds.

Finally, after emerging from his trance, Blake stepped from the shadows, merged with the crowd, walked to the front of the theater, and waited in line with all the other patrons until an usher opened the doors and allowed everyone to go inside. Once inside, he referred to his ticket, located his seat-for-the-evening, watched *Hamburg* from start to finish, and applauded Ava's performance until certain there would be no more curtain calls.

On any other night, Blake would have calmly exited the theater, walked around the corner, and concealed himself in the same shadows in which he had concealed himself earlier. But this was not any other night. This was *this* night, and on *this* night Blake did something new. Something different. Something he had never done before. He walked straight to his car, climbed inside, and waited for Ava to exit the theater's back door. He then watched her as she—*accompanied, as always, by Jack Smith*—waded through her throng of screaming and groping fans, gave them a final wave, and climbed into a taxi.

Blake turned the key, started the engine, and, in an effort to control his eagerness, drummed the fingertips of both hands on the steering wheel while staring at Ava's taxi. He watched Ava slide across the seat...watched Jack climb in behind her...and watched the taxi pull away from the curb.

Only then did Blake switch on his headlights, shift his transmission into drive, pull out of his parking space, and merge with the traffic. He cautiously followed Ava's taxi, always remaining close enough to keep it in sight, yet lagging far enough behind so as not to attract the driver's attention. Several blocks—and several turns—later, Blake, along with the car that filled the space between his car and Ava's taxi, got stopped by a red light. Angered by the fact he had no choice but to wait for the light to turn green, he balled his hands into fists and pounded the steering wheel.

Meanwhile, Ava's taxi proceeded down the next block.

Just when Blake thought he would lose sight of Ava's taxi, its driver double-parked in front of an apartment building. Jack and Ava climbed out, Jack pulled out his wallet, paid the driver, and the taxi pulled away.

Meanwhile, Blake's traffic light remained red.

And he, along with the car in front of him, had no choice but to continue sitting there while watching Ava's taxi motor away.

But Blake no longer cared where Ava's taxi was going.

Because, now, he knew where Ava Bechtel lived.

Blake's light finally turned green. To avoid detection, he pulled into a vacant parking space, shut down the engine, and turned off the lights. He then watched as Jack and Ava—who had paused a moment to speak to some friends—ascended the steps that led to the apartment building's entrance. Upon reaching the landing outside the door, Ava stepped aside and waited patiently while Jack reached inside his pocket, removed a key, and unlocked the door.

Blake was elated!

Because, now, he knew where Ava Bechtel lived!

Blake's elation quickly died the moment he saw Jack return the key to his pocket. *His* pocket. He did *not* give the key to Ava.

Because the key belonged to Jack.

Blake looked away, hoping, by doing so, it would lessen his pain. However, unable to resist the compulsion to continue watching, he again looked in Jack and Ava's direction.

What he saw next made his blood boil.

Jack had opened the door, and was holding it open while waiting for Ava to enter the building. However, instead of closing the door and walking away, Jack followed Ava inside...and the door closed behind them. Blake pursed his lips so tightly, and squeezed the steering wheel so firmly, that both his lips and his knuckles turned white as snow.

Thus began a new and sinister chapter in Blake Turner's life. From that night on, whether *Hamburg* showed or its theater remained dark, he drove to Jack and Ava's apartment. On some nights, he got lucky and found a parking space within view of their apartment. However, on most nights, he found it necessary to park his car two or three blocks away and walk to a secluded spot that provided a good view. And, every night, regardless of where he parked, and regardless of whether he sat inside his car or stood in a secluded spot, he stared at Jack and Ava's windows until they turned off all their lights, hoping, always hoping, to get one final glimpse of the beautiful Ava Bechtel before returning to his own apartment.

CHAPTER 9

Blake had never gotten close enough to Ava speak to her. And yet, each time he saw her, even if only from a distance—even if he saw nothing more than a fleeting glimpse of her shadow on a closed curtain—he experienced an indescribable feeling of euphoria. But that feeling of euphoria seldom lasted more than a second or two.

Because Jack Smith was always...*always*...at Ava's side.

Jack and Ava seemed inseparable. They rode together in the same taxi. They walked together when entering the theater. And they walked together when leaving the theater. They usually walked hand-in-hand—which was bad enough—but, sometimes, Ava clung to Jack, with her arm wrapped tightly around his waist, and his arm wrapped tightly, protectively...*and very possessively*...around her shoulders. Even the most casual observer could tell they were deeply, madly...*and totally*...in love with each other.

Without realizing it, Blake had become trapped in a strange paradox. The stronger his love grew for Ava, the more bitter and jealous he became of Ava's love for Jack. And the more bitter and jealous he became of Ava's love for Jack, the stronger his love grew for Ava.

Perhaps, Blake thought, *if I got a chance to speak to Ava...a chance to profess my love to her....*

A short time later, a single, explosive event made it clear to Blake that that would never happen. Actually, what Blake perceived to be a single event was, in reality, the culmination of a *series* of events spread over a twenty-four hour period.

The first event started early one evening only moments after Blake walked to the back of the theater, stepped into the chamber-like space beneath the exterior staircase, and waited for Ava's taxi to arrive. As always, he felt safe there, as he believed himself to be invisible in the dark shadows. And, for all practical purposes, he *was* invisible.

But only to those who didn't know he was there.

Little did Blake know that, on that particular evening, Zane Stevens, Jack Smith's fellow actor, closest friend, and trusted confidant, just happened to be looking directly at the chamber when a flash of light reflected off the window of a passing car. For a fleeting instant, Blake's face lit up as brightly as if someone had beamed a spotlight on it. And then, just as suddenly, Blake's face vanished into the chamber's darkness.

But not the total darkness he believed it to be.

Blake's face remained visible, if only barely, to someone who knew it was there. And, on this particular night, Zane Stevens just happened to be the someone who knew it was there.

Blake had become so focused upon Ava he failed to notice he had been discovered by—and was being observed by—Zane's watchful eye. So, as usual, he continued staring at Ava as she climbed out of her taxi, wrapped the fingers of her right hand around the bicep of Jack's left arm, and followed him through the clamoring crowd. In the meantime, while Blake was observing Ava, Zane was observing Blake...and Zane *continued* observing Blake until Jack and Ava had climbed the steps, entered the theater's back door, and disappeared inside. So intently had Blake been focused upon Jack and Ava he never realized Zane had discovered him—and had observed him.

The second event occurred later that same evening during the showing of *Hamburg.* Though Zane appeared to be concentrating on his role in the musical, he was actually studying the mental photographs he had taken of Blake hiding in the shadows and staring at Ava. Not until *Hamburg* entered its closing minutes did Zane finally realize why those images bothered him.

Not once had Zane seen Blake exhibit the excited gaze of an ordinary fan adoring a popular star as she walked to and from the back door of a theater. On the contrary, Blake had exhibited the emotionless and crazed stare of a perverted stalker lusting after his prey.

The third event occurred later that same night, moments after the show—and the final curtain call—had ended. As usual, Blake blended in with the crowd, exited through the theater's front door, and, very calmly, so as not to draw attention to himself, eased around the corner, stepped into the dark shadows beneath the exterior staircase, and waited for Ava to appear.

Unknown to Blake, Zane had walked to the same spot from which he had observed him earlier and was now peering into the shadows to see if he was there. Blake, of course, *was* there, and, as usual, was so focused upon Ava he failed to notice Zane was observing him—and his reactions—while Jack and Ava emerged from the theater's back door, descended the steps, waded through the crowd, and climbed into a taxi.

It took Zane but a matter of seconds to realize his earlier analysis of Blake had been correct. Most significant of his observations was the fact Blake stared at Ava, not with the gaze of an ordinary fan, but with the crazed expression of a madman.

The fourth event began even later that same night as Zane lay in bed trying, with almost no success, to get some sleep. He *wanted* to get some sleep, but three things about Blake kept pounding away inside his skull.

The first two things were Blake's eyes, which, Zane realized, had been fixated upon Ava. Not merely fixated upon Ava, but *fixated,* both before, and after, the show.

And there was a third thing, something Zane could not quite put his finger on, yet something his intuition told him was of the utmost importance. He lay there for many hours—with his head on his pillow, his eyes closed, and sleep refusing to come—while comparing Blake's behavior to the behavior of Ava's other fans. Finally, as the sky glowed with the start of another day, Zane realized all of Ava's fans were animated. Some, more animated, and some, less animated, than others. All of Ava's fans did something. A few simply smiled as she walked past. Some cheered. Others waved. Many reached out in an attempt to touch her. Some pushed and clawed their way through the crowd, hoping to get a better view. And some, their view completely obstructed by the crowd in front of them, jumped up and down, hoping to get one or two precious glimpses of Ava as she walked past.

The important thing...*the key to everything*...was the fact, in one way or another, all *of Ava's fans were animated. They all did something.* Even those who simply stood in one place—as Blake had done—were animated if only because their faces beamed with warm smiles of admiration.

All of Ava's fans were animated.

All of them.

All...

Except...

One.

Blake Turner.

Zane repeatedly studied the indelible images of Blake stored within his mind. In each image, Blake stood absolutely motionless...as rigid as a brick wall. Blake's body never moved. And Blake's face never revealed the slightest hint of emotion.

And Blake's eyes!

Suddenly, Zane sat bolt upright in his bed.

Blake Turner had never blinked.

Not...even...once.

Zane spent the night's final hour lying flat on his back. Looking upwards. Staring at the ceiling. Thinking about Blake. Finally, as it neared the time for Zane's alarm to go off, he gave up all hope of getting more sleep, threw off his covers, and crawled out of bed. His mind was filled with disturbing images of Blake. Images that would remain in his thoughts all morning long. Images that made clear one critical fact.

Blake Turner had never blinked.

Not...even...once.

Zane immediately phoned Jack, and Jack agreed to meet for lunch in a small hole-in-the-wall diner two blocks from his and Ava's apartment. He and Zane ordered their lunch at the counter, found an unoccupied table, and sat down. Zane immediately set the fifth event—a long, detailed discussion about Blake—into motion.

Later that evening Jack set the sixth event into motion the moment he arrived at the theater. Immediately upon climbing out of his taxi, he peered into the dark shadows beneath the exterior staircase. Sure enough, there stood Blake, in the same, exact spot in which Zane had seen him the previous evening. Also, just as Zane had described to Jack, Blake stared so intently at Ava he failed to realize he had been discovered...and was being observed. Jack had been thoroughly briefed by Zane during their lunch-time discussion and knew exactly what to look for—several things, actually—and he found each of them.

Blake never took his eyes off Ava.

Blake seemed oblivious to the world around him.

Blake had the lust-filled expression of a stalker.

And...

The most important thing of all...

Blake Turner never blinked.

Not...even...once.

Jack could think of nothing but Blake throughout that night's performance. Finally, as the show neared its end, he came to the same conclusion to which Zane had come: Blake did not have the gaze of an ordinary fan; he stared at his prey with the crazed expression of a madman.

And...

The most important thing of all...

Blake Turner never blinked.

Not...even...once.

Following that night's performance, Jack set the seventh and final event—the one Blake perceived to be a single, explosive event—into motion. He went straight to the men's dressing room...changed out of his costume...stepped out into the hallway...and waited for Ava to emerge from the ladies' dressing room. The moment she did, he took her hand into his, led her down the long hallway to the theater's back door, put on a wide, crowd-pleasing smile, and opened the door.

To Ava and all of her fans, it seemed Jack would continue doing everything as he had always done it. He led Ava down the steps, escorted her through her throng of screaming fans, opened the taxi's back door, and waited patiently while she crawled inside. Jack then did something that took everyone completely by surprise.

Everyone, that is, except Zane.

Instead of waiting for Ava to slide across the seat to make room for him, Jack slammed the door, dispensed with his fake, theatrical smile, spun away from the taxi, and sprinted across the sidewalk, straight toward the dark shadows beneath the staircase. The surprised crowd watched in disbelief as Jack cut through their midst from one direction, and Zane knifed through their midst from another direction. And then, side by side, the two men dove into the shadows, grabbed Blake by his arms and neck, and slammed him face down onto the concrete.

Ava, unable to see the action from her seat inside the taxi, opened the door, climbed out, and pushed her way through the shocked crowd. And then, in equally-shocked disbelief, she watched, along with all the other spectators, as Jack dug one of his knees into Blake's spine, leaned over, and placed his mouth within an inch of Blake's ear. Jack then whispered something to Blake...whispered it so softly that even Zane, who knelt only a couple of feet away, could not hear what he said.

Blake, however, heard every word.

"If either Zane...or I...see you stalking Ava again, you'll suffer consequences considerably worse than simply being shoved off your feet and pinned to the pavement. I swear, we'll break every bone in your body."

The crowd, which had stood and stared in rapt silence during Jack and Zane's take-down of Blake, continued standing in rapt silence while Jack and Zane rose to their feet, dusted off their hands, and turned away from Blake. And then, as if nothing out of the ordinary had happened, Zane squared his shoulders, took a deep breath, and disappeared into the crowd in one direction while Jack switched off his angry scowl, turned on his fake, theatrical smile, grabbed Ava by the arm, and escorted her back to the taxi.

Jack calmly opened the taxi's back door, waved goodbye to the stunned crowd, and gave Ava a nudge—along with a meaningful glance and a theatrical roll of his eyes toward the door—to let her know it was time for her to climb inside. He waited until she did so, then crawled in behind her and pulled the door shut.

And, with that, Jack and Zane considered the Blake issue to be settled once and for all. But they were badly mistaken. In fact, never had either man been more wrong about anything. Their action had the exact opposite effect upon Blake they had hoped it would have. Instead of discouraging Blake, it increased his passion for Ava. Instead of filling Blake with fear, it increased his resentment of—and intense hatred for—Jack and Zane.

Especially Jack.

Jack and Zane's action also made Blake more determined than ever to arrive at the theater long before the start of each show, and to remain at the theater long after the end of each show, so he could watch Ava, the love of his life, as she arrived at, performed in, and departed from the theater. But Blake no longer bothered to conceal himself in the shadows in the dark chamber beneath the stairwell behind the theater, because he knew that would be the first place Jack, Zane, and anyone else who had witnessed his take-down would look. So, instead of hiding *from* the crowd, Blake became an actor in his own right by disguising himself with wigs, fake beards, fake mustaches, and fake eyebrows and blending in *with* the crowd.

Jack and Zane thought their attack on Blake had put an end to the issue. Ava did not. As far as she was concerned, the issue had barely begun. In the days and weeks that followed Blake's take-down, she became increasingly passionate about Blake. Not passionate about Blake himself, but passionate about her *fear* of Blake.

Blake had never said a word to Ava. In fact, he had never made a move, innocent or otherwise, in Ava's direction. And yet, almost overnight, Ava developed a deep-seated fear of the man, a fear so powerful it gripped her entire being, even when Jack or Zane —and sometimes both—were nearby to protect her.

Especially when they were not.

Each time Ava ventured outside her apartment, and each time she entered or exited the theater, she half-consciously, and half-subconsciously, searched the crowd for Blake's face. Of course, Ava never found Blake's face, because Blake always wore a disguise that made his face impossible to recognize. But there was one feature, one *critical* feature, of Blake's anatomy he could not disguise.

His crazed...

His possessed...

And his unblinking...

Eyes.

Blake tried to think of something he could do to hide his eyes. He briefly...*but only briefly*...considered wearing sunglasses. He put on a pair, took one glance at his reflection in a mirror, and realized they would make him stand out in a crowd, especially at night, as if illuminated by a bright spotlight.

On most nights, Ava spied Blake's eyes in the midst of the crowd. Each time she saw them her stomach muscles tightened, her pulse increased, and her pace quickened. Even on the nights she could *not* find Blake's eyes, she reacted the same way.

Because she knew Blake was there.

She could feel his presence.

CHAPTER 10

On the outside, Blake Turner appeared to be the same person he had always been. Monday through Friday, he sat side-by-side with Fred Johnson in their tiny office at the Wexler and Ferguson Accounting Agency, each man staring at his respective computer screen eight hours a day, five days a week. Eight full hours in Blake's case; somewhat less than eight hours in Fred's case.

During those eight hours, Blake appeared so focused upon the accounts displayed on his screen...and so oblivious to the world around him...that Fred accused him of becoming one with the microchips inside his computer. In fact, Blake *did* become oblivious to the world around him, but not because he was obsessed by his work; he was obsessed by Ava and, try as he might, he could not get her out of his mind.

Every afternoon, the moment five o'clock arrived, Blake continued doing as he had done for more than ten years. He tidied his desk, rode the elevator down to the lobby, bought a newspaper on his way out of the Wexler Tower, grabbed a quick sandwich at a deli, and walked straight to one of New York City's many public libraries. Only on Monday nights, the nights *Hamburg* did not show, did he remain at the library, sitting alone and reading a book, until the library's closing time. On all the other nights, the nights *Hamburg did* show, he remained in the library only as long as it took to return one or more of the books he had finished reading, and to check out one or two more.

Blake's favorite library, and the one he frequented the most, was located less than two blocks from his office. He knew its every nook and cranny. Knew exactly where everything was. He even had a favorite table and a favorite chair. Of course, neither the table nor the chair had his name on it, and he never asked anyone to move to a different table or a different chair if they arrived before he did and were already using them. But, still, he always went straight to "his" table, and, if "his" chair remained unoccupied, he placed his books on "his" table, sat down in "his" chair, and claimed them for the remainder of the evening.

On the outside, Blake appeared to be the same Blake he had always been. On the inside, he no longer resembled that Blake at all. Accounting ledgers had kept his mind fully occupied eight hours a day, five days a week, for more than ten years. However, from the moment he first saw Ava perform, his accounting ledgers—and the numbers within those ledgers—had captured his attention for no more than one or two minutes at a time. To Fred or anyone else who entered their office, he appeared to be totally absorbed by those numbers...but his mind was somewhere else. As a result, both the quantity and the quality of his work suffered greatly.

Blake's passion for reading also suffered. In the past, the words in his newspapers, books, and magazines had reached out, grabbed him, and pulled him inside. His mind had become so focused upon the text in those newspapers, books, and magazines that he literally flew through their pages. But now, he found it necessary to plod through the paragraphs, often reading each sentence time and time again in an effort to comprehend its content and the meaning of its words. For as long as Blake could remember, columns of numbers had occupied his mind during work hours, and line after line of printed words had dominated every spare minute of his nights and weekends. But now, regardless of where he happened to be, and regardless of what he happened to be doing, he could think of one thing, and one thing only.

Ava Bechtel.

CHAPTER 11

Blake decided the time had come to purge Ava from his mind. Time to turn the page and move on to the next chapter of his life. So, he stopped going to the theater, made a serious attempt to concentrate on nothing but his work during the day, and spent his nights and weekends reading newspapers, books, and magazines.

Blake's efforts proved futile.

Regardless of where he happened to be, and regardless of what he happened to be doing, day after day, night after night, weekend after weekend, and week after week he constantly saw Ava's angelic face and heard Ava's angelic voice. So, he worked even harder during the day, and read harder than ever during nights and weekends.

But, again, regardless of how hard Blake tried, his efforts proved futile. It didn't matter where he happened to be, or what he happened to be doing, he simply could not fill his mind with anything but thoughts and images of Ava Bechtel.

Until...

Finally...

After several weeks of trying...

He succeeded.

Now, eight hours a day, Monday through Friday, he again focused all of his energy on his clients' spreadsheets. And now, night after night, weekend after weekend, he again became lost in the pages of his newspapers, books, and magazines. Every aspect of his life had returned to normal.

Or so it seemed.

Little did Blake know he had become a key player in a strange paradox. In the very moment he tamed his all-consuming passion for Ava, she teetered on the brink of a nervous breakdown because of her all-consuming fear of him. In the very moment Blake relegated thoughts of Ava to a dark and all-but-forgotten corner of his mind, thoughts about him took center stage in her mind.

It was in that pivotal moment that a strange event, foreseen by neither Blake nor Ava, brought them face to face. *Literally* face to face. Neither had imagined such an event could take place. As a result, neither was prepared for it.

The event occurred late on a Monday night, just before the library's closing time. The last thing Blake wanted to do was disturb those sitting nearby, so he took extra care to lift his chair instead of sliding its legs across the floor. He then carefully moved the chair away from the table, rose to his unimpressive five-foot seven-inch height, and did his equally unimpressive he-man pose to stretch the stiffness, caused by two and a half hours of sitting in an unpadded, straight-back chair, from his spine and shoulders.

Blake then leaned over the table, closed the reference book from which he had been taking notes, picked the book up, and walked to the far side of the room where thousands of books filled row after row of twenty-foot-long shelves. He stepped between two rows and returned the book from which he had been taking notes to the same spot on the same shelf from which he had removed it two and a half hours earlier. He carefully adjusted the book so it sat in perfect alignment with the books on either side of it. He then took one step back and glanced in both directions to see if any of the other books needed to be straightened. Finally, satisfied all was in order, he turned away and walked toward his chair.

But Blake stopped walking long before he reached the end of the row. Something—something that should have been a subtle event but would prove to be just the opposite—had captured his attention.

A second or two later, Blake heard it again: the sound of a disgruntled voice coming from the far side of the shelving unit that sat to his left. Intrigued by the tonal qualities of the voice—and sympathetic with the obvious frustration of whoever had spoken— he turned to face the shelf, bent his knees ever so slightly to lower his head a couple of inches, and peered through the narrow gap created by the tops of the books on one shelf and the bottom of the shelf sitting above them. There, directly in front of him, unaware she was being observed by Blake, stood a young, plainly dressed, black-headed woman.

Blake's first impulse was to pay as little attention to the woman as he possibly could. In fact, reason told him he had already paid far more attention to her than he should have. However, when she again complained under her breath—thus removing any doubt as to her frustration by not being able to find a particular book— Blake decided to offer his assistance. He rose to his full height, walked to the end of the bookshelf, rounded the corner, and, with a sincere yet humble air of confidence born of an in-depth knowledge of the library, approached the young woman.

Ava instantly recognized the eyes of the crazed and perverted madman who had been stalking her for the past several weeks. Acting purely on instinct, she spun away from Blake and broke into a run—only to find her escape route blocked by bookshelves on either side of her, a huge, heavily-laden book cart in front of her, and Blake behind her. Had Blake set a trap for her? With no route of escape—and believing Blake had intentionally cornered her—she inhaled deeply, spun around to face him, and opened her mouth to scream.

But Ava never made a sound.

Because Blake had seen through her disguise, had already started backing away from her, and was holding both hands out in front of him in a palms-outward gesture meant to calm her fears.

And it worked.

Almost.

Ava was, indeed, comforted by the increased gap between herself and Blake. And she did believe, for the moment at least, Blake no longer posed a threat to her. But she remained tense...continued taking rapid, heavy breaths...and continued backing away from him.

Until she bumped against the book cart and could go no farther.

Ava stared at Blake a moment, then spun away from him, leaned her shoulder against the heavily-laden cart, and gave it a powerful shove. The cart moved, just as she had hoped it would. But it moved only a few inches. The bump she had given it moments earlier had dislodged the stack of books sitting on its top shelf and sent several of those books toppling to the floor. Two of those books were now wedged underneath the cart's wheels....the wheels on the side of the cart farthest away from Ava...the same wheels that lay a few tantalizing inches beyond her reach.

Ava gave the cart a second, and more powerful shove, hoping to force its wheels over the books. Her spirits rose when the cart moved, then crashed when she realized the cart had moved but a fraction of an inch and would move no farther.

Ava gave the cart a third shove.

This time, the cart did not move at all.

She was trapped.

With shelves on either side...

The cart in front of her...

And Blake behind her.

Ava spun away from the cart and stared at Blake.

And Blake stared back.

But Blake's stare was not a cold stare. In fact, it was just the opposite. A warm smile spread across his face, and he spoke to Ava in a soft, soothing voice. After all, the last thing he wanted to do was upset his beloved Ava more than he had already upset her.

"I'm sorry, Miss Bechtel. Please forgive me. I did not mean to alarm you. *Honest* I didn't. In fact, for a moment there, I didn't even recognize you. I simply thought you were someone looking for a book and thought I might help you find it."

Ava remained motionless.

Paralyzed with fear.

Unable to breathe.

Unable to move.

She just stood there, frozen in place, staring at Blake. And Blake, not sure of what, if anything, he should do, continued his clumsy effort to make conversation.

"I, uh, I know my way around this place. So...if, uh...if I can be of any help..."

Ava never answered Blake. Nor did she wait for Blake to finish his sentence. Instead, she spun around to face the cart, selected a heavy book from its top shelf, and spun around again to face Blake. After pausing only as long as it took to take careful aim, she threw the book directly at Blake's face.

Acting purely on instinct, Blake raised his hands to protect himself from the book. A fraction of a second later, he leaned to one side in an effort to avoid the book altogether. And then, after another fraction of a second, it occurred to him the book's fall to the floor might crease its pages—or, even worse, damage its spine —so he attempted to catch it.

Blake's attempt to catch the book failed. If anything, it only served to increase the book's velocity on its downward plunge toward the floor. He stared at the open book, which now lay face down and bent backwards in the ninety degree angle formed by the floor and the base of the bookshelf. As he had feared, several of the book's pages were crumpled and creased, and it's spine had been irreparably damaged.

Ava shared none of Blake's concern about the book. She had only thought, by throwing the book directly at Blake's face, she might divert his attention long enough to escape the trap he had set for her. With that thought in mind, she broke into a run before the book left the tips of her fingers.

Blake glanced at Ava as she bolted past...glanced down at the damaged book...and then watched, in confused disbelief, as Ava sprinted across the room and vanished into a stairwell.

Ava never looked back. She never even glanced over her shoulder to see if Blake had followed her. Instead, she descended the stairs two-steps-at-a-time, dashed across the lobby, emerged onto the sidewalk, and ran as fast as she could until two city blocks lay between herself and the library.

CHAPTER 12

Fate had finally given Blake a chance to speak to his beloved Ava. In fact, h*e had* spoken to Ava...and she had not said a single word in return. She had not needed to. Her actions alone had made it quite clear to Blake she both feared and despised him.

Ava Bechtel had totally...

Entirely...

And completely...

Rejected Blake Turner.

For the first time in his life, Blake knew the true meaning of what it meant to be heartbroken. Simply going through the motions of his daily routine seemed more than he could bear. But bear his routine he must. And bear his routine he did.

The next morning, as he had always done, Blake listened to his kitchen radio while cooking and eating a hot breakfast. He listened to another radio while shaving and taking a shower...another radio while putting on his clothes...and yet another radio while driving to work. He listened attentively—more attentively than usual—hoping the music and the news would divert his thoughts from Ava.

But Blake's efforts proved futile.

No matter what he did, and no matter how hard he tried, the perfectly-focused image of Ava Bechtel's face remained constantly in the forefront of his mind. He found it impossible to concentrate on anything but her. Even at his office, where he tried to concentrate on the intricate spreadsheets and colorful ledgers that filled his computer screen, his thoughts repeatedly turned to Ava.

After several days of this, Blake resorted to something he had always avoided during work hours. He opened additional windows on his computer screen—windows that had nothing to do with his job—hoping, by shopping online, going to various news sites, and researching various topics in which he had an interest, he could fill his mind with something—*anything*—other than Ava.

At first, Blake's efforts were as fruitless as they had been in the past. Time and time again he glanced at his watch to discover he had been staring blindly at his computer screen, sometimes for as long as ten minutes, totally oblivious to the text, numbers, and graphics displayed before him while daydreaming about Ava.

Blake hoped evenings and weekends would bring relief, but evenings and weekends proved just as bad, if not even worse, than mornings and weekdays. No matter what he did, no matter where he did it, and no matter *when* he did it—day, night, weekday, or weekend—he could think of nothing but Ava. Even his favorite pastime—sitting alone while reading a book, his eyes moving back and forth across row after row of precisely-arranged text—proved incapable of diverting his thoughts from Ava. Time and time again, he scanned coal-black letters printed on snow-white pages. And, time and time again, he saw, not coal-black letters, and not snow-white pages, but the cream-colored face and silky-blond hair of Ava Bechtel.

Even sleep failed to liberate Blake's mind from thoughts about Ava. Seven nights a week, from the moment his head hit the pillow until his alarm awoke him the next morning, he either lay in his bed staring into the darkness while thinking about Ava, or tossing and turning while dreaming about Ava.

A few of Blake's dreams were blissful, but most were nightmares. *Recurrent* nightmares. Nightmares that held him captive while forcing him, over and over, to relive the moment in which fate had given him an opportunity to speak to Ava, only to be flatly, totally, and unequivocally rejected.

For two long weeks—day after day, and night after night—Blake forced himself to go through his daily routine. Each time Ava entered his mind he tried to think of something else—*anything* else—in an effort to push her out of his thoughts. At first, mere seconds passed from the time he stopped thinking about her until he thought about her again. But, finally, as days became weeks, he found it easier to think of other things...easier to concentrate on his work...easier to comprehend the text in his books.

Until...

Late one night...

As he sat in the library...

Totally lost in the text of one of his books...

At a moment when Ava was nowhere *near* his thoughts, let alone *in* his thoughts...

A young, red-headed woman dressed in a baggy, light-blue sweatsuit...

A sweatsuit that tried, but failed, to conceal the graceful curves of her petite body...

Walked across the room, placed her hands on the chair to the right of Blake's chair...

Quietly slid the chair out from under the table...

And sat down beside him.

Blake glanced briefly at the young woman...returned his attention to the book he had been reading...gave the woman another brief glance...and, once again, returned his attention to his book. He then cursed himself—not out loud, but inside his mind—and gave himself a mental tongue-lashing.

I can't believe this! I've tried so hard to stop thinking about

Ava—and thought I had succeeded—only to let this young woman's presence cause me to think about her again.

A vivid image of Ava's face filled Blake's thoughts. After resisting the temptation until he could no longer stand it, he turned his head to the right and took another look at the young woman. Moments earlier, he had given the woman only the briefest of glances. This time, however, he allowed his eyes to linger on her eyes...gave her a polite smile...and followed the smile with a nod of his head to acknowledge the presence of a kindred, book-loving spirit.

And then, Blake returned his eyes to his book.

However, no matter how hard he tried, he could not bring the book's text into focus.

Because his mind was focused elsewhere.

Focused on a mental image of Ava Bechtel's beautiful face.

Blake closed his eyes, smiled, chuckled softly, and gave a barely perceptible shake of his head.

I honestly thought I could stop thinking about Ava. And yet, here she is...dominating my every thought...transporting me to a different time...taking me to a different place.

For a moment, Blake forgot he was in a library...forgot he was staring at a book..and forgot a beautiful young woman had just sat down beside him. He struggled to pull his mind back to the present...struggled to focus his eyes on the text in his book. However, no matter how hard he tried, he could not stop thinking about Ava.

Blake again closed his eyes. He then rubbed his face and forehead with the palms of both hands, as if doing so would purge the vivid image of Ava's beautiful face from his mind.

But Ava's image refused to leave.

So Blake gave up, opened his eyes, and stared at the blurred pages of his book. He made another attempt—another *futile* attempt—to rearrange the blurred, jumbled, and senseless text into meaningful words.

Finally, after several failed attempts, Blake won the battle. He looked beyond Ava's image...brought the blurred text into focus...rearranged the jumbled letters...and, once again, became lost in the words of his book...so lost he completely forgot about Ava...completely forgot about the beautiful young woman that had sat down...*and was still sitting down...*in the chair next to his.

And yet, despite the fact Blake's conscious mind had stopped thinking about Ava, his subconscious mind knew she still existed. His subconscious mind also knew, despite the fact his conscious mind was trying to ignore the young woman who sat beside him, *she* still existed.

If Blake had paid more attention to the woman he would have noticed two important things. First, she had not placed anything on the table—no books...no magazines...*nothing*—because she had not come to the library to read a book or a magazine; she had come to the library to read Blake Turner's face. And second, after the woman had been sitting there a few minutes...and after she had carefully analyzed everything about Blake—*especially Blake's eyes*—she spoke to him.

"Blake?"

The woman spoke Blake's name in a soft, timid whisper—so soft, and so timid, Blake's preoccupied mind failed to register, not only the fact someone had spoken to him, but the fact someone had spoken his name.

The young woman again sat in silence, and again studied every detail of Blake's face.

Especially Blake's eyes.

She finally gathered up her courage, slid her chair a few inches closer to Blake's chair, and repeated his name. Only, this time, she spoke his name in a louder voice...a firmer voice...a voice filled with confidence.

"Blake!"

It took a couple of seconds, but Blake's mind finally registered the fact someone had spoken his name. He reluctantly pulled his mind out of his book, turned his head to the right, and stared blankly at the young woman.

Is it my imagination, or did she move her chair closer to mine?

Blake stared at the woman a few seconds, wondering how a stranger, someone he had never met, could possibly know his name. And then, when a tendril of blond hair snaked out from under the young woman's red wig, Blake studied her more closely.

And noticed more details.

Including the fact she had blond, not red, eyebrows.

Blake finally saw through the young woman's disguise.

"Ava?"

Blake's eyes opened wider and wider...his jaw dropped lower and lower...and he found himself at a total loss for words. He could only sit there, staring at Ava with his eyes agape, and his mouth wide open.

Meanwhile, Ava also sat there, intensely studying Blake's face.

Especially Blake's eyes.

And she said nothing.

It finally occurred to Blake he probably appeared dim-witted. He certainly *felt* dim-witted. He snapped his mouth shut, swallowed hard, and blinked his eyes a few times while trying to think of something to say. Finally, after a moment of thought, he managed a lame effort at conversation.

"Did you, uh, did you find what you...um...what you were looking for the other night?"

Blake sat right next to Ava—barely one inch separated their shoulders—and he could think of nothing to say. And, to make matters worse, Ava said nothing to him.

She just sat there.

Silent.

Motionless.

And strangely calm.

Blake continued staring at Ava.

And Ava continued studying Blake.

Especially Blake's bright blue eyes.

Ava finally decided they were not the eyes of the perverted stalker Jack and Zane had led her to believe he was.

Blake, of course, had no way of knowing Ava's thoughts, so he made another lame attempt at conversation.

"I, uh, I come to all of your plays. Well, not *all* of them, but I come to most of them."

"Yes, I know," cooed Ava in a soft voice while continuing her study of Blake's eyes.

"I've, um, I've hardly missed a performance since the night I first saw you."

"Yes, I know," cooed Ava a second time.

Blake took note of the fact Ava remained strangely calm, in stark contrast to the way she had reacted during their disastrously-awkward encounter of two weeks previous. He also noticed she appeared amazingly relaxed, despite the fact she sat right next to the man she had, for so many months, feared more than any other.

Blake continued his clumsy attempt to make conversation.

"Are you sure I can't help you find something?"

Blake waited for an answer...got none...and continued making a fool of himself.

"I, uh, I know this place backwards and forwards, so I can, um, probably find what you, uh, what you were looking for. Even if I can't find it, I, uh, I know who to ask."

Ava did not answer.

She simply sat there.

Silent.

And motionless.

A full fifteen seconds passed while Ava continued her calm-but-intense evaluation of Blake. Finally, just when Blake was about to speak again, her lips curled into a sweet smile.

Blake felt a strange sensation in his chest.

And then, figuratively...and almost literally...his heart melted.

He tried to say something, but nothing came out.

He *wanted* to say something—and again *tried* to say something—but words refused to come. Ava finally rescued him from the long and awkward silence.

"Can we go some place more private? Some place we can talk?"

"Sure," breathed Blake, trying to think of somewhere they could go. "There's, um, there's a garden behind the library."

Then Blake remembered how frightened Ava had been the night he cornered her in the aisle between two rows of bookshelves.

"Unless you'd rather go downstairs and sit in the lobby. It's more public there, but we can still talk."

Ava gave Blake a comfortable smile.

"No. The garden will be fine."

Ava's German accent excited Blake in a way it had never

excited him before.

"Uh, just, um, follow me," he stammered.

Blake slid his chair back from the table, and then rose to his feet. One minute later he led Ava into the garden, a garden in which he had sat and read hundreds, if not thousands, of times. He knew every square inch of it. Without wavering, he led Ava to a secluded...*and very private*...alcove. Sheltered inside the alcove were two small benches. Blake indicated on which bench Ava should sit...waited until she sat down...and then sat down directly across from her on the other bench. For almost a minute they just sat there, quietly staring at each other, Blake in utter disbelief that Ava had sought him out, and Ava continuing her evaluation of Blake. Finally, after another long and awkward silence—awkward for Blake, anyway—Ava broke the ice.

"I suppose you would like an explanation as to why I have come to the library in search of you."

"On the contrary, Ava. *I'm* the one who owes *you* an explanation. I at least owe you an apology."

"*You*?"

A perplexed expression replaced Ava's sweet smile.

"But *why*? What have *you* done that requires an explanation? What have *you* done that deserves an apology?"

"Well, the other night, for example, when I frightened you here in the library. I *swear*, Ava, I would never intentionally do anything to frighten you. You're the last person on Earth I would want to hurt."

"I *know* that, Blake!"

Ava punctuated her statement, first with a slight nod...then with a comfortable smile...and, finally, with a seductive tilt of her head accompanied by a long sigh.

Blake stared at Ava a few moments, still grappling with the fact she had come to the library, not to read a book, but to read him. He then pressed for more information.

"Ava, If all you say is true, why did you run away from me the other night?"

Though Blake did not mean to, he posed his question in such a manner, and with such a tone of voice, that it became clear to Ava her reaction to him on their previous encounter had hurt him deeply.

"I was frightened."

Ava looked directly into Blake's eyes and waited until he looked directly into hers.

"But that was *then*, Blake. I am not frightened *now.* As you Americans would say, I did my homework."

"You did your homework? I don't quite follow you."

"Jack and Zane convinced me you were stalking me. My deplorable behavior on the night we encountered each other inside the library was based on that belief. However, during the days following our encounter, I spent considerable time reflecting upon that moment and decided I should learn more about you. At first, I had no idea where to start. But, later, when I recalled how you so willingly...and so confidently...offered your assistance, I came to the conclusion you worked here. It took me until today to get brave enough to return. In fact, I arrived early this morning, just after the library opened, hoping to get a chance to speak to you. I roamed all over the building looking for you. Finally, when one of the librarians asked if she could assist me in finding something, I told her I was not looking for some *thing;* I was looking for some *one.* Even before I finished describing you, she knew who I was talking about. She told me your name.... It is Blake Turner. Yes? She then explained to me you do not work here, but come here almost every night of the week. And then, she told me something very odd. She said you also come here on weekends...*but only if the weather is bad.* You spend your weekends somewhere else when the weather is good."

"I, uh, I'd never really thought about it, but, yes, I, um, I suppose that's true."

Blake wanted to shrivel up and disappear. Ava...his beloved Ava...had come to the library, not to read a book, but to read *him*...to sit face to face with *him*...to talk to *him*...and all he could do was stutter and stammer and say things like, "I suppose that's true." Ava smiled, but said nothing more. A few moments later, when Blake realized Ava was waiting for additional details, he felt obliged to give her an explanation.

"Reading is, um, one of my hobbies."

Blake paused a moment, painfully aware Ava had noticed his stuttered uhs, stammered ums, and lame responses.

"In which genre are you most interested?" she asked calmly.

Blake raised his eyebrows. Earlier, Ava had impressed him by using the relatively-complex English word 'deplorable'." Now, she impressed him even more by using the word 'genre'.

But, then again, genre is a European word...not an English word...so it shouldn't surprise me at all.

Blake cleared his throat, and then, hoping Ava had not noticed his surprise, answered her question.

"It varies."

Without realizing it, Blake had begun to feel comfortable talking to Ava, mainly because their discussion had moved to one of his favorite topics. He was now able to speak in a stronger voice, and his words flowed freely and smoothly, with no more uhs, and no more ums.

"Sometimes, I get lost in fiction. I'll read something by a novelist, find I like his or her work, and read almost non-stop until I've read everything he or she has written. At other times, I find myself interested in a particular topic, a specific place, or a period in history, and read everything I can find about it. Lately, I've been interested in technical topics. To be more specific, I've been reading about whales, ships, boats, navigation, radar, engines..."

Blake smiled, embarrassed he had allowed himself to become selfishly carried away. He concluded, in an apologetic tone, by saying:

"My friends say I'm obsessed with the written word."

"Are you obsessed with *me*? Am I one of your '*hobbies*'?"

Ava's sudden...and painfully direct...line of questioning caught Blake completely off guard. He blushed, his face grew hot, and he looked away. A moment later, it occurred to him Ava seemed comfortable...*too* comfortable...as if determined to press home whatever point she was trying to make. He sat up straight, leaned out of the alcove, and craned his neck—first in one direction, and then the other—so he could study the garden's shadows.

"You do not need to worry, Blake."

Ava literally breathed the words in a soft, reassuring tone.

"I have not, as you Americans would say, set you up. Jack does not know I am here. And neither does his friend Zane."

Ava again spoke in a soothing tone, as if she had read Blake's innermost thoughts, understood his suspicions, and wanted to set his mind at ease.

"Zane would lecture me long and hard if he knew I had come to see you. As for Jack? He would rant and rave and pretend he wanted to kill me!"

Blake suddenly exploded.

"I haven't been stalking you, Ava!"

Blake blurted the words in an unmistakably hurt tone. His outburst surprised him as much as, if not even more than, it surprised Ava. He stared at her a moment, and then made an effort to recover from the awkward situation into which he had placed himself.

"Well...I guess...I suppose...*technically*...I *have* been stalking you. But I haven't meant anything by it. It's just...I just...well...I...."

Blake struggled for words, but none would come. Finally, words *did* come, and when he realized how comfortable he felt with what he was about to say, he relaxed a bit, and a big smile stretched across his face.

"Ava, you're the most wonderful actress I have ever had the pleasure of watching...you have the most beautiful voice I have ever heard...and...and...."

Blake's voice tapered off again, and he fell silent.

"And what, Blake?"

"Ava, you are the most beautiful woman I have ever seen."

Ava looked away, hoping Blake had not seen her blush. However, despite the garden's subdued, indirect lighting, Blake noted Ava's cream-colored face had turned several shades darker.

"How could a compliment like that embarrass someone like you? I'm willing to bet people say things like that to you all the time."

"Yes, they do. But most people who say such things have ulterior motives. You know? To get an interview...to get me to pose with them for a photograph...to get my autograph...to get *something*."

"I'll bet Jack tells you how wonderful and beautiful you are every day."

"No, not *every* day. Besides, it's *different* when Jack says it. Speaking of Jack!"

Ava suddenly stiffened and stood up.

"I should be going. I must not allow Jack to get suspicious."

Blake also stood up, and resisted the urge to reach out and take Ava by the hand. He wanted her to stay longer—wanted to take her into his arms, pull her body close to his, and give her a long, gentle kiss—and yet, he knew he had no choice but to let her go. Blake also knew that this, his first opportunity to speak to Ava, would probably be his last.

"Thanks for coming to see me, Ava."

"I am glad I did, Blake. In fact..."

Ava paused. And then, for the first time, as if embarrassed to reveal what was on her mind, she seemed unable to find the right words to express her thoughts.

"In fact, what?" asked Blake.

"I would like to see you again. That is, if you would like to see *me* again."

Blake's eyes opened wide...his mouth dropped open...and several seconds passed before he could speak again.

"Of *course* I would!"

It had been an exclamation—an explanation Blake wanted to shout to the world—but it came out of his mouth as little more than a squeaky whisper, his words barely audible. He and Ava agreed upon a time and place, and then Ava turned to leave. However, after taking only three steps, she stopped walking, hesitated a moment, and turned to face Blake.

"Blake, I need to say one more thing"

"Yes?"

"I do not mind you coming to see me perform. In fact, now

that I know you better, I look forward to seeing you in the audience. But please, Blake, *please* do not stand outside the theater waiting for me to arrive and leave. As you already know, Jack is terribly protective of me."

"Don't worry, Ava. Just knowing that, one week from now, I'll get another chance to be with you...to *sit* with you...and to *talk* with you..."

Blake finished his sentence, not with words, but with a smile and a sigh. Ava gave Blake a smile in return. And then, without further ado, she turned and walked away. Blake continued staring down the garden's rock-lined path—illuminated only by the soft, low-voltage lighting—long after Ava disappeared beyond the thick glass door that separated the library's dimly-lit garden from its brightly-lit lobby.

CHAPTER 13

Days came.

And days went.

And, with the passage of each day, Blake became more and more doubtful he would ever see Ava again. He just *knew* something would happen. Either Jack would discover Ava's plans, or Ava would get cold feet. Blake did not know *what* would happen, but he knew *something* would happen to prevent Ava from meeting him at the appointed time and the appointed place.

But Ava *did* meet Blake at the appointed time and the appointed place. In fact, she arrived long before he did. And she *continued* to meet Blake, week after week, and month after month, always arriving long before their agreed-upon time, and always remaining as long as she dared. Blake believed Ava looked forward to seeing him as much as he looked forward to seeing her. Of even more importance, he also believed their relationship grew stronger each time they met.

Blake and Ava did everything they could to keep their secret meetings a secret. First and foremost, they never met at the same place twice in a row. Sometimes, they met in a library. And, sometimes, they met at a secluded table in a coffee shop. But, usually, they met at one of Blake's favorite locations: the back corner of one of the many bookstores in New York City.

Ava always wore a disguise, a different disguise each time they met. Not to conceal her identity from Blake, but to enable her to go out in public without being recognized and mobbed by her fans. And, of even more importance, to avoid being followed by Jack or Zane.

However, despite their elaborate efforts, Blake and Ava were able to keep their secret affair a secret for only so long. When Jack suspected Ava had been sneaking out from under his watchful eye, he took immediate steps to confirm it. And, when he *did* confirm it —when he knew for a certainty Ava was, indeed, sneaking out—he confronted her and demanded she tell him the truth.

With Ava's secret revealed, she had no choice but to admit to Jack she had been spending time with Blake. She tried to explain herself to Jack, but Jack refused to listen. Like a fire-and-brimstone preacher, he lectured her long and hard about "the dangers of falling into that pervert's lair." Jack ended his lecture by insisting either he or Zane always accompany Ava whenever she stepped outside the apartment so at least one of them would be there to defend her from strangers. In closing, Jack made it absolutely clear to Ava he forbade her to see Blake again.

Blake, of course, had no way of knowing his and Ava's secret had been discovered. Nor did he have any way of knowing Jack had placed a twenty-four hour guard on Ava's every move. Unaware of these developments, his excitement continued to grow as the date and time of their next rendezvous drew near.

It seemed to take forever.

But...

Finally!

The date arrived.

And, as usual, Blake arrived fifteen minutes earlier than his and Ava's agreed-upon meeting time. And, as usual, Blake expected Ava to already be there.

But Ava was *not* there.

Fifteen minutes—and the appointed meeting time—came and went.

And still no Ava.

Blake continued waiting.

He waited thirty minutes.

Forty-five minutes.

An hour.

An hour and fifteen minutes.

Blake waited *another* fifteen minutes.

A full hour and a half beyond their appointed meeting time.

And still no Ava.

Hoping Ava had merely been delayed, Blake waited an additional thirty minutes.

A full two hours had passed beyond their agreed-upon meeting time.

And still no Ava.

A week went by. Two weeks. *Three* weeks. A full month passed and not once, during all that time, did Ava call Blake. Not once, during all that time, did Ava send Blake a text message. Why, he wondered, just *why*—when it seemed his and Ava's relationship as close friends had blossomed into something much greater—*why* had she stopped meeting him?

And why, Blake wondered, had Ava stopped communicating with him? Could she not call? Or send a text message?

Blake finally concluded Ava had gotten cold feet. But why*?* Did she no longer want to be with him? Did she feel they had become too serious about each other? Was she afraid to let their relationship advance to the next level? Or, even worse, had she become fearful of the damage a dead-end relationship with a nobody like Blake Turner might do to the career of a somebody like Ava Bechtel? Of all the possibilities, the fear that Ava had simply lost interest in him pained Blake the most.

Once again, Blake made a serious attempt to push Ava out of his mind. And, as before, his efforts fell miserably short of success. Whenever he tried to think about some *thing* or some *one* other than Ava, he only succeeded in thinking about her that much more. If he had only known the truth—that Jack had discovered his and Ava's secret relationship and taken steps to terminate it—he would not have blamed himself as the reason for their breakup. If he had only known the truth—how *desperately* Ava wanted to be with him...how *desperately* she wanted to call him and talk to him...and how *desperately* she wanted to send a text message to tell him where and when to meet....

Actually, Ava tried...*repeatedly* tried...but found it impossible to escape the watchful eyes of Jack, Zane, and all the others Jack and Zane had recruited to keep an eye on her.

Blake, of course, had no way of knowing the reason, the *true* reason, Ava had failed to meet him. He also had no way of knowing the reason Ava had cut off all communication with him. Unaware of the facts, he could only assume the worst: For whatever reason, Ava Bechtel, the highly popular actress from Berlin, Germany, had lost interest in Blake Turner, the shy, reclusive accountant from a small, nameless suburb of New York City.

Finally, after weeks and weeks of blaming himself for the death of his and Ava's blossoming relationship, Blake decided it was time for remorse and self-pity to come to an end. It was time to move forward. Time to get on with life.

And that's exactly what he intended to do.

On one hand, Blake found it hard to believe he was actually going to do what he was about to do. On the other hand, reason told him he had no choice but to do whatever proved necessary to push Ava, once and for all, out of his mind.

So...

He took a deep breath...

Held it a few moments...

Released an explosive sigh...

And placed his hand on top of his computer mouse.

And then, with a stiff upper lip, accompanied by an expression of resolute determination, he minimized the accounting window on his computer screen, moved the mouse's tiny arrow until it sat on the icon linked to the Wexler Tower's online phone directory, and, for several long moments, hovered his right index finger above the mouse's left button. And then, speaking aloud, he asked:

"Do I really want to do this?"

He hesitated a moment longer...

Took another deep breath...

Dropped his finger onto the button...

And double-clicked the icon.

After an incredibly long delay—both the Wexler Tower's computer and network were *badly* in need of an upgrade—the phone directory's window finally opened. Blake stared at the flashing cursor a few seconds, then typed a name into the search box. He stared at the name a few seconds, summoned the nerve to press "Enter", and waited for the employee's information to appear.

Blake waited...*and continued waiting*...for the Wexler Tower's computer to respond. Finally, after a pause of what he estimated to be at least ten seconds, an hourglass appeared. And then—with the blinding speed of an ancient mainframe computer dragged down to a frustratingly-slow crawl by the combined delays resulting from outdated software, obsolete hardware, and an overloaded network —the hourglass disappeared and the search screen morphed into a listing of all the public information about the employee who's name he had typed into the search box. Blake stared a few seconds at the four-digit phone extension, again shook his head in disbelief as to what he was about to do, and lifted the desk phone's handset from its cradle. He looked at the phone number one more time—and dialed the extension.

Blake allowed the phone to ring only once. And then, as if the handset had suddenly burst into flames, he slammed it down...*hard*...and withdrew his hand.

"Who am I *kidding*?" he asked aloud. "Have I gone *insane*?"

As if to say a prayer, Blake closed his eyes, bowed his head, and propped his chin atop steepled fingertips. After a long pause, he lifted his chin, lowered his hands, took yet another deep breath to steady his nerves, and extended his right arm. He paused one more time, picked up the handset, and redialed the extension.

Once again, the phone began ringing. And, this time, Blake resisted the urge to hang it up on the first ring. He forced himself to listen to the second ring...the third ring...and, finally, the fourth ring. Just when he was about to remove the handset from his ear and hang up the phone—he had no desire to leave voicemail—he heard a click, followed a second or two later by a woman's weak voice that sounded bored, distant, and detached.

"Hello?"

Blake said nothing in reply.

The woman spoke again, this time her voice a little stronger, less distant, and more energetic. She sang the second syllable half an octave higher than the first.

"Hell-OH?"

Once again, Blake said nothing in reply.

"Hell-OH-ohhhh."

This time, the woman's voice rose a full octave on the second syllable before dropping a third of an octave to a long, stretched-out third syllable. Blake again fought the urge to hang up the phone. And, again, he said nothing in reply.

After a short pause, the woman spoke again.

"Anyone there?"

Blake could tell the woman's patience was wearing thin, so he decided to speak.

"Gigi? This is Blake Turner. Yes, it *has* been a while. *Quite* a while. No, it wasn't your fault. Please, Gigi. Let's not talk about it. Yes, I know you didn't realize.... Yes, I know you're not that kind of.... Gigi! *Please!* Let's chalk that night up as past history. Okay? Let's just put it behind us, move on to something else, and make sure we never let that happen again. Yes, I suppose so. Yes, in retrospect it *is* kind of funny. But *please*, let's not talk about it. Not only now, but never again. Gigi! I said let's not talk about it! Okay? Yes, I accept your apology. Listen.... Yes! I've gotten over it. Gigi! I said don't talk about it. *Please,* Gigi. Let *me* say something. Okay? *Please*, Gigi. Just listen to me. I was wondering...I was wondering if...if you don't have any plans for Saturday night...? *Hamburg*? Are you sure? There's nothing else you'd rather do? There's nowhere else you'd rather go? Okay. Okay. You've never seen *Hamburg*? You *promise* you've never seen *Hamburg*? Okay. Okay. I'll take you to see *Hamburg*. I'll go online as soon as I hang up the phone. In fact, I'm clicking on *SpeedyOnlineTickets.com* even as we speak. I'll see if any seats are available. Are you *sure* there's nothing else you'd rather do? Some other place you'd rather go? Okay. Okay. I'll let you know if I'm able to get some tickets. Well, never mind about that. Regardless of whether or not I get tickets, plan for me to pick you up at six o'clock. Yes, at your apartment. Yes, I remember where you live. We'll have dinner on our way to the theater...unless the show is sold out. If that's the case, we'll still go out to dinner, and then do a movie or something. Until then? Okay? Bye."

Long before Blake hung up the phone, he knew he had made a mistake. A *big* mistake. A *terrible* mistake. He hung up the phone, placed his elbows on his desk, and cradled his face in the palms of his hands.

"What have I done?" he asked aloud.

And then, upon hearing a slight rustling sound behind him, he lifted his head, looked over his right shoulder, and saw Fred leaning against the door frame.

"Fred! How long have you been standing there?"

"Long enough, my friend. Long enough. So! You're going out with Gigi. Gonna give her another try?"

"Uh, yeah. I, uh...I guess I am. I think she deserves another chance."

"I think she does, too, Blake. I really do. You don't know how glad I am to know you're giving your social life a kick in the seat of the pants. Gigi must have made quite an impression on you. I'll be expecting a full report first thing Monday morning. In fact, looking forward to that report will be enough to get me here on time."

CHAPTER 14

As promised, Blake arrived at Gigi's apartment promptly at six o'clock. He asked the taxi driver to wait for him, then got out of the taxi, crossed the sidewalk, and climbed the steps to the doorway. Using the tip of the index finger of his right hand as a guide, he scanned the names listed on the large panel mounted beside the door. He found the button for Gigi's apartment, hesitated a couple of seconds, and then pressed the button with the tip of his index finger. When Gigi answered, he announced his arrival, stepped away from the panel, and waited until she came down the stairs. Gigi started talking the moment she opened the door.

"Whatever else you do, Blake, don't let me get drunk again. I *swear!* I am *not* like that! *Honestly,* Blake! I am *not* that kind of girl. I don't have the slightest clue what came over me that night. Oh, can you *ever* forgive me?"

"Please, Gigi. *Please!* We've been over this time and time again. Let's forget about *that* night and try to enjoy *this* night. Okay?"

"Well, okay. I'll try. But I feel just *terrible* about it. *Please!* Don't base your opinion about me on that one night. It wouldn't be fair. Oh, I am so excited. *Hamburg*! I've heard *so* much about it. I've been reading about it, too. And I've listened to all the music from it. But I've never gotten a chance to actually *see* it. This will be *so* exciting. Where do we plan to eat? I am absolutely starved! I skipped breakfast, and only had a small salad for lunch, and...my gosh! It seems like the last food I ate was yesterday. Isn't this a beautiful evening? As windy and rainy as it was this afternoon, I never expected tonight would be so beautiful. Oh, my! Just look at that moon. Doesn't it take your breath away? Have you ever seen the moon as big and bright as it is tonight? And it's not even dark yet! What were you thinking about? For supper, I mean. Steaks? Chinese? Or Italian!! I know a great little Italian restaurant not far from here. It has the best spaghetti I ever put in my mouth. Oh, I love that tie you're wearing. You were wearing that tie the day we rode the elevator together. You remember? The Monday after our first date? I'm sorry. No, *really*. I am so, so, *so* sorry. I promised not to mention that again. Well, if this is *not* the tie you were wearing, it's just like it. I notice things like that. Oh, gosh. I am *so* embarrassed. I can't believe I got drunk like that. And I can't believe I did all those crazy things. I am *not* like that, Blake. Can you ever forgive me? Oh, look! Isn't that a pretty car? I saw one just like it, just the other day...same color and everything. Well, I didn't see it on the street. I saw it in a magazine. But this is the first time I've seen one. Oh, you know what I mean. The first time I've *actually seen* one, like, in *real life*—not just a picture in a magazine. It looks really, *really* expensive. Oh, look over there! Have you ever seen...?"

Blake rolled his eyes while opening the door to the taxi. Though he and Gigi had not even left her apartment, he already knew their second date, like their first, would be memorable for all the wrong reasons. For a moment, he seriously considered jumping into the taxi, slamming the door, and ordering the driver to whisk him away from what promised to be a very long night.

But Blake did *not* jump into the taxi...he did *not* slam the door...and he did *not* order the driver to whisk him away. Instead, he politely held the door open and waited while Gigi climbed inside and slid across the seat. He then climbed in behind her, pulled his legs inside, and closed the door. Gigi immediately scooted across the seat, nestled up against him, leaned her head on his shoulder, and began chattering...*non-stop chattering*...about anything and everything that popped into her mind.

Oh, Lord in Heaven, thought Blake. *If You let me survive this night, I promise—I double-dog triple-dog promise—I will never, ever, ask anyone to go out on a date as long as I live.*

Gigi talked non-stop, without a single break, until Ava Bechtel stepped out of the wings, strolled across the stage, and opened her mouth to sing. Even Gigi had enough sense to recognize greatness when she heard it.

And Blake had enough sense to realize, despite all his efforts to the contrary, he was still hopelessly, helplessly, and indisputably in love with Ava Bechtel. He would *always* be in love with Ava Bechtel, and there was nothing he, nor anyone else—especially a motormouth like Gigi, cute though she may be—could do to change it.

For the next two and a half hours, Blake, along with Gigi and all the other patrons in the theater, sat spellbound in the semi-darkened room. Without exception, each patron underwent something akin to a religious experience while watching and listening to Ava's magnificent performance.

In Blake's case, that abruptly ended halfway through the first act when, purely by coincidence, Ava's eyes found his eyes. But Ava's eyes did not linger on Blake's eyes—not for even the slightest fraction of a second—because she had not been looking for them. Instead, as required by her role in *Hamburg*, her eyes continued scanning the dimly-lit audience.

Until...

A full two seconds later...

When her subconscious mind finally registered the fact her

eyes had seen Blake's eyes...

She stumbled in her performance.

It seemed Ava had forgotten both the words and the music for the song she was singing.

She snapped her head in Blake's direction, squinted her eyes to block out as much of the bright spotlights as possible, and searched the section in which she had seen him.

But Ava could not find Blake.

And then, just when Ava decided she only *thought* she had seen Blake, she saw him again. Just to be sure, she squinted her eyes even more, and looked with double the intensity of the first time she had looked.

It was, indeed, Blake Turner.

Ava stared at Blake another second or two, then forced herself to look away—recomposed herself, as any professional performer would have done—and returned to her inimitable form. Blake, always the realist, assumed Ava had merely been surprised to see him in the audience...had done a quick double-take...and then, just as quickly, put him out of her mind and moved on.

But Ava had *not* put Blake out of her mind.

Nor had she moved on.

She repeatedly stole glances in Blake's direction...repeatedly searched the crowd for Blake's face. And, each time she found Blake's face, she allowed her eyes to linger upon his eyes, sometimes for as long as two or three seconds, before tearing her eyes away from his and re-immersing herself in her role.

Each lingering glance from Ava fanned the fire in Blake's heart, causing it to burn brighter and hotter. Did Ava still care for him as much as he cared for her?

The next hour passed quickly—*too* quickly, as far as Blake was concerned. He wanted to linger after the play ended. However, with Gigi standing at his side—and with Gigi's arm wrapped tightly around his waist—he knew lingering was not an option. So, instead of waiting for the actors and actresses to return to the stage for their first curtain call, he peeled Gigi's arm from around his waist, took her by the hand, and fled the theater—partly to whisk Gigi away before Ava realized he had attended the play with another woman, and partly to get Gigi back to her apartment before she drove him absolutely insane with her constant, non-stop, rambling chatter.

CHAPTER 15

At eight o'clock—eight o'clock *sharp*—on Monday morning, Blake sat down at his desk and logged onto his computer. At one minute after eight—almost, but not quite, true to his word—Fred stormed into the room, eager to receive Blake's report about his date with Gigi. As usual, Fred started talking the instant he entered the doorway, and Fred continued talking while tossing his briefcase onto the top of his cluttered desktop.

"Well? Don't torture me another minute, Blake. I've been sitting on pins and needles all weekend. Quick! Tell me about your date with Gigi. And, *please* tell me it went better than your first date."

Without bothering to look up from his computer screen, Blake released a long, descending sigh—more of a groan, actually—which made it perfectly clear to Fred his evening with Gigi had not gone well.

"Uh-oh. *That* didn't sound good. I *know* that groan, and it didn't sound good at all."

"My date with Gigi was a *disaster,* Fred. A *total* disaster."

"A disaster? But why? What happened? Did Gigi get drunk again? Did she embarrass you again?"

"No, Fred, it wasn't *that* kind of disaster. It was a totally *different* kind of disaster. But still, even though it happened in a different way, my second date with Gigi was just as disastrous as the first."

"You're *killing* me, Blake. Stop teasing me. Tell me what happened. What did Gigi do this time? You promise she didn't embarrass you? Quick! Tell me, Blake! What did Gigi do to embarrass you?"

"I hate to disappoint you, Fred, but Gigi did nothing to embarrass me. She's actually a very cute—and a very sweet—girl. However, if you look closely at my ears.... Are they still red? Are they bleeding? No? Well, they *should* be. I swear, Fred, Gigi came close to talking my ears off. If someone had told me a human being can talk as much...and as fast...as Gigi—*without ever saying anything*—I would not have believed it in a million years."

Suddenly, totally out of character, Blake slammed his fist down onto his desktop. The coffee cup holding his pens and pencils went flying in one direction, and one of his clipboards flipped end-over-end in the opposite direction.

"Whoa!" exclaimed Fred, taken aback by Blake's never-before-exhibited display of emotion. After a long pause, Fred squeaked, "I take it...? Does this mean...? Are you finished with Gigi?"

"Fred, Gigi likes to talk as much as I like to read. And *that*, my friend, makes us totally...*totally and completely*...incompatible."

With that, Blake had told Fred all he cared to tell him. Without another word, he pushed away from his desk, got up from his chair, and knelt on one knee. It took him less than ten seconds to retrieve his clipboard from the floor and place it on top of his desk, but the better part of a minute to gather up his pens and pencils, return them to the coffee cup, rise to his feet, and place the cup in its customary place. Blake then recomposed himself, sat down in his chair, rolled up to his desk, and stared at his computer screen.

But Blake did not *see* his computer screen.

Because his thoughts had turned inward, to memories of the relationship he had briefly—*too* briefly—enjoyed with Ava. So, for the next several minutes he sat in silence while staring at an *imaginary* computer screen, and an imaginary balance sheet, inside his mind. The sheet had two columns on it: one column for Gigi; and one column for Ava.

Gigi could not sit still long enough to read a single paragraph, let alone read an entire page...and *certainly* not long enough to read an entire book. Ava, however, enjoyed reading almost as much as he did.

One check for Ava.

No checks for Gigi.

Gigi rattled on and on with mindless prattle. Ava said something only when she had something to say.

Two checks for Ava.

No checks for Gigi.

As Blake added more and more entries to his imaginary ledger, one thing became more and more clear to him: Never had two people been more perfect for each other than he and Ava. Which made him wonder: *Why did Ava so abruptly stop communicating with me?*

For the next three hours Blake made a lame attempt to accomplish some progress on his accounting files. However, try as he may, he could not push Ava out of his mind long enough, nor keep his eyes focused on his computer screen long enough, to concentrate on his job. So, just before lunch, he gave in to the urge, logged onto *SpeedyOnlineTickets.com*, purchased a ticket to the next showing of *Hamburg*, and made plans to attend.

Unlike in the past, when Blake had felt compelled to arrive at the theater early so he could witness Ava's arrival, and to remain late so he could witness her departure, he simply wanted to be near her...to see her perform...to be in the same room she was in. He simply wanted to feel Ava's presence, even if it meant sharing her with all the other patrons sitting in the subdued lighting of the theater.

Barely two minutes into the show, Blake realized Ava's performance seemed flatter than usual. He doubted any of the other patrons had noticed it, because he doubted any of the other patrons had seen Ava perform as many times as he had.

A quarter of an hour after that, Blake realized Ava's performance was not simply flat. It was *different.* In previous performances, she had been totally focused on her role. But not tonight. She seemed diverted.

It took a while for Blake to realize Ava was scanning the dimly-lit audience far and above that required by her role in *Hamburg*. She was not merely interacting with the audience; she was searching for someone.

Blake's mind took him back to Friday night...all the way back to the middle of Act I. On that night, Ava had been completely focused on her role—until she made eye contact with him. From that moment on she had repeatedly looked in his direction...and she had *continued* looking in his direction...until she found him. And, he recalled, each time she found him, she held her gaze on his gaze for as long as two or three seconds before focusing on her role again.

Blake pulled his mind back to the present.

Is Ava's performance off tonight, as it was on Friday night? Is she searching for me now, as she did then? Is she trying to pick my face out from all the other faces in the audience? Did she also search the audience during Saturday and Sunday's performances?

Blake's mind again took him back to Friday night's performance. In the early part of the show, Ava's every effort—her entire being—had been focused on nothing but her role in *Hamburg*. However, from the moment she realized Blake was sitting in the audience....

Blake again pulled his mind back to the present. For several minutes, he critiqued Ava's performance. And then, one last time, he allowed his mind to take him back to Friday night...back to the moment Ava stumbled in her performance...back to the moment she discovered he had come to the theater, was sitting in the audience, and was watching her perform.

It suddenly occurred to Blake he was smiling. But why? What did he have to smile about? He finally realized he was smiling because, on Friday night, from the moment Ava knew he was in the audience, from the moment she believed he had come to the theater to see her perform, she had repeatedly looked in his direction...had repeatedly searched among the patrons' dimly-lit faces—*especially their eyes*—until she found his eyes. And each time Ava found his eyes, she made him feel he was the most important person in the audience.

Blake again pulled his mind to the present...and, once again, critiqued Ava's performance. He doubted other patrons could tell she was having trouble focusing on her role. After all, her spoken lines *were* flawless. And her songs *were* note perfect. But Blake could tell she was not pouring her heart into her role as she usually did.

Blake studied Ava's performance a moment longer. He then looked beyond her performance, beyond her face, and studied her eyes. The first thing he noticed was—as required by her role—she repeatedly scanned the audience, randomly picked someone out from the crowd, and pretended she was either speaking or singing directly to that person, to that person only, and to no one else.

But Blake noticed Ava was doing something different. Something new. Something she had never done before. She repeatedly squinted her eyes to filter out the glare of the bright spotlights.

Blake finally realized Ava was not merely interacting with the crowd as she usually did. *She was searching for* someone. Not some *random* someone, but someone in particular. Blake asked himself the same questions he had asked himself moments earlier.

Is Ava looking for me?

Did she also look for me during Saturday and Sunday's performances?

Without realizing he was doing so, Blake leaned forward. And then, when he became aware of what he had done, he leaned forward even more. Finally, after leaning as far forward as he possibly could without toppling over, he shifted his weight, straightened his back, lifted his head, and leaned forward even more.

Perhaps this will make me stand out from the crowd...make me more visible from the stage...make it virtually impossible for Ava to miss me.

It worked!

The next time Ava scanned the section of the auditorium in which she thought she had seen Blake, her subconscious mind immediately registered the fact something was out of place. A couple of seconds later, when her conscious mind became aware of what her subconscious mind was telling it, she turned, not just her eyes, but her entire head in Blake's direction. And then, after squinting her eyes again to filter out the bright spotlights, she searched that section of the audience again. A second or so later, she found what had caught her attention.

A young man was leaning so far forward it appeared he was either falling out of his seat, or had been frozen mid-way in the process of standing up.

Ava squinted her eyes more tightly, studied the young man more intently, and concluded he was none other than Blake Turner. Blake gave Ava a wide smile, a deep bow-like nod of his head, a subtle wave of his hand, and leaned back in his seat. He then waited to see how she would react.

Ava no longer searched the audience—because she no longer *needed* to search the audience. She had found the someone for which she had been looking. She wanted to keep her eyes on Blake, to look at him, to *stare* at him, and no one else. However, mindful of the requirements of her role in *Hamburg*, she continued scanning the audience...continued picking out one or two people at random...and continued pretending to interact with them. However, between each unfocused scan of the audience, she turned her head toward Blake, focused her eyes on his eyes, and allowed her gaze to linger on his gaze—not just one or two seconds, but a full three or four seconds—before pouring herself back into her role.

Blake felt encouraged by the fact Ava's performance had become more focused, her acting more energetic, and her singing more emotional than it had been before she realized he was in the audience. She now acted and sang with the power and enthusiasm for which she had become known. Blake doubted other members of the audience had detected these subtle changes. The important thing—the thing that mattered the most—was the fact *he* had noticed.

Can it be possible? Has Ava returned to her inimitable form solely because she knows I'm in the audience? Because she knows I'm here to see her perform?

Can it be, all this time, Ava has missed me as much as I have missed her?

Has she wanted to be with me as much as I have wanted to be with her?

Blake's chest tightened.

And his heart skipped a beat.

Does Ava love me as much as I love her?

After the show ended, multiple times during each curtain call, Ava glanced in Blake's direction...found his eyes...and locked her gaze upon his gaze for as long as three or four seconds. During all that time Blake did the only thing he knew to do: He simply stood there, beaming from ear to ear, and clapping with all the other patrons.

Blake waited until absolutely certain there would be no more curtain calls. He then followed the crowd out the front door, walked around the corner, stepped into the dark chamber, and became one with the shadows. And then, he just stood there, his heart pounding in his ears, waiting for Ava to step outside.

Why is Ava taking so long?

Blake repeatedly pressed the button to illuminate the dial on his watch.

And why is time moving so slowly?

Blake finally realized Ava was not taking any longer than usual. He was simply more excited than usual. And, by repeatedly looking at his watch, he made time pass more slowly than usual.

Just when Blake swore he could no longer stand it, Ava switched on her beautiful smile, opened the back door, stepped outside, and waved to the crowd.

Exactly as she had always done.

However, Blake noticed, Ava did not pan her eyes across the crowd as she usually did; instead, she looked directly *into* the crowd, and carefully studied each and every face.

Is Ava looking for me?

Blake's spirits soared higher and higher.

And his heart beat harder and harder.

So hard he feared it would leap from his chest.

And then...

Jack Smith stepped through the open doorway...

And Blake's heart abruptly stopped beating.

His chest grew tighter.

And his spirits came crashing down.

Not once.

Not even twice.

But three times.

First, when Jack joined Ava on the small landing.

Again when Jack took Ava's hand into his hand.

And yet again when Ava made no effort to pull her hand away from Jack's hand.

Blake cursed under his breath. He wanted to know the truth. He *had* to know the truth. And he had to know the truth *right now*. He considered all the possible consequences, decided they were acceptable, and, despite knowing he might pay dearly for what he was about to do, squared his shoulders and stepped from the shadows.

The instant Ava saw Blake, her eyes sparkled like stars in the sky. And the instant Jack saw Blake, his eyes also sparkled.

Until they burst into flame.

For several long seconds, Jack just stood there, his theatrical smile replaced by an angry scowl. And then, while maintaining eye contact with Blake, he pulled Ava down the stairs, drug her through the crowd, and opened the back door of a waiting taxi. He pushed Ava inside, shoved her across the seat, rose to his full height, and turned to face Blake.

Jack glared at Blake with a stern *I dare you to come one step closer* look on his face. And then, when Jack realized Ava had slid back across the seat, was leaning outside the taxi, and was also looking at Blake, he leaned over, shoved her across the seat a second time, crawled in behind her, and slammed the door.

CHAPTER 16

Blake, always the analytical and ever-calculating accountant, began second guessing himself. *Why,* he wondered, *why would a high-profile actress, an actress with the star status and fast-rising fame of Ava Bechtel, want to spend her life with a no-profile, no-status accountant like Blake Turner?*

The days that followed crawled by with agonizing slowness. As Blake had done in the past, he did everything he could to avoid seeing, hearing...or even *thinking*...about *Hamburg*. And yet, despite all of his self-deprecating reasoning, he never went anywhere without his cell phone, hoping he might get a call, or at least a text message, from Ava. He eagerly glanced at his phone each time it rang, hoping the name displayed on its screen would be *Ava*.

But Ava's name never appeared.

Because Ava never called.

And Ava never sent a text message.

Please, Blake pleaded each time his phone rang. *Please let it be Ava.*

But it never was.

At first, Blake glanced at his cell phone every five or ten minutes, as if doing so, through some subliminal form of mental telepathy, might will Ava to either give him a call or send him a text message. He glanced at his phone each time he heard the Navy Choir sing *Anchors Aweigh,* his phone's ring song, to let him know he had received a call; and he glanced at his phone each time it *Toot-Toot*ed like a toy tugboat to let him know he had received a text. Each time, he hoped to see the word *AVA* in big, bold, black letters, but *Anchors Aweigh* never heralded a call from Ava; and *Toot-Toot* never announced a text from Ava.

Blake finally realized, if Ava *did* give him a call, she would likely make the call, not from her phone, but from a phone belonging to someone else in order to prevent Jack from finding out about it. So, he stopped looking at his phone's display each time it played its ring song or tooted its text whistle.

However, Blake *did* answer his phone whenever it rang. In fact, he *eagerly* answered his phone, usually reaching for it during the first measure of *Anchors Aweigh*, hoping the caller's voice would be Ava's voice. And he *still* read his text messages, hoping at least one of them would be from Ava. But none of the calls...and none of the texts...were from Ava.

This went on for two weeks...fourteen days that Blake swore were the longest fourteen days of his life. Finally, as he entered a third week, he abandoned all hope—both consciously and subconsciously—of getting another call from Ava. Abandoned all hope of getting another text from Ava. And abandoned all hope of getting another chance to be with Ava. It was in one of those moments, a moment when Ava was nowhere near Blake's thoughts, he heard his phone's ring song.

Anchors Aweigh, my boys...

A week or so earlier, a phone call...*any* phone call...would have sent Blake's heart into overdrive. He would have eagerly answered his phone the instant he heard the first note of its ring song, hoping against hope the voice he heard would be Ava's voice. But not today. He no longer placed any hope or expectation upon whom the caller might be, so he no longer had any reason to answer his phone the instant he heard the Navy Choir sing its first line. Instead, he calmly finished the paragraph he had been reading, just as calmly marked his place with an index card, and set his book on the table beside him. If he had known the call was from Ava—and, if he had known she had finally escaped the watchful eyes of her chaperon long enough to make that one, all-important...*that one, unsupervised*...phone call—he would have made a special effort to answer his phone as quickly as possible. But he did *not* know the call was from Ava, nor did he expect the call to *be* from Ava, so he listened to the remainder of the song's first stanza—the entirety of his ring song—before tapping the *Accept Call* icon on his phone.

Anchors Aweigh.
Farewell to foreign shores,
We sail at break of day-ay-ay-ay.
Through our last night on shore,
Drink to the foam.
Until we meet once more,
Here's wishing you a happy voyage home.

Blake finally tapped *Accept Call* and greeted the caller in a flat, unenthusiastic monotone.

"Hello."

Ava—who, moments earlier, had frantically dialed Blake's number and then waited, with her heart threatening to rip itself out of her chest, and her phone threatening to leap out of her shaking hands—could barely whisper his name.

"Blake?"

Blake's conscious mind fought to pull itself from the pages of the book he had been reading. Meanwhile, his subconscious mind noticed three things.

One, the caller was a woman.

Two, the woman had spoken his name.

And, three, the woman had spoken his name in little more than a whisper.

It took Blake's conscious mind a couple more seconds to transition from the passage in his book to the conversation with his caller...and a couple more seconds for his conscious mind to comprehend what his subconscious mind was telling it.

One: *The caller was a woman.*

Two: *The woman had spoken his name.*

And, three: *The woman had spoken his name in little more than a whisper.*

Blake finally realized to whom the woman's voice belonged. In an instant, his eyes opened wide, his chest muscles tightened, and he found it impossible to inhale his next breath.

"Ava!"

Though Blake had shouted Ava's name, it came out of his mouth in little more than a mouse-like squeak. He rose to his feet, swallowed hard, and struggled to inhale his next breath. Finally, when he started breathing again, he spoke in a more normal voice.

"Ava! I thought you had lost interest in me."

"No, Blake!"

Ava's voice seemed louder than before, but was still little more than a soft, guarded whisper. After the shortest of pauses, she continued with her explanation.

"Nothing could be farther from the truth. If I could have my way, I would be with you every minute of every day. However, since the moment Jack discovered that you and I have been seeing each other, he hardly lets me out of his sight. He makes certain either he, Zane, or one of their friends is with me twenty-four hours a day."

"Oh, Ava, it is *so* good to hear your voice. You can't imagine how much I've..."

"Shut up and listen, Blake. *Please!* Just *listen. Okay*? I have less than one minute, maybe only a few seconds, before Teresa comes back. If she finds out I'm on the phone.... Quick! Tell me a time and place I can meet you...a *private* place...a place *far out of town*...a place where neither Jack, nor Zane, *nor anyone else* can find us. You know the area around New York much better than I do, so tell me: Where and when do you want me to meet you. *Please*, Blake. I *promise*—no matter *where* you suggest...and no matter *when*—I'll do whatever it takes to be there. I *promise*. I *will* be there."

Blake's favorite place—a secluded place, far out of town—popped into his mind long before Ava finished talking. He immediately suggested a date and time, recited the address, gave a brief description of his hideaway, and began dictating instructions to Ava as to how to get there. Ava wrote frantically in an effort to keep up with Blake. She managed to scribble down the date, the time, the address, and key words from his description. However, before he finished the first line of instructions as to how to get there, she abruptly said, "Gotta go!"

And...

Just like that...

Ava was gone.

Blake, cut off in the middle of a sentence, just stood there a moment, staring into space, and holding his cell phone next to his ear. And he *continued* standing there, and *continued* holding his phone to his ear, long after Ava whispered, "Gotta go!"

Blake continued standing there...

Holding his phone to his ear...

And listening to dead silence...

For ten long seconds.

Until, finally...

After accepting the fact Ava had terminated their call...

He lowered his phone.

But he continued standing there.

And continued staring into empty space.

Why did Ava hang up before I told her how to get there? At least she got the address.

It seemed to Blake that Ava could have said something more thoughtful...something more pleasant...something more personal than an icy, "Gotta go!" *Anything* would have been better than that. A simple "Good Bye, Blake," or "I'll see you then" would have been better than "Gotta go!"

It finally occurred to Blake why Ava had so abruptly...so *very* abruptly...ended their conversation. It was not because she thought their conversation had reached a logical conclusion—it obviously had not—nor was it because she was ready to hang up the phone. It could only have been because someone—most likely Teresa, Ava's chaperon-for-the-evening—had entered the room.

Blake's anger grew stronger by the second. He gripped his cell phone so tightly his fingers turned white. But it was not Ava toward whom he directed his anger. Nor was it Ava's face that filled his thoughts. He could see nothing but the sneering face of Jack Smith.

CHAPTER 17

Blake had never been a clock-watcher. In fact, he had always frowned upon clock-watchers, believing the seconds, minutes, and hours they wasted watching the clock could be put to better use by concentrating on the job at hand. Nonetheless, from the moment Ava ended their phone call, he became deeply religious about the passage of time. In return, long before the night was over, the passage of time taught him a cruel lesson:

The more often one looks at a clock, the more slowly its hands seem to move.

Blake swore Sunday afternoon would never arrive. Of course, Sunday afternoon *did* arrive. And, the moment it did, the moment the final curtain call signaled the end of *Hamburg*'s matinee, he walked out of the theater, drove straight to the secluded site he had suggested to Ava for their Monday morning rendezvous, and began preparing his tiny cabin for her arrival. He had made a point to arrive there a full twelve hours early, on the evening before their agreed-upon meeting time, so he could make certain everything was set up exactly the way he wanted it to be. Everything, down to the tiniest of details, had to be absolutely perfect for Ava. Nothing less would do.

Blake worked on the cabin, both inside and outside, until long after dark. And then, early Monday morning, long before the sun's glow appeared on the eastern horizon, he crawled out of bed, shaved, and, since his secluded retreat had no shower or bath tub, took a quick sponge bath. He then prepared and ate a light breakfast.

The moment Blake finished his meal, he became a flurry of

activity. He washed his dirty dishes, dried them, and put them away. He cleaned the stove, the sink, and the counter top. And, finally, just to make certain everything was in order, he gave his cozy little cabin what he assumed would be its final inspection. However, a quick glance revealed a couple of cleanup jobs he had missed during the first go-round, as well as a maintenance item that begged his immediate attention.

On any other day, Blake would have eased himself onto one of his cabin's comfortably-padded seats and relaxed a few moments while enjoying a second cup of coffee and reading a few pages in one of his books. Today, however, instead of taking a break before finishing his chores, he tackled the two cleanup jobs he had missed earlier. And then, as soon as he finished those, he set about cleaning the entire cabin a second time—despite the fact he had already cleaned every item and polished every surface as much as humanly possible.

If I keep myself busy, time will go faster—and Ava will get here sooner—than if I just sit and wait. I'll also burn off some of this nervous energy that's making my heart beat double time.

With that thought in mind, Blake cleaned things he had already cleaned, polished things he had already polished, and organized things he had already organized. And then, even though he had already done it three times, he re-cleaned, re-polished, and re-organized everything a fourth time.

The hands on the shiny brass clock mounted above the sink indicated it was almost seven o'clock, the time he and Ava had agreed to meet. He looked outside the cabin, hoping to see her petite figure walking towards him. But she was not there. He again looked at the clock, looked outside the cabin, looked at the clock, looked outside the cabin, looked at the clock, looked outside the cabin, compared the time on the clock to the time on his watch…

Yes, the clock was running.

And, no, it was not running slow.

But, still, it seemed seven o'clock would never arrive.

Of course, seven o'clock *did* arrive.

And Ava did not.

Blake tried to maintain his heightened level of anticipation while waiting another fifteen minutes. Finally, at thirty minutes past the hour, his excitement began to fade. And, at forty-five minutes past the hour, he assumed Ava would be a no-show.

Blake realized he had been a flurry of activity for more than two hours and decided he should take a break.

So, he sat down at the table…

Opened his book…

And, instantly, the cabin became eerily quiet.

And the cabin remained quiet…

Until a single drop of water landed in a puddle.

"Bloop."

Only then did Blake remember the maintenance item he had yet to attend to. He got up from the table, opened the doors to the cabinet underneath the sink, got down on his knees, and ran his fingers along the pipes until he found the leak's source. It took but a few seconds to determine which fitting needed to be snugged up a bit. Blake grasped the large nut and tried to twist it with his bare hands.

The nut refused to turn.

Blake gave the matter a few seconds of thought, then reached for a paper towel, wiped the fitting dry, wiped his hands dry, and wrapped the damp towel around the nut. He then re-positioned his legs and torso…again wrapped the fingers of both hands around the nut...gripped the nut as tightly as he could...and twisted with all of his strength.

The nut refused to turn.

Blake watched...and listened...as another drop of water oozed from the fitting and landed in the puddle.

"Bloop."

Blake decided he would need a pipe wrench to do the job. He reached up with both hands, hooked his fingers over the rim of the sink, and pulled himself to his feet. He then walked to the far side of the cabin, opened a cabinet, selected the appropriate tool, returned to the sink, got down on his hands and knees, and adjusted the wrench until it fit snugly on the large nut. He turned the nut a quarter of a turn, rose to his feet, filled the sink half full of water, and allowed it to drain. He waited a minute—a *full* minute—just to make sure his effort had stopped the drip. And then, for good measure, he got down on his knees one more time, turned the nut a tiny bit more, hooked his fingers over the rim of the sink, and pulled himself to his feet.

Blake placed the wrench on the counter beside the sink. He then tore three sheets of paper towels off the roll, leaned inside the cabinet, and sopped up the puddle of water beneath the drain's P-trap.

Meanwhile, one hundred and fifty yards away, the driver of Ava's taxi braked to a stop. Ava hesitated a moment, stepped out of the taxi, and just stood there, staring in disbelief at the idyllic setting Blake had chosen as their meeting place. She finally reached into her pocket, removed the small sheet of paper she had torn off the notepad, unfolded it, and double-checked the address Blake had dictated to her on the phone. Yes, she was definitely in the right place. She refolded the sheet of paper, returned it to her pocket, and stepped up to the taxi driver's window. While thanking him for his trouble, she opened her purse and asked how much she owed him. The driver read his meter and told Ava the amount. She paid him the full fare, did some quick mental arithmetic, and added a twenty percent tip.

Ava waited until the taxi motored away and vanished beyond a line of trees. She stared at the empty road a moment, then turned away from it, and stepped onto a long pier that jutted out from the west bank of the Hudson River.

Ava stood on the end of the pier a moment...not long, but long enough to take in a sweeping, panoramic, view of the harbor. She then began walking along a line of boats she swore reached halfway across the river. Sailboats and powerboats, some as short as fourteen feet, and the longest measuring more than fifty feet, sat absolutely motionless on glass-smooth water in the calm morning air.

Ava again reached into her pocket, pulled out the small sheet of paper, and referred to the information she had scribbled on it while talking to Blake on Saturday afternoon. She then lifted her eyes from the paper, took another look at the long line of boats, and searched for one that matched the description Blake had given her during their short phone conversation. Sure enough, tied up on the left side of the pier, midway down the line of boats, sat an antique, thirty-five-foot wooden cabin cruiser, exactly as Blake had described.

The boat, painted gleaming white except for its highly-varnished, natural-wood trim, literally sparkled in the early-morning sun. Ava knew nothing about boats, but she sensed this boat was to be admired as much as, if not more than, any of the other boats moored nearby. Even her untrained eye could see it was an old boat.

A *very* old boat.

But a highly prized boat.

And a lovingly cared-for boat.

Ava approached the boat until its stern came into full view. The name across the transom confirmed it was, indeed, the boat on which Blake said he would be waiting. She walked the remaining twenty-five feet, and then, speaking no louder than she thought absolutely necessary, called out Blake's name.

"Blake?"

Blake, who had just lifted the pipe wrench from the counter and was about to return it to the cabinet on the far side of the cabin, froze the instant he heard someone call out his name. He turned away from the counter, looked up through the companionway hatch, and scanned the deck.

No one was there.

Had the voice Blake heard been nothing more than wishful thinking? Just to make sure, he stood up straighter, leaned his torso to the right, twisted his head to the left, and looked up, beyond the deck, and onto the pier.

And then...

Blake just stood there, gazing up at the beautiful young woman gazing down at him. He finally gave the woman a smile, a smile that grew wider and wider until an elated grin spread all the way across his face. He ducked inside the cabin, returned the pipe wrench to the counter beside the sink, and bounded up the narrow companionway ladder to the boat's open cockpit.

"You *came*!" he exclaimed in a loud whisper.

Blake had spoken to Ava in a hushed tone—as hushed as the tone she had used to call out his name—as if he feared Jack might hear him over the hustle and bustle of New York City, despite the fact New York City lay on the opposite side of the river more than twenty miles away.

"I had begun to think you weren't coming."

Ava again spoke in a soft voice, somewhat louder than before, but still little more than a hushed whisper.

"I would have gotten here sooner, but several complications delayed me. First, I had trouble sneaking out of my apartment; my roommate has been watching me like a hawk! And then, as if that was not enough, the taxi driver had to stop for gas and a quart of oil. On top of all that, the driver took a wrong turn and got lost. It wasn't *your* fault, Blake. You gave me the correct address. The taxi driver either misunderstood me, or he selected 'Flotilla Ct' in his GPS instead of 'Flotilla Cir'. I would have been here on time—in fact, I would have been here early—if I had not had trouble leaving my apartment, the driver had not stopped for gas and oil, and...."

Ava finished her sentence by heaving a sigh and giving Blake a heart-melting, sincere smile.

"Can you forgive me for being late?"

"Of *course* I can, Ava. You *know* I can."

Blake stepped across the deck, extended his left hand palm upward, and waited until Ava placed her hand in his. He then helped her step down from the dock, onto the gunwale, and from the gunwale into the roomy cockpit. Finally, without wasting the time it would have taken to give Ava a hug, he tugged her across the deck, down the ladder, and into the main cabin.

Ava stepped to the center of the cabin and, one item at a time, took everything in. Through a small door, which sat slightly ajar, she could see a portion of the forward cabin...including the V-berth on which Blake had slept the night before. To her right lay a small but well-equipped galley, in the center of which sat a tiny but fully-functioning sink; to the left of the sink sat a small, two-burner propane stove; and, to the right of the sink, sat the small counter. Storage cabinets filled every spare inch on both the forward and aft bulkheads, as well as the boat's hull, both above and below the galley. And, finally, a small gas-electric refrigerator sat in the corner next to the bulkhead that separated the main cabin from the smaller forward cabin.

Ava turned her attention to the port, or left side, of the cabin. Directly across from the galley, oriented at a ninety degree angle to the boat's hull, sat a pair of padded benches. A small table, mounted on a pair of shiny, stainless steel posts, sat between the benches. Ava correctly assumed the posts could be removed, the table could be lowered to the level of the benches, and the backrests could be placed on top of the table to form a small bed. Storage cabinets lined the hull above the dining area, and drawers filled the spaces below the benches. It amazed Ava how the boat's designer had put every inch of the boat into use for one purpose or another.

Ava wanted to study more of the cabin's details, but returned her attention to Blake. Only then did she realize Blake had wasted no time getting her into the cabin so they would be hidden from the nosy eyes of the other boats' owners. Blake stepped up to her, placed his hands on her waist, and gently pulled her body towards his body. Ava instantly forgot her curiosity about the boat, gazed into Blake's eyes—those bright, sky-blue eyes—wrapped her arms around his waist, and allowed herself to be drawn into his eager embrace.

Blake and Ava never got a chance to share a kiss, intimate or otherwise. Just when their lips were about to touch, they stiffened their backs, pushed away from each other, and snapped their heads toward the open companionway hatch to glare at the man who had jumped off the dock and landed onto the cockpit's deck with a heavy, boat-jarring thud.

For several long seconds, Blake just stood there, staring into the eyes of his uninvited guest. Meanwhile, Blake's uninvited guest also stood there, staring straight down the ladder...straight at Blake. Ava opened her mouth to speak, but the man staring down the ladder spoke before she could utter a single word.

"Hello, Blake. It is *so* good to see you."

Blake felt surprise, anger, and embarrassment...all at the same time. He glared at Ava, glared at Jack again, and searched the cabin for a weapon. Not just any weapon would do. He wanted a murder weapon. And there, just inches from his hand, lay the pipe wrench he had used only moments before.

In a single fluid movement, Blake wrapped his fingers around the wrench, snatched it off the counter, bounded up the ladder, lunged at Jack, and swung with all his might. For a moment, Jack just stood there, motionless, with a dazed and surprised expression on his face. A few seconds later, while staring with sightless eyes into nothingness, he sagged to his knees, slumped forward, and fell face down in the ever-widening pool of crimson flowing from the gaping hole in his skull.

Blake stood above Jack's lifeless body for several long seconds, gloating over the fact he had finally eliminated his most despised and hated adversary. And then, driven by unbridled rage, he dropped to one knee, raised the wrench high above his head, tensed every muscle in his body, and delivered another crushing blow. Again and again he delivered blow after blow, each time shattering more bone, and shredding more flesh.

CHAPTER 18

Blake ground his teeth while shaking the gruesome image of Jack's shattered skull and blood-splattered brains out of his mind. Only his strong sense of reason had prevented him from becoming the uncontrolled killing machine his mind had imagined him to be. Though he would never reveal to Ava, Jack, or anyone else the macabre vision his imagination had so vividly created for him, he would forever be ashamed of it. He glared up at Jack for several long seconds, glanced down at the pipe wrench that lay on the counter, and glared up at Jack again. A few seconds later, he abruptly spun away from Jack and glared at Ava.

To think, all this time, I trusted Ava. I totally trusted Ava. But now? I don't know what to think.

Blake could only assume Ava had brought Jack...brought Jack *here,* to *his* boat...despite her claim she had gone to great effort...and taken great risk...to prevent Jack from finding them. After struggling with that contradictory thought a few moments, Blake finally concluded there was nothing he could do to change the facts and accepted them as they were. But still, how could Ava, in whom he had placed his utmost trust, have betrayed him and invited Jack to come along?

Blake continued glaring at Ava...who continued staring at him with a helpless expression. Blake glared at Ava a moment longer, then turned his head toward the companionway hatch and glared up at Jack...who had not moved a single muscle. Jack glared down the ladder a moment longer, and then continued the one-sided conversation.

"I am *so* glad Ava asked me to join you."

Jack took his eyes off Blake's eyes just long enough to give Ava an *I'll deal with you later* look. He then turned his eyes toward Blake again, resumed his sinister glare, and continued the one-sided conversation.

"That's right, Blake. You can thank Ava for my presence. She *insisted* I come along. After being repeatedly warned about the kind of person you are, she came to her senses and decided it would be best if someone accompanied her. You know? As a chaperon. So, here I am, just in case you try something she may not like."

ANCHOR
PART TWO
CHAPTER 19

"Dammit, Jack! Get the hell off my boat!"

The anger, bitterness, jealousy, and hatred Blake had harbored toward Jack for so many months erupted in an uncharacteristic fit of fury that took Ava completely by surprise. Jack, however, enjoyed every second of it.

Jack smiled a moment, then gave Blake a wide, taunting grin that made two things perfectly clear, not only to Blake, but also to Ava. First, it had been his intention to make Blake lose his temper; and, second, he had derived great pleasure by doing so. When satisfied that he had made his point, Jack stepped through the hatch, descended the companionway ladder, and entered the main cabin. He glared defiantly at Blake a moment, then reached out his left hand, gruffly took Ava by her right hand, and dragged her up the ladder, through the hatch, and onto the cockpit deck.

Jack whispered something into Ava's ear. And then, before she could utter a word in reply, he pushed her to the rear of the cockpit and forced her to sit down on the padded bench. After pausing a moment to recompose himself, Jack returned to the companionway hatch, looked down at Blake, and smiled...

As if nothing had happened.

"As I said earlier, Blakey Boy: This is one nice rig you've got. And it is *so* kind of you to take Ava and me on a cruise. I've been wanting to go on a cruise since I was a little kid, but I never had the time, nor the money. You can't imagine how excited I am."

Jack looked over his shoulder, glared briefly at Ava, and then turned his head toward the front of the boat again. And then, one more time, he looked downward through the companionway hatch, switched on his fake smile, and glared defiantly at Blake.

"Well, Captain. What are you waiting for? Don't just stand there! Raise some steam...weigh the anchor...avast, ye mates...and all that other good sailor talk. Get this tub underway."

Blake stared angrily at Jack a few moments, then gave the pipe wrench another long, lingering look while thinking seriously about using it. He then glared at Jack again...looked beyond Jack...and glared at Ava.

I can't believe Ava asked Jack to come along. And yet, she did ask Jack to come along. And here he is.

Blake continued glaring at Ava, and Ava continued staring at Blake, her face twisted into a strange, helpless expression.

An expression she had never displayed.

An expression Blake could not interpret.

Perhaps Ava feels guilty about the fact she betrayed me.

Blake glared at Ava a moment longer. And then, while glaring up the ladder at Jack, his anger rose to an all-time high. Even more vividly than the first time, he imagined himself grabbing the pipe wrench, leaping from the cabin, lunging at Jack, and beating his skull to an unrecognizable pulp. In this vision, however, unlike the first one—in which he just stood and stared at Jack's lifeless and blood-drenched body—he imagined himself picking up Jack's headless body, tossing it overboard, and watching it sink deeper and deeper into the black depths of the Hudson River.

Meanwhile, Jack, who was blissfully unaware of Blake's homicidal thoughts, continued glaring down the ladder through the companionway hatch. Finally, satisfied he had made it clear to Blake he was here to stay, Jack turned his back to the hatch, walked to the rear of the cockpit, sat down beside Ava, draped his arm around her shoulders, and pulled her body firmly against his.

All three people aboard the *Mary Beth*—none more than Jack—were fortunate that the calm, reasoning, and mild-mannered accountant Blake Turner actually was had prevailed over the emotional, out-of-control, and murderous Blake Turner who wanted nothing more than to destroy Jack Smith. It required the greatest of efforts, but Blake finally rejected the notion of killing his unworthy opponent and pulled his mind back to reality.

Blake took...and held...a long, deep breath to steady his nerves. He then gradually exhaled that breath in an effort to slow his pulse and lower his blood pressure. And finally, with extreme deliberation—as if it required great effort—he climbed the ladder, exited the cabin, took a couple of steps across the cockpit deck, and stepped up onto an elevated platform that sat to the right of the companionway hatch. After taking a final, lingering look at Jack and Ava—glaring first at Jack, and then at Ava—he turned his back to them and faced forward.

Blake now stood in front of a set of weatherproof controls mounted on the starboard aft bulkhead of the cabin. He had not planned to take the *Mary Beth* away from the dock. However, having been distracted by Jack's sudden and unexpected arrival, he made the spur-of-the-moment decision to do exactly that. After all, with Jack on board—thus no chance for intimacy with Ava—he no longer had a reason *not* to take the *Mary Beth* out for a short cruise.

Blake reached into his right-front pants pocket and pulled out a small, orange-colored float. A single key hung on its short chain.

He inserted the key into a switch labeled *Master* and turned it from the *off* position to the *on* position. He then flipped another switch—this one labeled *Ventilator*—to the *on* position. From somewhere near the stern of the boat came the sound of an exhaust fan gradually revving up to speed. Blake glanced at his watch, noted the time, and began putting check marks beside the various tasks on his mental checklist.

Master Switch On?
Check.
Ventilator On and Running?
Check.

While Jack and Ava critiqued his every move, Blake stepped up and onto the gunwale, and, from the gunwale, onto the dock. He then stepped over to a short pedestal mounted beside the boat and unplugged an electrical cord.

Shore Power Disconnected?
Check.

That done, Blake stepped onto the gunwale again, eased himself down into the cockpit, coiled up the electrical cord, and stowed it in a small compartment made just for that purpose.

Cable Secured?
Check.

Blake returned to the elevated platform and, one by one, studied the various dials and gauges arrayed on the instrument panel. His eyes moved slowly, pausing a second or two at each dial and each gauge while he made certain each and every needle sat in its normal, engine-off position.

Right Fuel Tank?
    Full.
Left Fuel Tank?
    Full.
Fresh Water?
    Just below the full mark.
Black Water?
    Just above the empty mark.
Battery Voltage?
    Just under Thirteen.
RPM?
    Resting on the zero peg.
Speed?
    Three knots.

Blake tapped the decades-old gauge until its needle dropped to the zero peg.

Engine Temp?
    Resting on the peg.
Oil Pressure?
    On the peg.
Bilge Pump?
    In the auto position.

Blake switched the bilge pump to the *on* position, listened to the satisfying whine of an electric motor coming to life, allowed the motor to run a couple of seconds, then returned the switch to the *auto* position.

Running Lights?
Off.
Anchor Light?
Off.
Radio?
Off.

Blake switched the radio to the *on* position, lifted the microphone off its bracket, and pressed the transmit button. Normally, he would have called the local yacht club and requested a radio check. Today, however, flustered by Jack's unexpected intrusion, he took the movement of the needle on the radio's power meter—combined with the click he heard from the weatherproof speaker—as sufficient evidence that both the microphone and the transmitter were working. A moment later he heard some chatter between two boats, which confirmed the receiver was working. Satisfied that both the transmitter and receiver were doing their jobs, he turned the volume down. On any other day, he would have left the volume up. Today, however, listening to marine chatter—virtually none of which would be of any concern to him—would be more than he could handle while dealing with Jack Smith.

Blake glanced at his watch. The exhaust fan had been running four minutes. Standard procedure called for running the fan five minutes prior to starting the engine to ensure all the toxic, flammable—and highly explosive—fuel and battery fumes had been expelled from the engine compartment. To pass the time while waiting for the fifth minute to tick by, he returned his attention to the instrument panel. And then, as methodically as the first time, he scanned all the dials and gauges, again pausing at each one to make sure it still sat in its proper engine-off position. When finished, he glanced at his watch. The exhaust fan had run the recommended five minutes, but he decided to let it run an extra minute before starting the engine.

Always err on the side of caution and safety.

His father's favorite mantra bore repeating—which he did, placing special emphasis on key words.

Always...always...err on the side of caution—and safety.

Blake checked his watch one more time, waited until a full six minutes had passed, and then pushed a large black button, labeled *Start,* just to the right of the master switch. From somewhere deep inside the bowels of the boat came the slow, grinding moan of a starter motor.

The engine failed to start.

But Blake did not want the engine to start. Not yet, anyway. His father had taught him to turn the engine over slowly a few times to pump some oil through it. So, he allowed the starter to run two or three seconds, and then, while still holding down the starter button, he pushed a second button, this one labeled *Choke.* The starter cranked another two or three seconds before the boat's single—and, like the boat, very ancient—one-hundred horsepower gasoline engine came to life with a throaty roar.

Blake's eyes continued scanning the various gauges and needles until each one remained steady. He then scanned the engine-related gauges one more time to assure himself each one sat inside the green arc of its normal operating range. Only when satisfied everything was in proper order did he step up from the platform, onto the gunwale, and, from the gunwale, onto the dock. He untied the mooring lines, returned to the cockpit, glanced one more time at each engine gauge, and then, very slowly...and with extreme caution...eased the *Mary Beth* out of her slip.

Jack and Ava had remained seated, absolutely spellbound, throughout the time Blake had prepared the Mary Beth for her unplanned, spur-of-the-moment cruise. And now, they remained seated—and spellbound—neither saying a word while observing Blake as he skillfully maneuvered his boat out of the crowded marina, pointed her bow toward the open waters of the Hudson River, and eased the throttle halfway forward.

Unable to constrain herself any longer, Ava squirmed out from under Jack's arm, walked to the front of the cockpit, stood next to Blake, and tried to strike up a conversation.

"You never told me you owned a boat."

At first, Blake felt encouraged by the fact Ava had gotten up from her seat, walked away from Jack, and come forward to stand next to him. But, he then realized her voice had sounded shaky, as if she was nervous. He also noticed she kept glancing over her shoulder at Jack. Blake glanced over his own shoulder and noted, for the moment at least, Jack remained seated at the rear of the cockpit. He finally addressed Ava's comment.

"I don't."

Ava turned her back to Jack, took a moment to compose what she was about to say, and spoke in a low voice so as to prevent Jack from hearing her.

"Blake, I did not.... I do not want you to think...."

Ava never finished her sentence, because Jack had gotten up from his seat, sauntered across the cockpit, and cut short her conversation by putting his arm around her waist and pulling her body tightly against his—and, Blake noted, Jack had done so, not with a romantic and gentle tug, but with a violent and possessive snap. Jack glared at Blake, and then glared at Ava, to make certain both understood the unspoken message he had just delivered to them.

Blake's bitterness returned in an instant. And then, while watching Jack drag Ava to the rear of the cockpit, his bitterness yielded to another bout of anger. He stood helpless, barely able to restrain himself, as Jack forced Ava to sit down on the bench, sat down beside her, draped his arm around her shoulders, and, with another possessive snap, pulled her body snugly against his body.

Blake found it unbearably painful to see Ava so totally controlled by Jack. He glared at her a moment...glared at Jack a moment...then turned his body to face forward again. A moment later, somewhat consciously, but mostly out of habit, he scanned his instruments, pausing at each one to make certain its needle sat in the green arc of its normal operating range. And then, again somewhat consciously, but mostly out of habit, he scanned the hundred-eighty-degree arc that started abeam on the port side of the boat, swept across the bow, and ended abeam on the starboard side. Even though Blake was incensed about Jack's presence and his domination of Ava, he retained enough of his wits to make certain there were no objects floating in the *Mary Beth*'s path, and no boat on a course convergent to the *Mary Beth*'s course.

Finally, after several moments of repressed silence, Ava spoke to Blake. Unlike moments earlier, when she had stood right beside him and could make herself heard by speaking in a lowered voice, she now had to talk very loudly in order for Blake to hear her words above the throbbing growl of the poorly-muffled engine.

"Blake, you said this boat does not belong to you. If not to you, then who *does* it belong to?"

While continuing to hold the wheel with his right hand, Blake twisted his torso to the left until he could look straight aft...straight at Ava. At first, he just glared at her with an accusatory *How could you do this to me?* expression. And then, after transferring his glare to Jack, he pursed his lips and scrunched down his eyes until they were little more than narrow slits. For a moment, Jack simply glared back at Blake. Jack then pursed his own lips—and scrunched down his own eyes—to make clear to Blake that his threatening posture did not intimidate him in any way. And then, to drive home his point, Jack pulled Ava's body even more tightly against his own body—as if it were possible to do so.

Blake chewed his lower lip a moment, then used a combination of eye, head, and hand signals to indicate to both Jack and Ava they should come forward and sit near the front of the cockpit. Blake considered his invitation a fair compromise, as it would place Jack and Ava close enough for the three of them to converse more easily over the roar of the engine's loud exhaust, yet far enough away so Jack would not consider Blake to be a threat to Ava.

Jack glanced down at Ava, and then glared up at Blake. After mulling over Blake's non-verbal invitation a few seconds, he shrugged his shoulders, as if to say, "What harm can that do?" Jack then rose to his feet, motioned for Ava to do the same, and led her to the front of the cockpit. Blake waited until they were comfortably seated on the forward end of the port-side bench before answering Ava's question.

"I guess you could argue the *Mary Beth* does, in fact, belong to me...although she belongs to me in a strange and convoluted way. My great-grandfather purchased her when she was brand new, and named her after his wife, my great-grandmother. Several years later, when my great-grandparents died, my grandfather, being the only surviving child, inherited their entire estate—which included the *Mary Beth*. Some years after that, my grandfather died and my father inherited the estate—which, of course, included the *Mary Beth*. And, finally, about ten years ago, *my* father died and my mother inherited what was left of the estate...which still includes the *Mary Beth*."

"So, your mother owns it now?"

Blake glanced at Ava, scanned the gauges, and then looked forward again.

"Yes—and no. According to Mom, Dad always wanted *me* to have the *Mary Beth*, but he never got around to stating so in his will. Mom and Dad, like my grandparents, had one of those standard wills in which everything passes to the wife upon the husband's death, and vice versa, or, if the husband and wife should die at the same time, everything goes to their children—in my case, their child."

Blake laughed to himself, and then shook his head.

"I'm sorry. I didn't mean to get side-tracked on the specifics of my ancestors' wills. Suffice it to say Mom inherited the entirety of Dad's estate, which made her the sole owner of the *Mary Beth*. Since she knew Dad wanted *me* to have the *Mary Beth*, she proposed we have the title changed over to my name. The first lawyer we talked to argued it would be in Mom's best interest to leave things exactly as they were. That way, if something should happen to me before she died, she would still own the *Mary Beth*, could sell the *Mary Beth*, and use the money however she saw fit. The lawyer explained to her, if she transferred ownership of the *Mary Beth* to me, and if I died before she died, she would have no rights to it and would be lucky to net a single dime from its sale after the court finished probating my estate, paying off the lawyer fees, the court costs, and so on.

"Luckily for us, Fred Johnson—Fred is the guy I work with—encouraged me to talk to a different lawyer...to get a second opinion. As it turned out, Fred's suggestion to talk to a different lawyer was a good one. The second lawyer advised us to have the *Mary Beth*'s title changed to list Mom *and* me as joint owners with rights of survivorship. We took his advice, not only with the *Mary Beth*, but with *all* of Mom's stuff. Her house...her jewelry...her car...everything of value. That way, I won't have to worry about probating her will if she dies before I do, and she'll still own everything...including the *Mary Beth*...if I die before she does."

Blake laughed—and then shook his head.

"I'm sorry. Once again, I allowed myself to get side-tracked. Anyway, to come full circle...and to answer your question...no, the *Mary Beth* is *not* mine, and yet, at the same time, she *is* mine. I take her out every weekend...unless the weather is bad. As you already know, I spend those weekends in the library."

Ava smiled and nodded. And then, when she understood the meaning of the librarian's strange statement about weekends and weather, she smiled and nodded a second time. Finally, after all these months, she understood Blake spent his weekends in the library—*but only if the weather was bad.* He went somewhere else —to the *Mary Beth*—when the weather was good.

"Do you take your boat out alone?"

"Yes, I do. Most of the time. But not always. Sometimes, Mom goes with me. Sometimes, she brings one or two of her friends along. And, sometimes, I take Fred Johnson for a ride. As I said, Fred and I work together at Wexler. He's my office-mate, and I guess you would say he's also my best friend. Usually, it's just me. Or Fred and me. And, sometimes, Fred brings his wife and kids along."

Blake smiled. And then, when his mind carried him back to the distant past, he became glassy-eyed.

"On one occasion, I took Mom, two of her friends, plus Fred's entire family...*all at the same time*. That made for one full boat!"

Blake stopped smiling, refocused his eyes, and pulled his mind back to the present. He then cleared his throat.

"But, usually, it's just me and the *Mary Beth*."

Jack chose this moment to butt into a conversation he knew he was not welcome to join...and he did so with words and tone-of-voice clearly meant to irritate Blake.

"Do you just ride around in circles for a while, or do you actually *do* something? You know? Like go somewhere...do some fishing...or do *something*."

Blake turned his head to the left and noted the smirk on Jack's face. And Jack, aware Blake was watching him, planted a kiss on Ava's cheek to flaunt the fact—and to make the fact perfectly clear to Blake—that Ava Bechtel belonged to Jack Smith, *not* Blake Turner.

Blake, angered by Jack's blatant gesture of ownership and affection—and stung by the fact Ava had made no effort to fend off Jack's kiss—turned to face forward again.

"Sometimes, I..."

Blake's voice trailed off. And then, while chewing on his upper lip, he viewed a mental replay of Jack kissing Ava...and Ava showing no effort to fend off Jack's kiss.

Ava allowed Jack to kiss her.

And Ava seemed relaxed, as if she had been kissed by Jack many times before.

Ava made no effort—none whatsoever—to fend off Jack's kiss.

This bothered Blake.

This bothered Blake a *lot*.

"Usually, I..."

Blake, still stinging from how comfortable Ava had seemed when Jack kissed her, allowed his voice to trail off. He then just stood there, staring straight ahead at nothing in particular. Finally, when he realized both Jack and Ava were waiting for an explanation, he turned his head toward them and started over.

"Sometimes, I take the *Mary Beth* out for a local run on the Hudson River. And, sometimes, I cruise her all the way down the river, motor past Manhattan, and enter the open sea. But, usually, I just find a quiet cove on the Hudson, drop the anchor, and either work on my boat or relax while reading a book."

"Have you ever gone whale watching?"

Blake turned his head to the left and looked at Ava, who was trying to pry herself out from under Jack's arm. Her strength, of course, was no match for Jack's; he simply tightened his grip and resisted her effort. However, the moment Jack realized Blake was watching, he relaxed his arm and allowed Ava to wriggle free. She immediately rose to her feet and looked across the cockpit at Blake. She then looked down at Jack, who immediately pointed to the spot where she had been sitting.

Ava clearly wanted to do otherwise, but she obediently sat down beside Jack...who, once again, draped his arm around her shoulder and pulled her close. This time, Ava made no attempt to shrug her body out from under Jack's arm. Nor did she make an effort to push away from him when he pulled her body closer to his. However, after peering briefly into Jack's eyes, she turned her head toward Blake and stared into *his* eyes. Blake stared back, and watched Ava's face twist into a strange, helpless expression.

Confused by what he had just seen, Blake turned his head forward and pretended the exchange he had witnessed between Jack and Ava had not affected him in any way. But the exchange *had* affected him. So, he again turned his head toward Jack and Ava, pursed his lips, and glared at Jack.

Almost a minute passed from the time Ava asked her question until Blake answered it.

"Sure, Ava. I've done some whale watching. In fact, I've done *lots* of whale watching."

"Could we go whale watching today?"

Blake realized Ava had made an effort to sound enthusiastic, despite Jack's obvious, heavy-handed—and seemingly total—control over her.

"I've never seen a whale," she continued, speaking in a relaxed tone for the first time since Jack had leapt aboard the *Mary Beth*. "Well, I *have* seen whales and porpoises in theme parks, but I've never had an opportunity to actually *see* one. You know? In the wild. In its natural habitat."

Blake glanced at his fuel gauges. Not that he needed to. He already knew both tanks were full, because he had topped them off at the end of his last cruise.

"I suppose we could go whale watching..."

Blake paused a moment to glance at his watch and run a series of mental calculations involving speed, distance, and time. He then completed his sentence.

"...but we won't get back to the dock until late tonight. *Very* late. It may even be after sunrise tomorrow morning."

Ava shrugged her shoulders.

"I don't mind. I think it will be fun."

Ava exchanged another glance with Jack. She then continued

speaking, halfway making a statement to Blake, and halfway seeking approval from Jack.

"We don't perform tonight, so it doesn't matter how late we get back."

Jack, aware Ava had asked him a question, gave the issue a moment of thought. He finally nodded his head, tightened his arm around her shoulders, pulled her body tightly against his body, and gave her a *But you still belong to me, and don't you ever forget it* look.

Jack glared at Ava until certain she understood who was boss. He then looked up at Blake. The two men stared at each other for several long seconds before Blake turned forward, gave the wheel a half turn to starboard, placed his right hand on the throttle, increased the power a bit, and coaxed the *Mary Beth* into a wide, sweeping, right-hand turn. He did not center the rudder until the *Mary Beth*'s bow pointed straight down the middle of the Hudson River.

CHAPTER 20

Blake adjusted the *Mary Beth*'s throttle until she cruised at an engine-saving and fuel-conserving fourteen knots. And then, for the next hour and a half, he steered her down the middle of the Hudson River, which allowed Jack and Ava to enjoy the various sights along both shores. Blake cruised past the busy waterfront of New York Harbor...motored along the shores of Ellis Island...circled the Statue of Liberty...crossed the wake of the Staten Island Ferry...continued downstream to the mouth of the Hudson River...and, from there, left all land in the *Mary Beth*'s wake and entered the open sea.

Only then did something occur to Blake: If he could not get Jack *off* his boat, he would put Jack to work *on* his boat.

"Hey, Jack? How about going below and putting on a pot of coffee? You'll find both the coffee and the pot in a storage locker directly above the sink."

"Sure, Blakey Boy. I'd be more than glad to."

Blake smiled, finding it hard to believe how easy it had been to get rid of Jack. With Jack gone, it would only be a matter of seconds until he and Ava got an opportunity to spend some time alone. His smile quickly faded, however, when Jack took Ava by the hand, snatched her to her feet, and drug her toward the companionway hatch.

"*You* are coming with *me*, Ava."

Jack literally growled the words.

"No, Jack. *You* go. I will stay up *here*."

Ava resisted Jack's effort for a moment, but quickly realized her diminutive strength was no match for his. Meanwhile, Blake watched...and listened...while Jack snarled at Ava through tightly clenched teeth.

"You are *not* staying up here. Like I said: *You* are coming with *me.*"

Jack placed his mouth next to Ava's ear and spoke to her in a soft voice. Despite the loud roar of the M*ary Beth's* growling exhaust, their close proximity to Blake allowed him to hear every word Jack said.

"*You* are going down into the cabin with *me.* I've told you this a thousand times. Wherever *you* go, *I* go...and wherever *I* go, *you* go. I'm doing this for *your* sake, Ava. Don't you *ever* forget that."

Jack muscled Ava through the companionway hatch, then followed her down the ladder.

Blake stared into the shadows beyond the open companionway hatch. He couldn't decide at whom he should be more angry: Jack, for tagging along with Ava; or Ava, who had deceived him into believing she wanted to meet in secret, only to bring Jack along as a chaperon. For a brief moment, Blake considered following them down the ladder. However, mindful of his duties, he glanced at the *Mary Beth*'s compass, adjusted her course to starboard a few degrees, noted the time on his watch, and eased the throttle back fifty rpm.

Right now, at this very moment, Jack and Ava are belowdeck...in my cabin...just the two of them...alone...in my cabin...while I am topside...also alone...and there is absolutely nothing I can do about it.

A scowl formed on Blake's face as he stared forward. And then, his down-turned lips curled upward into a mischievous smile.

"Then again," he thought aloud, "perhaps there *is* something I can do about it."

Blake conceded the fact he had no control over what Jack and

Ava did elsewhere. Today, however, they were *not* elsewhere. They were *here*...on *his* boat...and, as captain of his boat, he had every right to know what was going on from bow to stern. He abruptly snatched the throttle back to idle, shifted the transmission into neutral, leapt through the companionway hatch, and landed with a heavy thud on the cabin floor. Jack and Ava, still off balance after being startled and thrown forward by the sudden deceleration of the boat, were startled a second time by Blake's unexpected—and very dramatic—entrance.

Jack and Ava stared wild-eyed at Blake for a long moment, then gave each other a meaningful glance that said, *We'll continue this conversation later*. Blake, pretending he had not noticed the unspoken message exchanged between them, spoke in a high-spirited voice as if he were in a jovial mood.

"I sure could use a cup of coffee! Is it ready?"

"No!"

Jack snapped out his answer, making no effort to hide the fact he was *not* in a jovial mood. And then, after a moment of thought, he added:

"Ava, *you* make the coffee. Blake and I are going outside."

Jack maneuvered himself into a strategic position between Blake and Ava, assumed a protective posture, and nodded toward the ladder—an unspoken command to Blake that he was to be the first one to climb the ladder. Only after Blake ascended from the enclosed cabin, stepped outside onto the open deck, and walked to the center of the cockpit did Jack also climb the ladder, emerge from the cabin's dark shadows, and join Blake in the bright sunlight.

For the next four hours Jack made certain Blake was never allowed to spend any time, not even the briefest of moments, alone with Ava. Only when a pod of whales came into view did Blake finally accept defeat and concentrate his efforts on giving his passengers a good, close-up view of the gargantuan, sea-dwelling mammals.

CHAPTER 21

So intent was everyone on watching the whales that no one noticed the solid bank of dark clouds rolling in from the west. Thanks to a lifetime of nautical experience, Blake was the first to become aware of the precarious situation into which he had placed his boat and his passengers.

But it was not the dark clouds approaching from the west that captured Blake's attention. For the past half hour, both he and his passengers had been looking toward the east, where a few fluffy white clouds drifted across a wide expanse of brilliant blue sky. What *did* capture Blake's attention was the sudden and startling fact that a following sea had lifted the *Mary Beth*'s stern to an alarmingly high angle. Even before the boat's stern began to settle, Blake snapped his head around and scanned the dark clouds. He then noticed the angry white-capped waves that stood out in stark contrast against an ink-black sky that stretched all the way across...and far beyond...the western horizon.

While maintaining a tight grip on the wheel with his right hand, Blake released his left hand, spun his body around, and stared open-mouthed at the angry black monster rolling in from the west. He figured he had but a matter of seconds, a minute at most, before the storm's leading edge would roll across the *Mary Beth* with all its fury.

The last thing Blake wanted to happen was to have the *Mary Beth* present her stern to the giant waves about to overtake her. In less than five seconds he assessed the situation, evaluated all the options, and concluded his best course of action—indeed, his *only* course of action—was to turn the *Mary Beth*'s bow directly into the massive storm and hope she could ride it out.

Jack and Ava, neither of whom had ever stepped foot on boats other than the rock-stable ferries that cruised upon Germany's placid inland waters, were not yet aware of how serious their situation had become. However, the moment they noted Blake's rigid posture—and the unveiled look of concern on his face—they sensed something was wrong. And then, a moment later, when Blake turned his body forward again, spun the wheel hard a-port, and rammed the throttle as far forward as it would go, they *knew* something was wrong.

Not just wrong, but *terribly* wrong.

The under-powered *Mary Beth* could not have chosen a more inopportune moment to rebel against one of her skipper's commands. For the past hour and a half her engine had been running smoothly at little more than a slow idle; however, the instant Blake rammed the throttle to its maximum setting, her engine began spitting and sputtering. At first, this puzzled Blake, but he quickly realized the engine had become flooded due to the ancient carburetor's inability to match the abrupt increase in fuel flow with a corresponding increase in air flow. So he eased the throttle back a bit. And then, failing to get the desired results, he eased the throttle back a bit more. The air-to-fuel ratio finally stabilized, the spitting and sputtering stopped, and the engine ran smoothly.

Blake again pushed the throttle full forward, but, this time, he made a conscious effort to push the lever gradually, over the span of two or three seconds, instead of an abrupt fraction of a second as he had done before. Now, able to comply with Blake's command without spitting and sputtering, the *Mary Beth*'s engine increased its rpm until it produced all the horsepower it had to offer.

Even so, the *Mary Beth* failed to surge forward as Blake had hoped she would. Instead, she raised her bow high into the air, lowered her stern deeply into the sea, and just just sat there—much like a rebellious child that drops to the floor, folds its arms across its chest, and pouts with a loud "Harrumph."

But the *Mary Beth* was a boat, not a rebellious child, so her tantrum lasted but a few seconds...seconds during which she underwent several major changes.

The first change involved the *Mary Beth*'s propeller. For the past hour, it had lazily chopped the sea into a mottled, greenish-white wake. It now churned the water into a frothy, snow-white foam.

The second change occurred a second or so later when the *Mary Beth* leaned lazily to port and began what Jack and Ava assumed would be a gentle and gradual left-hand turn. However, when the *Mary Beth* began dropping her bow, lifting her stern, and turning in earnest, they realized there would be nothing gentle or gradual about it.

For a moment, Jack and Ava simply sat there, their wide-eyed expressions exhibiting a combination of fear and wonder. But then their instincts took over, and they tightened their grip on the rail and braced themselves against the powerful centrifugal force doing all it could to sling them off the seat.

All morning long—from the moment the *Mary Beth* eased away from the dock, during her scenic cruise down the middle of the Hudson River, and throughout her lazy and uneventful trek across the tranquil and seemingly endless blue waters of the Atlantic Ocean—Blake had stood in a calm, relaxed posture off to one side of the steering wheel, with most of his weight supported by one leg, and the fingertips of one hand resting lightly on the wheel. However, the instant Blake realized a storm was about to overtake the *Mary Beth*, he became an entirely different person. He no longer stood off to one side of the console...no longer supported most of his weight on one leg...and no longer rested one hand lightly on the wheel. He now stood squarely in front of the console, his feet set wide apart, his legs bent at the knees, and the white-knuckled fingers of both hands wrapped tightly around two of the wheel's wooden spokes.

Jack and Ava, momentarily confused by Blake's drastic maneuver, quickly realized he intended to meet the storm head-on. They exchanged quick glances with each other, but neither said a word. They communicated only with their eyes, each telling the other they understood two things: first, their lives lay in Blake's hands; and second, they were in for a long and tempestuous ride back to port...assuming they were fortunate enough to get back to port. Meanwhile, relying more on instinct than conscious thought, they gritted their teeth and gripped the rail more tightly than ever.

Just a few seconds more, everyone thought, *and the Mary Beth will complete her turn.*

But the *Mary Beth* did *not* complete her turn, because a huge wave—a massive wave, a wave much bigger than the one that, only moments before, had caught Blake's attention by lifting her stern high into the air—crashed broadside onto her port beam. Instantly, the *Mary Beth* heeled over to starboard at a frighteningly steep angle. Somehow, Jack and Ava managed to maintain their grip on the rail—and, somehow, Blake managed to remain standing, his legs locked in place, and the fingers of both hands wrapped tightly, with an iron-like grip, around two of the steering wheel's spokes.

Blake tried to move, but was unable to coax a single muscle

into action. He could only stand there, literally frozen in place, while listening to the *Mary Beth*'s over-revving engine. The rpm quickly reached, and then went far beyond, the tachometer's red line. Blake's brain screamed at him to release his right hand from the wheel, place it on the throttle, and reduce power. His instinct, however, told him it was far more important, no matter what may come, that he use both hands to maintain his grip on the wheel and remain on board.

What good will you be to the Mary Beth and her passengers if you fall into the sea?

Blake's brain immediately countered his instinct's argument.

But what good will the Mary Beth be if you let her engine chew itself to pieces?

Blake continued arguing with himself...

The seconds continued ticking by...

And the *Mary Beth*'s engine revved higher and higher.

To everyone's good fortune, Blake's brain won the argument. Even though his natural impulse told him to do otherwise, he released his right hand from the wheel, placed it on the throttle, and snatched it all the way back. The instant he did so, his body, now secured to the wheel with only one hand, surrendered to the force of gravity and fell toward the starboard rail—which, by virtue of the fact the *Mary Beth* lay on her starboard side, was now situated, not beside him where it normally sat, but almost directly below him.

Jack and Ava gasped, and then held their breaths, certain that they, along with Blake, were about to fall overboard. Only when they saw Blake slap the palm of his right hand onto the rail—thus breaking his fall—did they begin breathing again.

Despite the gravity of his and the *Mary Beth*'s situation, Blake had the presence of mind to turn his head, glance over his shoulder, and look up—*almost straight* up—at Jack and Ava. He then stared at them in amazed wonder. They were suspended in mid air, directly above him, with their legs dangling straight down. Technically, they were still aboard the *Mary Beth,* but only because their arms remained tightly wrapped around the rail. The scene would have been quite humorous if it had been posed for the purpose of taking a photograph. But the scene had *not* been posed, and Blake considered it far from humorous.

Jack and Ava, with their eyes bulged to twice their normal size, stared in horror at Blake, who, like them, was certain the *Mary Beth* would continue her rollover and turn upside down.

However…

To everyone's relief…

The *Mary Beth* stabilized…

At an incredible eighty degree angle…

And just sat there…

As if patiently waiting for the crest of the wave to pass beneath her hull.

Several tantalizing seconds later the *Mary Beth* began righting herself. Finally, when it became obvious she would remain top-side-up, everyone relaxed a bit, breathed a collective sigh of relief, and muttered silent prayers of thanks.

And yet, despite their relief, all three of the *Mary Beth*'s passengers knew her troubles…*and theirs*…were far from over. The *Mary Beth* had lost virtually all of her forward speed…had stopped turning…and, though she was, indeed, in the process of righting herself, remained heeled over on her starboard side at an alarmingly-steep angle.

Like the proverbial weak-jawed boxer, the *Mary Beth* had been knocked to her knees by a single punch in the first seconds of the first round. Jack and Ava—and, more importantly, Blake himself—believed the *Mary Beth* had given up the fight without throwing any punches of her own.

Blake's lips curled downward into a deep frown. He was disappointed, mainly with himself for not paying closer attention to the weather, but also with the *Mary Beth.* Never had he imagined his boat, having survived the elements for decades on end, would surrender so easily to a single wave.

And then, Blake 's lips slowly curled upward. Though the *Mary Beth* was still reeling from the punch Mother Nature had thrown at her, she let it be known she was not ready to throw in the towel. Not yet, anyway. Very slowly and very deliberately, just as the proverbial boxer rises from the mat to avoid the ten count, she continued righting herself...eased her propeller and rudder into the water...and patiently awaited her captain's next command.

When Blake realized his faithful boat was eager to throw a few punches of her own, the corners of his lips curled upward even more, and his smile grew even wider. With renewed energy, he pushed himself away from the rail and placed his right hand on the throttle. And then, mindful of the lesson he had learned seconds earlier, he *gradually* pushed the lever all the way forward. This time, thanks to his patience with the throttle, he avoided flooding the engine with excess fuel, and the engine ran smoothly throughout its crescendo from a slow, rumbling idle to a loud and roaring full power. He gave the throttle a second shove, just to make certain he had pushed the lever as far forward as it would go.

Tentatively at first, and then with dogged determination, the *Mary Beth* pressed her stern low into the water...lifted her bow high into the air...leaned to port...and resumed her turn. Slowly at first, but then faster and faster, the bow dropped, the stern rose, and she accelerated toward the next wave.

Finally, with the turn completed, Blake centered the rudder, placed his right hand on the throttle, and used the combined strength of his left arm and both legs to brace himself for the *Mary Beth*'s impact with the rapidly-approaching wall of water. He had been woefully unprepared for the wave that almost turned his boat over. Now, however, he was several seconds older, had learned a new lesson, was much wiser, and was well prepared for the next wave.

Despite having a lifetime of nautical experience, Blake had never encountered waves anywhere near as big as these. Not even *half* as big. And yet, *because* he had a lifetime of nautical experience, he quickly figured out what needed to be done...waited until just the right moment...eased the throttle half-way back...and returned his right hand to the steering wheel. He then held on as tightly as he could...and prayed the *Mary Beth*'s hull would endure the storm's incredible power.

Blake gripped the wheel as tightly as ever, the fingers of his left hand wrapped around the spoke at the ten o'clock position, and the fingers of his right hand wrapped around the spoke at the two o'clock position. He spread his feet even wider apart, and bent his knees into a half-standing, half-squatting stance. Thousands of hours aboard boats had taught him that spreading his feet wide apart made it easier to maintain his balance, and the spring-like effect of partially-bent legs increased his ability to absorb the forces generated by a boat's impact with the face of an oncoming wave.

And, with that, Blake had done all he could to prepare the *Mary Beth*...and himself...for the boat's impact with the towering wall of water. Or so he thought. Though totally unaware he was doing so, he did two additional things:

He clinched his teeth;

And he stared in wide-eyed wonder.

Meanwhile, Jack and Ava did the two things *they* knew to do:

They held their breaths;

And they gripped the rail as tightly as they could.

A second or two later, the *Mary Beth*'s bow pierced the face of the oncoming wave. In rapid succession, a powerful jolt threatened to tear her hull apart...a towering wall of water rolled across the roof of her cabin...and icy seawater soaked every stitch of her passengers' clothing.

It seemed the *Mary Beth* would remain beneath the water forever. However, after a seemingly-endless struggle that, in reality, lasted but a few seconds, she fought her way to the surface and emerged triumphantly from the back side of the wave. She hovered there a moment, the front half of her hull suspended in mid air.

And then...

She abruptly dropped her bow.

Blake was a super-fast learner...*especially* when it came to things nautical. He relaxed his knees...tightened the fingers of his left hand around the wheel's ten o'clock spoke...released the fingers of his right hand from the two o'clock spoke...and reached for the throttle.

And then...

Blake just stood there.

And waited.

But not for long.

The instant the *Mary Beth* lifted her propeller from the water, he pulled the throttle back to prevent the engine from over-revving as it had done before.

And then…

Blake again just stood there.

And waited.

But only until he sensed the *Mary Beth* had thrust her propeller back into the water. He then eased the throttle forward as far as it would go, removed his right hand from the throttle, wrapped his fingers around the wheel's two o'clock spoke, and tightened his grip. The *Mary Beth*—halfway pulled by gravity, and halfway thrust forward by her propeller—rapidly gained speed as she accelerated down the backside of the wave.

Not until the *Mary Beth* reached the trough lying between two waves did Blake, Jack, and Ava realize they had been holding their collective breaths. In perfect unison, they expelled the stale air from their lungs, took a few short breaths, then took one, big, deep breath, and braced themselves for the *Mary Beth*'s impact with the next wave.

And the next wave.

And the next wave.

And the next wave.

And the next wave.

This monotonous, exhausting pattern continued, wave after wave, for ten brutal minutes. Time and time again Blake used his right hand to jockey the throttle forward and backward while constantly using his left hand to saw the wheel clockwise, counter-clockwise, and back again—all in an effort to keep the *Mary Beth*'s bow pointed into the storm.

While Blake did the things *he* knew to do, Jack and Ava did the things *they* knew to do.

They gritted their teeth…

Held their breaths…

And gripped the rail as tightly as they could.

Meanwhile, the *Mary Beth*, oblivious to the plight of her passengers, plodded onward while repeatedly absorbing wave after wave and exchanging punch after punch with her deadly opponent.

She throbbed with life from stem to stern...

Obediently complied with each of her captain's commands...

And, above all...

She, like her passengers, displayed a desperate will to live.

Until...

Without warning...

Without any warning whatsoever...

The *Mary Beth*'s engine...

The *Mary Beth*'s one and *only* engine...

Quit running.

One second, the roar of the *Mary Beth*'s poorly-muffled engine, running at full throttle, drowned out all the other sounds. Her propeller, spinning at its maximum rpm, whipped the sea into a frothy, snow-white wake.

One second later...

Indeed, one-*thousandth* of a second later...

The *Mary Beth*'s engine became silent...

Her propeller stopped spinning...

And her bow, no longer held high with pride, dropped down

and plowed into the sea.

Over the span of a single second, the *Mary Beth* had become a lifeless hulk.

And, within two boat lengths, came to a complete stop.

For ten minutes Blake had been standing in the classic pose, immortalized in countless paintings and statues, of the determined sea captain.

Feet set wide apart.

Both hands gripping the ship's wheel.

A face as resolute as stone.

And eyes staring straight ahead.

Not once during those ten minutes had it occurred to Blake the *Mary Beth*'s engine might fail. But the *Mary Beth*'s engine *did* fail. And, the instant it did, the irrefutable laws of physics set into motion two significant events.

The first event involved the *Mary Beth* herself. As already noted, her bow dropped down, she plowed into the sea, and, within an incredibly short distance, decelerated from full speed to no speed.

The second event involved anything and everything not physically attached to the *Mary Beth*...which, of course, included her three passengers. During the moment the Mary Beth underwent a rapid deceleration, her passengers' bodies continued moving forward at virtually the same speed they had been moving.

Bake's body crashed into, and then smashed through, the steering wheel...his head and left shoulder collided with the solid, unyielding surface of the cabin's aft bulkhead...and his limp, unconscious body slumped to the deck directly below the shattered remains of the *Mary Beth*'s power console.

CHAPTER 22

A full minute passed before Blake regained consciousness. But he did not simply open his eyes, sit up, and yawn as if awaking from a restful nap. Instead, he awoke slowly...and in several stages.

When he first opened his eyes, Blake saw nothing but a thick, translucent blur. And his mind, like his vision, was a virtual blank. He just lay there a moment, unable to *see* anything, unable to *hear* anything, and unable to *think* anything. However, as he awakened a bit more, and progressed to the next stage, he asked himself the same questions, and in the same order, those waking up from a period of unconsciousness have asked themselves for millennia.

Where am I?

Blake instinctively shook his head and blinked his eyes in an effort to clear the fuzzy cobwebs from his mind and the translucent curtains from his eyes. No sooner did he dislodge the old cobwebs and curtains than new ones formed.

He then asked himself the next question.

What happened?

Blake again shook his head and blinked his eyes.

And then, he shook his head and blinked his eyes again.

And again.

And yet again.

Each time Blake shook his head, he shook it a little harder.

Each time he blinked his eyes, he blinked them a little longer.

He then asked himself the same questions he had just asked himself, but from a different angle.

Where had he been?

What had he been doing?

And what had been done to him?

Blake continued sitting there.

Continued shaking his head.

And continued blinking his eyes.

If only I could bring something—anything—into focus.

He again shook his head.

And again blinked his eyes.

Perhaps, if I can locate...and identify...just one visual cue, I can determine where I am.

By this time, Blake had regained enough of his senses to realize massive waves were crashing into the *Mary Beth*'s bow. He could feel the powerful shudder each wave sent from one end of her hull to the other. And, with each wave, tons of seawater flowed across the roof of her cabin and crashed down on top of him. At first, he considered the waves to be little more than a nuisance. However, when a wave he swore was bigger, wetter, and colder than all the others crashed down on top of him, a multitude of questions...and answers...cascaded through his mind.

Where am I?

On the *Mary Beth*, of course.

But where is the Mary Beth? Is she tied to a dock?

The extreme pitching, rolling, and yawing of the deck told Blake the *Mary Beth* was not tied to a dock. She was not tied to anything.

But where, exactly, are we? On the Hudson?

Blake quickly ruled out that possibility, as well. The Hudson could never be this rough.

Are we alone?

Blake looked all around, but could see nothing through the translucent curtain that shrouded his eyes. He then asked himself the same question, but with different words.

Is it just the Mary Beth and me?

On most days, Blake took no one with him. So why should today be any different?

Yes. It's just the Mary Beth and me. I came out here alone.

A vision of Ava placing her hand in his, and then descending from the dock to the gunwale, flashed through Blake's mind.

No! I did not come out here alone!

A lightening bolt could not have given Blake a more powerful jolt.

Ava is here! Ava came out here with me!

Blake shook the latest batch of cobwebs from his mind.

Is it just Ava and me? Are we the Mary Beth's only two passengers?

Blake shook more cobwebs from his mind.

He then recalled the moment Jack landed, with a dramatic thud, on the cockpit deck.

Okay. I have two passengers on board. So, where are they?

Blake again shook his head and blinked his eyes. However, despite all of his efforts, his thoughts and vision remained fuzzy.

Think, Blake! Think!

Blake shook more cobwebs from his mind...

And blinked more curtains from his eyes.

He then lifted his head...

Looked up, out, and over the stern...

And saw nothing but water.

Blake *again* shook his head...

And *again* blinked his eyes.

He then looked up, out, and over the port gunwale.

Nothing but water.

Blake *again* shook his head..

And *again* blinked his eyes.

And then—*again*—he looked up and out, this time over the starboard gunwale.

Still nothing but water.

Not a single landmark from which Blake could get his bearings.

For a brief moment, he considered pulling himself to his feet so he could look up, out, and over the roof of the cabin. However, when he considered the size of the waves that were curling, one after the other, across the roof of the cabin, he realized looking over the bow would be a waste of time and effort...because he already knew what he would see.

Nothing but water.

Lots of water.

Because, he finally realized, the *Mary Beth* was surrounded by ocean in every direction.

Another wave curled across the roof of the cabin and filled the cockpit's deck with water.

And filled Blake's mind with more details.

At Ava's request, and with Jack's approval, he had taken the *Mary Beth* out for a cruise. Not a cruise on the calm waters of the Hudson River, but a cruise on the open sea. A cruise to observe whales. So why, he asked himself, was he lying in a crumpled heap in the middle of the deck? And why, he asked himself, did he feel the flames of a hot fire in his rib cage every time he took a breath?

In the meantime, while Blake contemplated these and other questions, gigantic waves continued crashing into the *Mary Beth*'s bow and curling across her cabin. Each wave filled Blake's mind with more details...and raised more questions.

Blake finally realized a massive storm had overtaken the Mary Beth. He also realized this was not just any storm. It was, by far, the worst storm he had ever encountered.

Another wave crashed into the *Mary Beth*'s bow...
Curled across the roof of her cabin...
Crashed down upon Blake...
And filled his mind with more questions.

When did this storm begin?
How long has it lasted?
And how long have I been sitting here?
Has it been minutes?
Or hours?

Another wave.
Another detail.
I remember...
I remember pushing the throttle full forward...
As far as it would go.

Another wave.
Another detail.

I remember turning the Mary Beth directly into the storm...
Exactly as I should have done.

Another wave.
Another detail.

And I remember being so proud of her...
Each time she plowed through one of those waves.

Another wave.
Another de...

"*Damn* these waves!"

Blake again swore they were the biggest waves either he or the *Mary Beth* had ever encountered. In fact, they were larger than any wave he had ever *imagined* he would encounter. And yet, despite his pain and misery, he could not help but smile—because the *Mary Beth* had performed far beyond what he had ever dreamed her capable of.

And then...
Another wave...

And another detail...

Washed the smile off Blake's face.

Because he now remembered the most important point of all.

The *Mary Beth*'s engine had failed.
Failed without warning.
Gone from full power...
To no power...
In an instant of time.

Another wave...

This time a truly massive wave...

Crashed into the *Mary Beth*'s bow...

And with it came a virtual flood of details.

In ultra-fast motion, Blake's mind ran through the entirety of the fateful event. And then, in ultra-slow motion, one frame at a time, his analytical mind reviewed the event in the minutest of detail. First, he reviewed what happened to his boat. And then, he reviewed what happened to himself.

The *Mary Beth*'s instantaneous engine failure had caught him completely by surprise. Fate had denied him even the tiniest fraction of a second to brace his body against the *Mary Beth*'s sudden deceleration. In an incredibly short amount of time, and within an incredibly short distance—as small boats are wont to do—the *Mary Beth* had gone from full speed to no speed. While the *Mary Beth* underwent an almost-instantaneous deceleration, the unforgiving laws of physics—in particular the Law of Momentum—carried Blake's body forward at virtually the same speed it had been moving when the *Mary Beth*'s engine quit running.

Blake studied the power console and quickly realized why his rib cage burned as if it had been set on fire. His torso had crashed through the steering wheel at a speed of almost twenty knots. And then, a mere fraction of a second later, his head and left shoulder had slammed into the cabin's aft bulkhead. Blake knew all this was true because his head and shoulder throbbed as badly as his rib cage burned.

Another wave rolled across the roof of the *Mary Beth*'s cabin...poured more water into her cockpit...and flooded Blake's mind with more details. He finally realized how fortunate he had been. Fortunate because his rib cage and shoulder had absorbed most of the energy. And fortunate because, if his head had been the first part of his body to hit the bulkhead, the impact would have broken his neck or split his skull wide open..and perhaps both.

Blake made a quick but thorough assessment of his injuries.

Did I break any ribs?

He tested them by taking slow, steady, and deep breaths. He felt pain. *Lots* of pain. *Serious* pain. But nothing moved. And nothing popped. He could tolerate the pain, but needed to know, within the limits of a self examination, whether or not anything had been broken. So, he tested his ribs again, this time taking faster and deeper breaths than he did before. Again, nothing moved. And again, nothing popped.

The good news is, I don't think I broke a rib. The bad news is, it's still possible I broke a rib.

Blake spent a full thirty seconds reviewing the conundrum presented to him by his self-examination and resulting diagnosis.

If I broke a rib, I should feel something move or pop. Right?

Just to make sure, Blake tested his ribs again by taking several deep breaths. He then tested his shoulder again by raising his left arm high above his head and moving it from side to side as if waving to someone.

Once again, nothing moved.

And nothing popped.

Blake finally decided his ribs were okay. Badly bruised, maybe. Perhaps even cracked. But not broken. And he decided his shoulder, though badly bruised, had not been broken, nor had anything been torn.

Blake stared in wonder at the steering wheel. Or, to be more correct, he stared at what *remained* of the steering wheel. Until moments ago, the wheel had possessed eight spokes. It now had but four. The entire left side of the wheel...along with a portion of the hub...had been completely torn away by Blake's rib cage when his body crashed through it.

Blake panned his eyes across the shattered instrument panel. For three quarters of a century the *Mary Beth*'s instruments had been neatly arrayed on the cabin's aft bulkhead in an attractive arc that began on one side of the wheel, curved gracefully across it, and ended on the other side. The instruments were still arrayed in an arc, but the arc was no longer attractive, nor was the curve graceful. The glass on all but one of the gauges had been shattered, and one of the gauges had been torn free from the bulkhead and now dangled on a pair of wires beneath the gaping hole where it had previously been mounted.

Blake leaned his head back until it rested against the cabin.

He closed his eyes.

And winced.

He winced, not because of the various pains he felt, but because he had finally pieced together the full sequence of events that placed him and the *Mary Beth* in their present predicament.

And then...

Blake winced again.

And, this time, he did wince because of pain: a searing, white-hot pain that shot through his rib cage. He instinctively pressed the palms of both hands against his left side. And then, when the pain in his rib cage paled in comparison to a massive explosion that occurred deep inside his brain, he removed his hands from his ribs, placed his palms on the sides of his head, and squeezed his skull as if doing so would prevent it from blowing apart.

Do I have a concussion?

Blake squeezed his head for several seconds, then chuckled out loud.

Of course I have a concussion. I was knocked unconscious, wasn't I? That tells me, not only do I have a concussion, I have a bad concussion. How long was I unconscious?

Blake removed his hands from his temples and looked at his watch. Unlike all but one of the instruments on the power console, his watch had not been smashed. It was still running. However, Blake quickly realized it would do him little good. His watch would yield no useful information other than the present date and time. It could not tell him when the disaster had taken place, nor could it tell him how long he had been lying there, unconscious, on the deck.

I should get up.

And Blake *tried* to get up.

However, the moment he attempted to rise to his feet, everything around him started spinning...his body became limp again...and he sagged to the deck.

Perhaps.... Perhaps I moved too quickly. I'll try again. But, this time, I'll move more slowly. And more cautiously. But, first, I'll reassess my injuries, just to make certain none of them are serious.

Blake again took several deep breaths...again raised his left arm...again moved his shoulder through its full range of motion...and again concluded nothing had been broken or torn.

Blake made another attempt to get up. As with his previous attempt, everything around him started spinning. And, this time, he also experienced a powerful wave of nausea.

Blake again closed his eyes, allowed his body to sag to the deck, and leaned back until his head and shoulders rested against the cabin's aft bulkhead.

I need to rest. Perhaps I'll just sit here a few minutes.

And Blake did rest.

But only for a few short seconds.

No! I can't allow myself to rest. At least, not right now. It's more important that I check on my passengers.

Instantly, Blake's body stiffened.

Passengers!!!

Blake entered panic mode the moment he remembered other people were on board. He snapped his eyes wide open. And then, when he remembered how vertigo and nausea had taken over his entire being the last time he opened his eyes, he snapped them shut again. This time, however, thanks to a sudden surge of adrenaline, he experienced neither vertigo nor nausea.

Blake already had more than enough to worry about: the *Mary Beth*'s struggle with the raging storm...the inferno blazing inside his rib cage...the pulsating throb in his shoulder...

And a head he swore would explode at any moment.

Blake pushed all that to the back of his mind and tried to concentrate on nothing but Jack and Ava. Had they been washed overboard? Fearing the worst, he swiveled his head from side to side and searched the deck.

If only I could focus my eyes!

Blake blinked his eyes several times.

And then, he blinked them again.

And yet again.

He finally cleared his vision enough to see that neither Jack nor Ava had been washed overboard. They were lying in a shallow pool of foamy seawater on the cockpit deck. He inhaled deeply, and was about to heave a sigh of relief, when It occurred to him their bodies—*their limp bodies*—lay face-down, rocking back and forth, and from side to side, in concert with the boat's movements.

Are they injured?

Blake's eyes darted back and forth between Jack and Ava.

Neither showed the slightest sign of voluntary movement.

Seconds earlier, Blake had been relieved to discover Jack and Ava remained on board the *Mary Beth*. However, now that he realized they were unconscious—and possibly even worse—his relief yielded to another bout of panic, panic that grew stronger and stronger as he shifted his eyes back and forth between their limp bodies.

Blake's mental video rewound itself all the way back to the start. He watched the video again, this time one frame at a time, each frame adding newly-discovered details to his mental tally of recent events.

First, the *Mary Beth*'s engine quit, her bow dipped into the sea, and she underwent a rapid, almost instantaneous deceleration. Meanwhile, everything not tied down or otherwise secured continued moving forward at virtually the same speed it had been moving before the engine quit. In the span of a single second, Blake crashed through the steering wheel and smashed the gauges on the cabin's starboard bulkhead, while Jack and Ava crashed into the cabin's port-side bulkhead.

Blake took a long look at Jack and Ava, who, he realized, had been more fortunate than he had been. Fortunate because they had been sitting down instead of standing up...and fortunate because their arms had been wrapped around the port-side rail. If they had been standing up, or had not been gripping the rail, the differential between the speed of their bodies and the speed of the bulkhead at the time of impact would have been much greater than it actually was, and they would have crashed into the bulkhead with far greater force than they actually did. They would have received many broken bones—and may have even been killed—by their impact with the solid, unforgiving bulkhead. Blake prayed they had only been stunned.

As if on cue, Jack and Ava opened their eyes. Blake watched them survey their surroundings, and assumed they were asking themselves the same age-old questions he had recently asked himself. He watched a moment longer, and then asked:

"Are you two okay?"

Blake had tried to speak his words in a raised voice. However, due to the myriad of sharp pains shooting through multiple parts of his body, the words trickled out of his mouth in little more than a weak whisper, nowhere near his normal speaking voice.

"I think so."

Jack's voice, like Blake's, sounded very weak. Blake watched Jack whisper something to Ava, then shared Jack's alarm when Ava simply turned her head in Jack's direction and stared at him with a blank expression. At first, Blake feared Ava might be suffering from shock, but held on to the belief she was simply taking a moment to process what Jack had said to her. When Ava finally nodded, and the latter proved true, Blake puffed the air out of his lungs.

Ava had paused a moment before replying to Jack's question. First, to process his question, and again to reassess her injuries. Finally, after giving Jack additional nods of her head, she gave him an answer.

"Yes, Jack, I am okay. At least, I *think* I am okay."

Blake studied Jack's eyes while Jack studied Ava's eyes. Jack finally agreed with Ava's assessment, and turned his head toward Blake.

"Yeah, Blake, I think we're okay. What about you?"

Jack's voice sounded much stronger than it had a moment earlier. Blake took that to be a positive sign, an indication Jack had not been seriously injured.

"Yeah, Jack. I'm okay. Well, I *do* have a few bruises...a cracked rib or two...and I think I have a concussion. In fact, I think all three of us have concussions."

Blake rolled his eyes and nodded his head toward the wrecked console.

"I crashed through that wheel as if it were made of balsa. Of course, it's *not* made of balsa. That's solid teak. Well, what's *left* of it is solid."

Blake remained seated on the cockpit deck. Actually, in the truest sense of the word, he was not seated; he still lay in a crumpled heap. He made another effort to get up...watched the world, along with everything in it, start spinning again...and decided he should remain crumpled a while longer. He closed his eyes and reassessed his injuries while waiting for his head to clear. He then opened his eyes, looked across the cockpit at Jack and Ava, and reassessed *their* injuries. He decided all three would be okay.

Well, I checked out my status, and I checked out my passengers' status. Now it's time to check out the Mary Beth's status.

Earlier, Jack and Ava had marveled at the mental and physical bonds that connected Blake and the *Mary Beth*. No matter what Blake had asked the *Mary Beth* to do, she had done it. But now, those bonds no longer existed...because the *Mary Beth* lay dead in the water.

Literally...

Dead...

In the water.

She was helpless, *absolutely helpless*, unable to defend herself against the angry, violent sea. Wave after wave battered the *Mary Beth*'s hull, twisting it on all three axes. Each wave lifted her bow high into the air, rolled her deck to starboard forty-five degrees, and slued her hull into a sharp, right-hand turn. And then, as soon as that wave passed beneath her hull, her bow crashed down, her deck rolled forty-five degrees to port, and she slued into a sharp left-hand turn. Seconds later, another wave lifted her bow high into the air and the process started all over again. Time and time again the *Mary Beth* and her helpless passengers experienced an angry, violent, twisting-and-turning ride aboard a storm-tossed roller coaster.

CHAPTER 23

Blake knew his boat—and its three passengers—were in serious trouble. His mind screamed at him...demanded he spring into action...insisted he take immediate steps to ensure the safety of the *Mary Beth* and everyone on board.

But Blake's body also screamed at him...demanded he remain seated...and insisted, in no uncertain terms, that springing into action was not an option. His ribs stung, his shoulder ached, and his head throbbed—each pain a vivid reminder of his collision with the steering wheel and the cabin's aft bulkhead.

Blake wrapped his arms around his torso and clutched his rib cage, as if doing so would keep his insides from pouring out through some unseen hole. Again and again he shook his head in an effort to remove the stubborn cobwebs from his skull. And, again and again, he blinked his eyes in an effort to wipe away the translucent film that shrouded his vision.

I should get up. I should do something. I don't know what I should do, but I should do something.

Blake made another attempt to get up...another attempt to lift his body off the deck...another attempt to rise to his feet. But the pain was more than he could bear. So, once again, he slumped to the deck, leaned back, and rested his head against the cabin's aft bulkhead.

A new set of cobwebs formed inside Blake's brain, and a new translucent film obscured his vision. Once again, he shook his head, blinked his eyes, and clutched his rib cage.

I'll just sit here and rest a while longer. Another minute or two won't make that much of a difference.

Blake turned his head and watched Jack lift himself onto his hands and knees. Jack's first attempt failed, and his second attempt didn't do much better. But Jack finally succeeded, crawled across the deck to Ava, placed his right hand on her shoulder, and shook it gently. Ava opened her eyes and looked up at Jack...but said nothing. Jack looked into her eyes a moment, said something to her, and helped her rise from the deck and onto her hands and knees.

More cobwebs formed inside Blake's head, and another translucent film shrouded his eyes. He tried....but failed...to keep Jack and Ava in focus.

Blake finally decided, at least for the present, his eyes would do him no good. So, he closed them, and, within seconds, his thoughts turned inward. But only until another wave of pain started in his rib cage, moved upwards through his shoulder, and exploded inside his head.

When the pain subsided, Blake cursed himself for having placed the *Mary Beth*, along with himself and his passengers, in such a terrible dilemma. He shook his head again...and blinked his eyes again...all to no avail. He tried...tried hard...but was unable to see anything except a fuzzy blur.

So, Blake again closed his eyes.

And, this time, he lectured himself.

Listen, Blake. You have a choice. You can either sit here and feel sorry for yourself...like you're doing right now...or you can pick yourself up, tend to your boat, and take care of your passengers. Which is it going to be?

Blake shook the latest batch of cobwebs from his mind, then blinked the latest translucent curtain from his eyes. With his head and vision momentarily cleared, he returned his attention to Jack, who was now helping Ava crawl to the bench-like seat that stretched across the aft-most part of the cockpit. Jack waited patiently until Ava pulled herself up from the deck, seated herself on the cushion, and wrapped her arms around the rail. Jack then pulled himself up, sat down beside her, and wrapped his own arms around the rail.

Blake studied Jack. Meanwhile, Jack studied Ava. Like Blake, Jack wanted to make certain Ava was securely anchored to the rail. He also wanted to make certain she had not been seriously injured. Not until Jack believed he had done all he could for Ava did he remove his eyes from hers and turn his head towards Blake.

"What happened, Blake? Did we run out of gas?"

Blake did not answer Jack's question. Instead, he braced himself for the next cycle of the *Mary Beth*'s three-axis roller-coaster ride. He then studied Jack and Ava to make certain they were also braced. It was then that he noticed something new. Something different.

Jack's skin is white as a sheet.

At first, Blake considered the possibility Jack had been seriously injured, and was now showing the tell-tale signs of shock and internal bleeding. However, no sooner had that thought passed through Blake's mind than Jack twisted his torso around, leaned over the rail, and vomited. Jack's vomit had no blood in it—which told Blake the rough seas had taken their toll. A suppressed smile tugged at the corners of his mouth.

Jack was seasick!

Blake wanted to celebrate, but realized he had no time to do so. Instead of taking a moment to gloat in a small victory—but a victory nonetheless—he braced himself while the Mary Beth rode out another wave and Jack finished heaving. He then answered

Jack's question.

"No, Jack. We did not run out of gas. In fact, enough fuel remains on board to return to port, cruise all the way out here again, and return to port a second time."

Blake watched...and waited...while Jack again twisted his torso around, leaned over the rail, and underwent a second session of violent vomiting. For a brief moment, Blake considered going to Jack's aid, but quickly decided it would be wiser to brace himself for the merciless onslaught of the angry sea.

Besides, at this stage, there isn't much I can do for the man.

Jack and Ava braced themselves as the *Mary Beth*'s bow rose high into the air and she began climbing the face of another massive wave. Meanwhile, Blake's body began sliding down the steeply-sloping deck toward the stern.

Not until the *Mary Beth* reached the crest of the wave did her bow come down...she sat on an even keel for a couple of seconds...her bow dropped even more...and she began her long, plummeting descent down the back side of the wave.

And Blake's body again slid down the steeply-sloping deck.

Only, this time, down was toward the bow, not the stern.

Jack twisted his torso a third time, leaned over the rail, and endured another session of violent vomiting. Blake again considered whether or not he should do something to ease the man's discomfort. Should he go inside the cabin, open the first aid kit, and get Jack some pills for his motion sickness? No, Blake decided, it was too late to help Jack. Besides, Blake Turner had more pressing matters to worry about than a seasick passenger.

An uninvited seasick passenger, at that.

"No, Jack, we don't have a fuel problem. Our tanks are three-quarters full, perhaps even more. Nor do we have a problem with

186

the carburetor or any other part of the fuel system. If the problem had been fuel-related, the *Mary Beth*'s engine would have surged and sagged a few times before shutting down. At the very least, it would have sputtered once or twice. But it went from full power to no power...*instantly*...which tells me we either broke something, or we have an electrical problem. I didn't feel any unusual thuds or vibrations, nor did I hear any unusual sounds, so I'm betting we have an electrical problem—most likely a loose connection, considering how badly this sea is battering us around. I'll take a look and see if I can fix it."

Blake crawled over to the bench beside the wrecked steering console, reached up with one arm, grabbed the rail, and began pulling himself to his feet. Meanwhile, Ava noticed a wisp of smoke streaming from the engine compartment. She stared at it a few seconds, then unwrapped her left arm from the rail, swung an outstretched finger towards the smoke, and opened her mouth to say something. However, the moment she realized Blake had noticed the alarm on her face and was already looking in the direction her trembling finger was pointing, she closed her mouth, returned her left arm to the rail, and braced herself for the next wave.

The wisp of smoke grew thicker.

And blacker.

It took a moment, but Blake's groggy mind finally realized the *Mary Beth* was on fire.

Which caused a second burst of adrenaline to course through his bloodstream.

In an instant, the surge of hormone-induced energy cleared the remaining cobwebs from Blake's mind, flung wide the film-like curtain that obscured his vision, and muted the stings and aches in his rib cage and shoulder. He surprised everyone...including himself...with how quickly he sprang into action. Even before Ava finished withdrawing her left left arm and wrapping it around the rail, Blake had twisted his body around and was reaching for the nearest fire extinguisher—which had been conveniently mounted on the cabin's exterior bulkhead just below the steering console, a well-thought-out position easily reached from both inside and outside the cabin.

Jack and Ava watched with awe and admiration as Blake snatched the fire extinguisher from its storage bracket, rammed his index finger through a small loop, and removed the safety pin. It reminded them of the mandatory scene in all war movies...the scene in which a soldier pulls a nearly identical pin from a hand grenade. However, what Blake held in his hand was not a hand grenade, nor did he have any intention of throwing it. Instead, he used his left hand to cradle the fire extinguisher against his chest and abdomen while using his right hand to sidle across the deck like a crab missing one of its legs.

Upon reaching the center of the cockpit, Blake shifted his weight, thrust the fingers of his right hand through a large D-ring that lay in a depression on the deck, pulled the ring upward, and flung open the engine compartment's heavy hatch. Instantly, thick black smoke, tinged with dirty orange flames, erupted from the now-exposed engine compartment.

Jack and Ava, literally frozen in place by shock and fear, continued watching as Blake calmly, confidently...and with focused efficiency...raised the fire extinguisher, aimed its nozzle at the base of the flames, squeezed the trigger, and methodically swept the nozzle from side to side until all the chemicals in the tank had been completely emptied...and, to everyone's good fortune, the fire had been extinguished.

Blake stared at the smoldering engine and prayed it would not burst into flames again. When satisfied the fire would not reignite, he looked up just in time to see Jack and Ava communicate, each to the other with a single nod of their heads, their mutual acknowledgment and sincerest admiration of his cool-headed performance.

Not once had Blake demonstrated the slightest hint of panic or hesitation.

No one moved...and no one said a word...until the wind blew away the mixture of pitch-black smoke and snow-white fire-suppressing chemicals. Only then did Jack and Ava, no longer frozen with fear, unwrap their arms from the handrail, slide off the bench, get down on their hands and knees, and crawl across the wildly gyrating deck to the edge of the engine compartment. Though neither of them had a clue as to what they were looking at, they, along with Blake, surveyed the extent of the fire's damage. Even though a thick coating of white powder, speckled here and there with black dots of soot, covered everything in sight, all three could tell the engine had been severely damaged. Only Blake knew the extent of that damage, and how severe it actually was.

The fire had destroyed all but the largest of the wires attached to the engine. Even those had been damaged, with only a hint of charred insulation remaining on their thick copper cores; most of the smaller wires had melted in two; and some of the wires no longer existed. They had been completely vaporized. Further inspection revealed everything made of plastic, rubber, or thin metal had either been consumed by the fire, burned beyond recognition, or warped into absolute uselessness.

As far as Blake was concerned, the collective damage had

rendered the engine inoperable and, for all practical purposes, irreparable. He felt confident he *could* repair it, but only if someone towed the *Mary Beth* into a port and he had access to all the parts, tools, and wires necessary to complete the job. At sea, with only the limited tools and materials he had on board, there was nothing he could do to repair the *Mary Beth*.

Jack and Ava panned their eyes away from the engine...

And looked at Blake...

Who appeared oblivious to their presence.

Indeed, Blake *was* oblivious to Jack and Ava's presence. At the moment, he saw nothing but the *Mary Beth*'s wrecked engine—an engine that, only minutes before, had been her life force...her throbbing heartbeat. Such was no longer the case. The fire had rendered the engine both lifeless and useless.

Blake was staring at a dead carcass.

Jack and Ava, not yet aware of the totality of the damage, innocently thought Blake was evaluating what needed to be done to bring the *Mary Beth* back to life. They had no way of knowing he was taking a few extra moments to accept the fact her engine, without proper tools, shop supplies—and a substantial inventory of new parts—was beyond saving.

"Well," Blake sighed with a tone of finality.

And then, again becoming aware of Jack and Ava, and aware they were waiting for his next move—or, at least, waiting for him to give them some additional information—Blake spoke with carefully chosen words. The last thing he wanted to do was alarm his passengers; and yet, at the same time, he wanted to make the severity of the situation, and the extent of his disappointment, perfectly clear to both of them.

"It's obvious we won't get *this* engine running again."

Slowly, gently, and very reverently, as if closing the lid on the casket of one of his closest friends or a much-loved member of the family—and, to Blake, the *Mary Beth*'s engine had been both—he lowered the hatch and folded the D-ring into the recess her designer and builder had specifically provided for it. And then, during the few seconds of relative calm between waves, he stood up, walked wearily to the starboard side of the cockpit, and sat down on the bench beside the shattered remains of the steering console.

Jack and Ava, still on their hands and knees, watched Blake wrap his left arm around the rail and lean his head back against the cabin's aft bulkhead. They stared at him a moment longer...tried to imagine what was going on inside his mind...and returned their attention to the closed hatch cover. Only then did it occur to them the cover actually *did* conceal a grave...a grave in which Blake had, not just symbolically, but in reality, laid to rest the body of one of his closest friends. With that image in their minds, they did exactly as mourners at a funeral do upon realizing their physical eyes will never again see their loved one's body: They used their memories, along with their imaginations, to envision the entombed body.

Jack and Ava lingered a few more seconds to pay their last respects. And then, they turned away from the final resting place of the *Mary Beth*'s dead engine...crawled on their hands and knees to the rear of the cockpit...pulled themselves up and onto the bench...and wrapped their arms around the rail.

A moment later, Jack and Ava gave each other a somber look.

Neither needed to be told their situation had progressed from serious...

To hopeless.

CHAPTER 24

Blake began studying Jack and Ava the moment he sat down. He watched as they paid their last respects to the *Mary Beth*'s dead engine...felt pity for them as they turned their backs to the engine compartment and wearily crawled across the deck...and empathized with them as they struggled to pull themselves up from the deck and onto the bench. Not until they secured themselves to the *Mary Beth* by wrapping their arms around the rail did he feel the tension drain from his body.

And Blake *continued* studying Jack and Ava, even when he realized they had fixed their gaze directly upon him. He used the opportunity to study their eyes. First, he studied Jack's eyes. And then, he studied Ava's eyes. He wanted to look directly into their eyes for two reasons. First and foremost, to evaluate their mental state. But he also wanted to communicate an unspoken apology to each of them.

Next, Blake studied Jack and Eva's facial expressions. And, finally, he studied their body language. In the end, he concluded they were okay. Okay, at least, on the outside. On the inside, he still felt their collision with the cabin's aft bulkhead had given each of them a concussion.

It occurred to Blake that Jack and Ava seemed remarkably calm—*too* calm—considering all they had seen and experienced during the last few minutes. Were they in shock? Not just physical shock, but also emotional shock? Or were they simply not aware of how serious the situation had become? Whatever the case, he decided it was time to move on.

"I should send out a distress signal."

Blake leaned toward the console, reached for the weatherproof microphone, and lifted it off its hook. He then turned the radio's volume half-way up, rested his right hand...and the microphone...in his lap, and composed the message he was about to send. A moment later, he lifted the microphone, pressed the black button located on it's right-hand side, and listened to the speaker.

He heard nothing.

No clicks.

No static.

Nothing.

Blake stared at the microphone a moment, reached over to the console, and turned the radio's volume to its maximum level. And then, he pressed the microphone's button several times, just as he had done before leaving the dock. As before...

He heard nothing.

No clicks.

No static.

Nothing.

Blake checked to make certain he had turned on the radio and set the volume to its maximum level. And then, just as he had done a moment earlier, he keyed the microphone several times.

Still nothing.

No clicks.

No static.

Nothing.

Not a sound emanated from the console's weatherproof speaker. Blake pressed the transmit button one more time and, while holding it down, leaned forward, placed his ear against the speaker, and repeatedly tapped the microphone with the nails of the middle and index fingers of his right hand.

Still nothing.

Blake keyed the microphone several more times while staring at the radio's power meter.

The needle never moved.

Blake stared at the dead speaker. He then stared at the useless microphone. He felt the strong temptation to vent his frustration by slinging the microphone to the deck. Instead, he took a deep breath to calm his nerves, slowly released his breath, and, with an outward display of calmness that concealed his inner turmoil, returned the microphone to its hook.

"I was afraid of that."

Blake had spoken his words in a soft, matter-of-fact voice, as he had not intended to be overheard by Jack and Ava. However, when he realized they *had* overheard him, he turned his head directly towards them, lowered his chin, furrowed his brow, and paused a moment—as if to give them the non-verbal message: *You need to hear this*. He held that pose until he had their full attention.

"We don't have any power. *None.* As you already know, the engine is dead. Well, now you know the battery is dead. I'm guessing a loose connection...or perhaps a frayed wire...caused a short circuit; the short circuit caused the fire; and the fire, combined with the short circuit, drained all the power from the battery."

At a loss for additional words, Blake shrugged his shoulders, rose to his feet, and removed the cushion from the bench upon which he had been sitting. His cushion, like all the other cushions aboard the *Mary Beth*, served double duty: first, as a seat; and, second, as the cover on a storage compartment. Fully aware Jack and Ava had been—and still were—watching his every move, he leaned over, opened a tool box, and selected a long screwdriver. He then walked to the center of the cockpit, knelt on one knee, and grasped the D-ring on top of the engine compartment's hatch.

The same hatch he had so reverently...

And with absolute finality...

Closed only moments earlier.

As if reluctant to expose the cadaver he had so recently buried, Blake closed his eyes, took a deep breath, and held it a moment. He then whooshed the air from his lungs, lifted the hatch, and stared at the dead engine, just as one would stare at a recently exhumed body. A moment later, he leaned over, reached down into the compartment, and used the long metal shaft of the screwdriver to bridge the gap between the battery's positive and negative terminals.

From Jack and Ava's vantage point, it appeared nothing happened. They did not *hear* anything, nor did they *see* anything. They could only watch Blake as he stared at the battery a few moments, and then heard him mumble something under his breath. Blake had again spoken his words softly, with no intention of being overheard. However, upon realizing he should share his thoughts, he repeated them in a louder voice for Jack and Ava's benefit.

"I've seen static electricity make stronger sparks than that."

Blake looked up at Jack and Ava...gave them another apologetic grimace...took a final, farewell glance at the charred engine...and lowered the hatch. He then rose to his feet, returned the screwdriver to its toolbox, replaced the cushion on top of the storage compartment, and sat down on top of the cushion. Finally, he wrapped his left arm around the rail, gently leaned his head and shoulders back until they rested against the cabin's aft bulkhead, and contemplated his next move.

Meanwhile...

The seconds ticked by...

The weather grew worse...

Clouds turned blacker...

Winds blew stronger....

And seas grew taller.

A full minute passed before Blake rose to his feet, stepped across the cockpit, and lifted another seat cushion, this time exposing the contents of the port-side storage compartment. And then, doing something he should have done long ago, he retrieved three life jackets and replaced the cushion on top of the storage compartment.

As always, Blake placed his passengers' safety above his own. First, he helped Ava put on her life jacket. He then helped Jack put on his. Only after tending to his passengers' needs did he tend to his own by slipping the third life jacket over his shoulders. He then went around the trio a second time. First, he adjusted the straps on Ava's life jacket; then the straps on Jack's life jacket; and, finally, the straps on his own life jacket.

As they had done several times before, Jack and Ava gave each other a slight nod, this time to acknowledge they had noticed...and approved of...the fact Blake had taken care of them before he had taken care of himself.

Only when Blake was satisfied he had made his passengers as safe as he could did he return to the front of the cockpit, place his hand on the top frame of the companionway hatch, and brace himself against the *Mary Beth*'s tossing and turning. A few seconds later, during a moment of relative calm, he stepped through the hatch, descended the ladder, and disappeared into the cabin's dark interior. He remained there a full minute, then reappeared with an armload of bedding. Without bothering to climb the ladder, he tossed the bedding into the cockpit, turned around, and disappeared into the cabin's dark interior a second time...a third time...and a fourth. Jack and Ava stared in uncomprehending disbelief as Blake repeatedly tossed armload after armload of mattresses, cushions, and pillows onto the pile of sheets and blankets he had tossed out earlier.

Blake finally climbed the ladder, removed the seat cushion from the port-side bench, retrieved a coil of rope, and replaced the cushion. And then, confusing Jack and Ava even more, he tied the cushions, blankets, sheets, pillows, and mattresses into something that resembled an over-sized and over-stuffed version of the strips of cloth children tie onto the tails of kites.

And *then*, when Blake finished doing that, he added even more to Jack and Ava's confusion by crawling out onto the bow and securing the free end of the rope—which, unknown to them, ceased being a rope and became what sailors refer to as a line the instant he attached it to the cleat mounted on the deck at the extreme front end of the boat.

And, finally, as if Blake had not confused Jack and Ava enough, he returned to the cockpit and heaved the entire mound of bedding overboard. Jack was no longer able to contain his curiosity.

"What in the world did you just do? And why, *in the name of Insanity*, did you do it?"

Blake smiled, sat down on the bench beside the wrecked steering console, wrapped his left arm around the railing, leaned back, and rested his head and shoulders against the cabin's aft bulkhead. After a long pause—during which Jack assumed Blake had either not heard his question or had chosen to ignore it—Blake lifted his head, looked straight into Jack's eyes, and gave both him and Ava a brief, but very informative, lesson in basic seamanship.

"It's called a sea anchor."

While thinking out loud, Blake attempted to put a positive spin on things.

"When we get back home, I'll record this in my log book as *The first time I used a sea anchor*."

Blake didn't bother to tell Jack and Ava he carried an informal, spiral-bound, temporary log on the Mary Beth; not until later, after returning from a cruise, did he transcribe his notes and unrecorded thoughts to the formal, leather-bound book he kept safe and dry inside his apartment.

"To be perfectly honest with you, I've never even *seen* a sea anchor. I've read about sea anchors, and I've seen pictures and drawings of them, but I've never had an opportunity to actually *see* one. So, it stands to reason, I have never come close to using one. Of course…*now*…I *have* seen one…I have *made* one…and I am *using* one. It should only take a minute or two for us to find out, first hand, if mine actually works. I'll be the first to admit it doesn't look like much, but, assuming it works—and I'm confident it will—it should create enough drag to keep our bow pointed directly into the storm. If these waves get much taller than they are right now, and if the *Mary Beth* gets turned backwards or sideways, she'll either get swamped or turn turtle and roll over…neither of which will do us any good. That's why it's important we keep her bow pointed into the storm."

Jack and Ava no longer appeared confused. However, Blake could clearly see neither of them shared his confidence in the seemingly futile exercise of tossing all the boat's mattresses, pillows, cushions, and bedding overboard—despite the fact they had been tied together with a long rope and remained attached to the boat.

Blake again leaned his head back, closed his eyes, and tried to relax. Less than ten seconds later, his eyes flew open and his face lit up, suggesting to Jack and Ava a new idea had popped into his mind. He rose to his feet, strode with purpose to the rear of the cockpit, reached between Jack and Ava, and removed the small American flag from the short flagpole mounted on the stern. Jack and Ava watched in uncomprehending disbelief when Blake turned the flag over and rehung it upside down. Jack continued staring at the flag—*the upside-down flag*—long after Blake returned to his seat next to the console. Finally, again overcome by curiosity, Jack asked Blake to explain his actions.

"I don't mean to ask so many questions, Blake, but why—*why in the name of Insanity*—did you do *that*? Just what do you hope to accomplish by hanging the American flag upside down?"

"It's not a protest, Jack, if that's what you're thinking. It's a universal distress signal. It means we're in a dire emergency and need immediate assistance."

Though Jack and Ava did not say it out loud, they agreed with Blake—they were, indeed, in a dire emergency—but neither of them realized just how dire the emergency was. Nor did they realize how much more serious the emergency would become.

Throughout the remaining hours of daylight, the *Mary Beth*'s passengers did little but hold on while the storm continued battering her hull. Blake had hoped the captain of another boat—or, perhaps, the crew of a passing ship—might see them dead in the water, notice their upside-down flag, and come rushing to their rescue. Instead, the only things he saw during his brief, periodic sweeps of the horizon were huge, white-capped waves and towering seas. He saw no other boats. Nor did he see any passing ships.

As night began to fall, Blake rose from his seat, reached inside the cabin, and removed a flashlight from a hook on the aft bulkhead.

He switched on the light...

The light came on, though very weakly...

Flickered a time or two...

And went out.

Blake shook the flashlight. He then tapped it a couple of times against the open palm of his opposite hand. And, finally, he gave it a hard slap. The bulb never lit up again. Not even a weak flicker. He toggled the switch a few times...again slapped the flashlight's case —this time *really* hard—and cursed himself. Normally, he kept spare batteries *and* a spare flashlight on board the *Mary Beth.* Unfortunately, he had recently loaned both to the owner of another boat and forgot to replace them.

Blake returned the flashlight to its hook and went below. A minute or so later, he brightened the main cabin's darkness with a pair of kerosene lanterns, their wicks burning with feeble, yellow flames. He hung one of the lanterns on a hook, which existed just for that purpose, in the center of the ceiling of the cabin. He used the light of the second lantern to examine the water level in the bilge. He then emerged from the cabin, climbed onto its roof, and hung the second lantern on a hook attached to the top of a short mast.

After returning to the cockpit, Blake pointed the index finger of his right hand toward Jack, rotated his wrist palm-upward, and used the age-old signal of curling one's forefinger a few times to motion for Jack to come forward and join him.

At first, Jack hesitated to leave the relative safety of the stern handrail. However, when Blake again motioned for him to come forward—this time curling his entire arm with a sense of urgency—Jack unwrapped his arms from the rail and zigzagged across the deck to the front of the cockpit. Blake turned his back to Ava in order to prevent her from hearing what he was about to say. He then leaned closer to Jack, placed his mouth right next to Jack's ear, and spoke in a lowered voice.

"Listen, Jack. Listen very carefully. I'm sure you've already noticed this, but I'm going to tell you anyway. The *Mary Beth* is an old girl. She's a *very* old girl."

Blake turned his head just enough to look over his shoulder and steal a glance at Ava. And then, deciding he and Jack were far enough away from Ava to prevent her from hearing his words over the sounds of the storm, he stood up straight, looked Jack eye-to-eye, swallowed hard, and cut straight to the point.

"We're taking on water, Jack, and we're taking it on fast. Not so much from the occasional wave that rolls over the cabin and into the cockpit; most of that water is draining across the deck, through the scuppers, and back into the sea. The main problem is this: We're leaking below the waterline."

Blake stared more deeply...and more intensely...into Jack's eyes. And he *continued* staring into Jack's eyes until absolutely certain he had Jack's full attention.

"The *Mary Beth* is coming apart at the seams, Jack. And I don't mean that in a figurative sense. She is *literally* coming apart. She may hold together until morning, but I have my doubts."

Blake turned his head away from Jack and stole another glance at Ava—who appeared terrified, with her arms wrapped tightly around the rail and her frightened eyes staring laser-like straight into Blake's eyes. Blake allowed his eyes to linger on hers a moment longer, then turned his head forward again, looked into Jack's eyes, and waited until he had Jack's full attention.

"Jack, I'll do what I can for the *Mary Beth*. In the meantime, you do what you can for Ava."

Jack, no longer seasick—but considerably weakened by his bout with the landlubber's malady—lifted his eyes, looked beyond Blake, and studied Ava. He then lowered his eyes until he again stared directly into Blake's eyes. Blake stared back, with his head slightly cocked, and his eyebrows slightly raised—a clear signal to Jack he was waiting for a response. Jack finally gave Blake a few shallow nods to indicate he understood the seriousness of their situation, and began walking towards the rear of the cockpit.

Blake immediately reached out with his right hand, grabbed Jack's left arm, and gripped it firmly. Jack looked down, stared at Blake's hand a moment, and then peered into Blake's eyes. Blake spoke more loudly this time, making no effort to prevent Ava from hearing what he had to say.

Because...*this* time...Blake *wanted* Ava to hear every word.

"I'm sorry this happened, Jack. It's *my* fault. *All* of it is *my* fault. *Entirely* my fault. With my experience, I knew better than to pull away from the dock, let alone go out to sea, without first checking the weather forecast."

Actually, Blake had made several mistakes only a rookie skipper should make—mistakes he would have never made had his reasoning not been clouded by his all-consuming preoccupation with Jack's unannounced...and unwelcome...arrival. First and foremost, as Blake had already explained to Jack, he had failed to check the weather. That omission alone was bad enough. But he had also failed to file a float plan. And thirdly, he had made a conscious decision not to monitor radio traffic. If he had done those three things—if he had done just *one* of those things...and it didn't matter which—neither the *Mary Beth,* nor her passengers, would be in their present situation.

Jack squared his body with Blake's body, placed both hands on Blake's shoulders, and turned Blake's body until the two men stood face to face. And then, to Blake's complete surprise, Jack spoke to him as if they had been life-long friends.

"Don't be so hard on yourself, Blake. We're in this boat together...no pun intended. As I'm sure you figured out early on, I don't know the first thing about boats, but I'll do all I can to help you take care of the *Mary Beth.* Just tell me what to do."

"Right now, Jack, your main responsibility is to take care of Ava. For the moment, *your* girl needs *you* more than ever...and *my* girl needs *me* more than ever."

Jack stared at Blake a moment...opened his mouth as if to say something...and then closed his mouth. He finally gave Blake a simple nod, removed his hands from Blake's shoulders, and walked away.

Blake watched Jack zigzag across the gyrating deck, sit down beside Ava, and wrap his arms around the rail. Only after Blake felt certain his passengers were safe—or as safe as he could make them—did he descend the companionway ladder and disappear into the cabin to see what, if anything, he could do to help the *Mary Beth.*

CHAPTER 25

Blake extended his left arm and braced himself against one of the cabinets. Two seconds later, a massive wave crashed into the *Mary Beth*'s bow, a powerful shudder ran the full length of her hull, and her deck tilted steeply bow-up as she climbed the face of the wave. Her deck leveled off a moment as she rode across the wave's crest, and then tilted bow-down—*steeply* bow-down—as she raced down the wave's back side.

For a few brief seconds, the *Mary Bath* sat on an even keel in the deceptively calm water in the deep trough that separated the wave that had just passed underneath her hull and the wave about to crash into her bow. And then, time and time again, as steady and predictable as a pendulum swinging beneath a clock, she repeated her violent dance with the angry sea.

Blake had been correct about his sea anchor. Though it did not look like much, it did its job and created sufficient drag to keep the *Mary Beth*'s bow pointed directly into the waves. As a result, she no longer tortured her passengers with violent, twisting and turning, side-to-side, rolling and yawing motions—but she more than made up for it by increasing the amplitude of her bow-up and bow-down pitching motions.

Blake continued bracing himself against one of the cabinets with his left hand while using his right hand to open a small storage locker. He reached inside the locker, retrieved a galvanized bucket, closed the locker, and secured its latch. He remained in that position, braced against the cabinet with his left hand while holding the bucket with his right hand, until the *Mary Beth* neared the crest of a wave and began leveling off. He then pushed away from the cabinet, returned to the companionway hatch, and paused just long enough to glance across the cockpit to check on Jack and Ava. They still sat on the stern bench, exactly where he had last seen them, and they still had their arms wrapped tightly around the rail. Blake quickly decided, except for the frightened looks on Jack and Ava's faces, they were okay.

Blake leaned over, lowered the bucket to his ankles, laid it on its side, and waited for it to fill with water. He then lifted the bucket chest high, extended it beyond the edge of the cabin's companionway hatch, and poured its contents out of the cabin and onto the cockpit deck. Each time he lifted the bucket, two gallons—sixteen pounds—of water flowed from the *Mary Beth*'s bilge, across the cockpit deck, through the scuppers, and back into the sea from which they had come.

Relentlessly—and ever so slowly—the minutes ticked by. A glance at the galley clock told Blake he had bailed water for almost an hour. During that hour he had become increasingly weary from filling, lifting, and emptying the bucket...the gaps in the *Mary Beth*'s hull had grown wider and more numerous...and water had leaked through her hull at a faster and faster rate. He finally realized, despite the fact he had bailed water as fast as he could, the *Mary Beth* had settled another three inches into the sea.

Always...*always*...the analytical accountant, Blake refused to be deceived by his gallant efforts. He had known, even before he started bailing, water would flow into the *Mary Beth* faster than he could bail it out. He had also known, from the very start, it would be just a matter of time before the *Mary Beth* would sink. However, determined to keep her afloat as long as possible—and aware that even the shortest pause would hasten her demise—he continued bailing water...and swore he would never stop.

But Blake's efforts took their toll.

In less than an hour he became exhausted. His shoulders ached. His arms trembled. And the muscles in his upper back contracted into a tight knot. The combination of fatigue and pain forced him to slow down. And yet, despite all this, he again swore he would never stop.

Meanwhile, Jack realized Blake had reached the limits of what he could do. Though hesitant to leave Ava's side, he rose to his feet, walked to the front of the cockpit, and lowered himself through the companionway hatch.

For a long, uncomfortable moment Jack and Blake stood face to face, in knee-deep water, simply staring at each other. Jack finally glanced over his shoulder to check on Ava, turned to face Blake again, and extended an open, upturned palm—an unspoken request for Blake to hand him the bucket. Blake stared at Jack's palm a moment, lifted the bucket from the water, and placed its bail across Jack's outstretched fingers.

Just like that, with neither man saying a word, an informal ceremony—a ceremony the two would repeat several times during the long, stormy night—had been completed. Jack lifted the partially-filled bucket above the level of the companionway hatch and poured its contents onto the cockpit deck. He then leaned over, laid the bucket on its side, and waited for it to refill.

Exhausted, cramped, and in serious pain, Blake watched in a daze while Jack filled and emptied the bucket several times. He finally gathered enough strength to step past Jack, climb the ladder, stumble across the cockpit deck, and collapse onto the starboard bench next to the shattered remains of the steering console. A moment later, with barely enough energy to do so, he lifted his left arm, flopped it over the rail, and braced himself.

And not a moment too soon.

An instant after Blake wrapped his arm around the rail, another massive wave crashed into the *Mary Beth*'s bow. In rapid succession, the wave unleashed every ounce of its thunderous fury, curled across the top of the *Mary Beth*'s cabin, dumped hundreds of gallons of water onto her cockpit deck, and lifted her bow to a frighteningly steep angle.

Ava, who still sat on the bench that stretched across the stern, waited until the *Mary Beth*'s bow dropped, she rode across the crest of the wave, made a mad descent down the wave's backside, and her deck leveled off in the trough between two waves. And then, in a single, fluid motion, Ava unwrapped her arms, pushed away from the rail, rose from her seat, ran across the cockpit, and threw herself onto the starboard bench next to Blake. She paused only as long as it took to glance into his surprised eyes, and then wrapped her arms around the starboard rail to brace herself a split second before the next wave crashed into the *Mary Beth*'s bow. As had happened so many times before—and, as would happen so many times more—the *Mary Beth* shuddered from stem to stern, a wall of water rolled across the roof of her cabin, and her bow lifted high into the air. Ava waited until the crest of the wave passed beneath the *Mary Beth*'s hull. And then, the instant the bow began to drop, she unwrapped her left arm from the rail and indicated to Blake, with a swirling motion of her index finger, she wanted him to twist his body around and face forward.

Blake gave Ava a puzzled look, his way of telling her he did not understand what she had in mind. In an unspoken reply, even in the middle of the *Mary Beth*'s race down the backside of the wave, Ava furrowed her brow, pursed her lips, and *again* twirled her finger in the air...this time twirling it twice as fast, and with double the urgency, as she had twirled it a moment earlier. Blake finally understood what Ava wanted him to do, but he didn't understand *why* she wanted him to do it. He wrinkled his brow and shrugged his shoulders to let her know he was confused as to her intentions, then obediently released the rail and twisted his torso.

Finally, and just in time, both Blake and Ava wrapped their arms around the rail and braced themselves for the violent impact of the next wave. As had happened so many times before, the *Mary Beth* shuddered from stem to stern...a wall of water curled over the roof of her cabin...her bow lifted high into the air...and she began her climb toward the crest of the wave.

Ava again waited until the *Mary Beth*'s bow began to drop. The instant it did, without wasting a single second, she unwrapped her arms from the rail, shifted her weight, slapped her hands down onto Blake's shoulders, and pressed her thumbs and fingers deeply into his flesh. For almost ten seconds—the length of time it took the *Mary Beth* to level off on the crest of one wave, drop her bow, race down the wave's backside, and level off in its trough—she kneaded Blake's cramped and aching muscles. Not until the last possible moment did she release Blake's shoulders, throw her arms around the rail, and brace herself for the explosive collision with the next wave. She quickly lost count of how many times she rode out one wave, released the rail, dug her thumbs and fingers into Blake's flesh, massaged his cramped and aching muscles, and then released Blake's flesh, wrapped her arms around the rail, and braced herself for the next wave.

Despite Ava's previous lack of nautical experience, she impressed Blake with how quickly she learned—as all good sailors learn—to time her movements with the movements of the sea. Ava impressed Blake even more with how effectively and efficiently she took advantage of each moment of relative calm to knead his aching shoulders and massage his cramped back.

After fifteen minutes of rest and massage, Blake rose to his feet, walked to the port side of the cockpit, lifted one of the seat cushions, and removed a large, water-proof bag. Even from the far side of the cockpit, and with no light other than the soft, yellow glow provided by the kerosene lanterns, Ava easily made out the words *Marine Emergency Kit* boldly stenciled in broad, black letters on the side of the bright yellow bag. She then noticed, stenciled in smaller letters below *Marine Emergency Kit*, the words *Mary Beth*.

Blake rummaged through the bag's contents and removed a large, orange, toy-like, pistol. And then, after rummaging through the bag's contents a second time, he pulled out a cardboard card with what appeared to Ava to be six shotgun shells attached to it. Blake resealed the yellow bag, stuffed it into the storage compartment, replaced the cushion, and removed one of the cartridges from the card. He inserted that cartridge into the pistol, then removed the five remaining cartridges and put them in his pants pockets—two in the right front pocket, and three in the left front pocket.

Blake tossed the empty card overboard, climbed atop the cabin, pulled back the pistol's hammer, pointed its barrel almost straight up, and pulled the trigger.

A loud "WHOOM" startled Ava and made her blink.

She opened her eyes to see a bright, reddish-orange ball of light ascend high into the sky, arc over the top of its trajectory, and plummet toward the sea. The instant the ball of light disappeared, she returned her attention to Blake watched as he intensely...and repeatedly...scanned the full, three-hundred-sixty-degree circle of the dark horizon.

Blake had hoped to see the arcing glow of an answering flare...flashes of light from the signal lamp on another boat...or, even better, the powerful beam from the spotlight mounted high atop a ship's bridge. The only things Blake saw, and the only things Blake heard, were the sights and sounds of wind, rain, and sea.

CHAPTER 26

Without any discussion whatsoever, Blake, Jack, and Ava settled into a routine they followed for the next eight hours. Blake bailed water forty-five minutes to an hour while Jack rested and Ava massaged his arms, back, and shoulders. And then, Jack took a turn with the bucket and bailed water forty-five minutes to an hour while Blake rested and Ava massaged *his* arms, back, and shoulders. Following each session of rest and massage, Blake climbed atop the cabin, fired another flare, spent five to ten minutes scanning the black horizon for the arc of an answering flare, the flashes from a signal lamp, or the powerful beam of a spotlight—none of which ever appeared. He then went below, took the bucket from Jack, and started the cycle over again.

An hour after Blake fired the last flare, daylight came. However, with the storm still raging as strongly as ever—and showing no signs of letting up—daylight proved to be little more than a lighter shade of black.

At times, rain came down so hard Blake could barely see the length of the *Mary Beth*'s hull. The wind, howling constantly, swirled and shrieked through the *Mary Beth*'s open hatch. And the waves, some of which towered more than fifty feet above the troughs between them, continued battering the old girl's hull with relentless fury. Sinking and drowning—both of which seemed inevitable—drew closer by the minute.

Blake twisted his torso to the left and looked into Ava's eyes. He then gave her a deep nod: first, to thank her for the massage she had been giving him; and second, to signal he was about to get up.

Though much less spryly than when their ordeal had first begun, Blake climbed atop the cabin and scanned the horizon. On a normal day, the ocean in this part of the Atlantic would have been dotted with boats and ships. But not today. Blake remained on top of the cabin long enough to make a second...and then a third...three-hundred-and-sixty-degree scan of the horizon. Finally, disappointed and discouraged, he eased himself down from the roof of the cabin, stepped onto the gunwale, and lowered himself into the cockpit. After giving Ava a brief glance, he stepped through the hatch, descended the companionway ladder, and extended his hand to take the bucket from Jack.

Jack, now exhausted beyond exhaustion, gratefully relinquished the bucket without showing the slightest hint of hesitation. He then turned around, placed a foot on the ladder, and attempted to climb it. However, initially weakened by his bout of seasickness, and further weakened by the long night of grueling sessions with the bucket, he paused halfway up the ladder to gather what little strength remained in his body. Upon reaching the last rung and stepping out onto the deck, he again paused, partly to catch his breath, and partly to scan the horizon...just as Blake had done a minute or two earlier.

And, like Blake, Jack saw nothing but white-capped waves.

Blake emptied a bucketful of water just as Jack completed his survey of the horizon and began his short walk toward the rear of the cockpit. While waiting for the bucket to empty, Blake glanced up at Jack, then leaned over to refill the bucket.

Blake never dipped the bucket underneath the water.

And Jack never reached the rear of the cockpit.

Because a monstrous wave...

A wave that came from a different direction than all the other waves...

Hammered the *Mary Beth*.

Neither Blake nor his passengers had prepared themselves for the rogue wave. As a result, none of them were prepared for the terrifying sequence of events the wave set into motion. For several hours they had repeatedly braced themselves against the rhythmic —and predictable—fore and aft pitching motions caused by waves hitting the *Mary Beth* bow-on. But the rogue wave did not hit the *Mary Beth* bow-on. It crashed full-abeam, on her starboard side. And it did so with the sound and power of a tremendous explosion. Almost in the same instant, it roared across the *Mary Beth*'s open cockpit.

The sudden and unexpected impact of water—tons and tons of it—hit Ava so hard it ripped her arms away from the rail, washed her off the bench, carried her across the cockpit, and slammed her against the base of the port-side bench. An instant after that, the *Mary Beth* heeled over to port a full eighty degrees.

Under normal circumstances, Blake would have simply braced himself, ridden out the wave, and waited for the *Mary Beth*'s deck to return to a more comfortable angle. But this had not been a normal circumstance—and Blake had not been aware the wave was coming—so he made no effort to brace himself for the wave's impact. As a result, he sailed across the interior of the cabin while half-consciously and half-instinctively flailing both arms in an effort to grab onto something. But his fingers found nothing...nothing but empty air...nothing to slow him down. His head and body slammed into the row of cabinets that lined the upper part of the cabin's port-side hull.

Blake's life jacket cushioned his body against the impact, which prevented additional damage to his ribs and shoulder. His head, however, absorbed the full impact of its collision with one of the cabinets. Knocked senseless a second time, he slumped to the deck and remained there, unconscious, for more than a minute. He would have drowned had his life jacket not kept his face above the water.

After regaining consciousness, Blake spent another minute figuring out where he was and piecing together what had happened. Once he accomplished that, he turned his thoughts, as all good captains do, to the safety of his passengers.

Passengers!!!

As had happened earlier, Blake suddenly remembered he was not alone. He immediately snapped his eyes open and tried to stand up.

And immediately recalled the pain and nausea he had experienced following his first concussion. So, he clamped his eyes shut again, and allowed his body to relax. He rested a moment, and then, slowly and cautiously, opened his eyes and raised himself to his feet. He stood there a moment, determined he would not allow himself to become nauseous again, and before wading across the cabin to the companionway ladder. He then grabbed the top rung with both hands to brace himself, leaned forward, and peered through the open hatch.

Blake immediately saw Ava, and noticed she was lying face down on the port side of the cockpit. He stared at her for several long seconds before he realized, not only was she not moving, her arms and legs were folded at odd angles.

A tight knot formed deep inside Blake's stomach.

Has Ava been hurt?

Blake held his breath…

And continued staring at Ava…

As the knot grow tighter…

And tighter.

Is Ava dead?

The knot grew even tighter.

If only Ava would move!

The knot grew tighter…

And tighter…

Until…

Finally!

Ava moved.

At first, she only raised her head.

But then…

She pulled her arms underneath her body…

Lifted herself onto her elbows…

And rolled over onto her back.

The knot in Blake's stomach relaxed a bit.

Ava is alive!

Blake continued staring at Ava…

Meanwhile, Ava stared straight up into the ink-black sky.

Suddenly, Blake became aware of two things:

One, the intense pounding inside his head;

And two, the fact he had been holding his breath.

The stale air whooshed from Blake's lungs. He then took several deep breaths in an unconscious effort to expel the carbon dioxide from his bloodstream and saturate it with oxygen.

Throughout this time, Blake had been focused on nothing but Ava. But now, knowing she was safe, he closed his eyes and concentrated the efforts of both his conscious and subconscious minds to make sense of what had happened.

It took a few seconds, but Blake finally realized Ava had flown across the cockpit and crashed, either into the port-side bench or the port-side rail, during the same moment he had flown across the cabin and crashed into one of the cabinets that lined the upper part of the *Mary Beth*'s port-side hull. He then realized that Ava, like himself, had been knocked unconscious a second time.

Blake opened his eyes and studied Ava again. She seemed groggy. And a bit confused. But, otherwise, she appeared to be okay. Blake fought his natural impulse to rush to her side, take her into his arms, comfort her, and reassure her that everything would be okay.

And then, as if struck by a bolt of lightning, Blake remembered he had a second passenger...a passenger whose status he had yet to determine. He looked away from Ava and searched every inch of the deck for Jack.

He, glanced at Ava, then searched the deck a second time.

And then, he searched the deck a third.

Jack was nowhere to be seen.

Blake returned his attention to Ava, studied her a moment, and decided she would be okay. His present and foremost concern was no longer with her, a passenger he *could* see, but with Jack, a passenger he could *not* see.

Once again, Blake's heart urged him to climb the ladder, rush to Ava's side, and give her as much aid and comfort as he possibly could.

But Blake's mind reminded him his top priority was *not* to rush to Ava's side; at the moment, his top priority was to determine Jack's status.

Blake's mind finally won the battle over his heart. He blinked his eyes to clear his vision...scanned every inch of the cockpit a fourth time...and then scanned the cockpit a fifth time.

Jack was nowhere to be seen.

Blake gave his head a hard shake to clear the latest batch of cobwebs from his mind...blinked his eyes to clear the newest translucent curtain that obscured his vision...and scanned the cockpit a sixth time.

Jack was *still* nowhere to be seen.

Blake returned his attention to Ava. She was now lying flat on her back...no longer staring upward into the sky. During the time he had been looking for Jack, she had rolled over onto her right side, lifted herself onto her right elbow, and was now staring in the direction of the companionway hatch.

Ava is staring directly at me.

This time, it was Ava who shook *her* head, and Ava who blinked *her* eyes in an effort to clear away the cobwebs and wipe away the curtains. She shook her head and blinked her eyes a second time. And then, a third time. Finally, with her mind and vision temporarily cleared, she looked one more time at Blake before making a thorough search of every corner of the cockpit.

Not just once, but twice.

Ava reached the same conclusion Blake had reached.

Jack was nowhere to be seen.

Ava again turned her head toward the companionway hatch. This time, however, she didn't simply stare in Blake's direction; she stared directly into Blake's eyes. She, like Blake, was still dazed and confused...and she, like Blake, thought Jack might miraculously reappear in a spot where she had already looked...so she tore her eyes away from Blake's eyes and scanned the cockpit a third time. Of course, despite her and Blake's multiple scans, and despite their unfounded belief Jack might reappear, he simply was not there.

In the same second, Blake and Ava realized Jack had been

washed overboard. Another second passed. And then, a burst of adrenaline surged through their bloodstreams. Their eyes, which had been glazed over the past few minutes, were suddenly clear and sharply focused. And their expressions, which had been dazed and confused during those minutes, now exhibited a combination of terror and panic.

Ava reacted differently to the rush of adrenaline than Blake did. Whereas Blake became calmly but intensely focused on the situation at hand, Ava became wildly hysterical. She repeatedly screamed Jack's name while frantically scanning back and forth between the deck and the ocean.

In an instant, the surge of adrenaline cleared Blake's mind of all confusion and propelled his body through the barriers of pain and exhaustion. He half climbed, and half leapt, up the companionway ladder...catapulted through the hatch as if shot from a canon...and dashed across the deck to the rear of the cockpit. He then leaned forward, removed one of the cushions from the bench, and, without slowing down—not even pausing a second or two to take aim—he heaved the cushion as far as he could throw it in Jack's general direction. He then heaved the second cushion as far as he could throw it.

On any other day, Blake would have waited...and watched...to see where the cushions landed. But not today. Long before the first cushion hit the water, even as the second cushion was still climbing toward the top of its arc, he looked downward and began surveying the pair of storage compartments he had just uncovered. He then leaned over, reached inside one of the compartments, and grabbed a large, brightly-colored, orange life ring. Ava noticed the words *Mary Beth* stenciled on its side in big, bold, black letters.

Blake lifted the life ring with his right hand, lifted the neatly coiled line with his left hand, and gave the line two sharp tugs. The first tug assured him one end was firmly attached to the life ring; the second tug assured him the other end was firmly attached to a fitting inside the storage compartment. When satisfied everything was as it should be, he took one step back, anchored the outside edge of his left foot against the base of the storage compartment, spread his legs wide apart, and tensed every muscle in his body.

Moments earlier, without wasting the tiniest fraction of a second to take aim, Blake had blindly tossed the seat cushions in Jack's general direction. However, before tossing the life ring, he took several seconds...several *long* seconds...first, to gauge the distance between Jack and the *Mary Beth*, and, second, to estimate the wind speed and wind direction. He adjusted his aim accordingly, made several practice swings, and, when everything felt just right, used every ounce of his adrenaline-induced strength to heave the ring.

Ava held her breath and watched in horror as the momentum generated by Blake's powerful toss carried his body aft. For a moment, she thought Blake's throwing motion would propel him up and over the rail—which led her to believe he was about to join Jack in the sea. Blake, however, by virtue of the fact both of his arms were already stretched out in front of him, simply slapped the palms of his hands onto the rail and used the combined strength of his arms and upper body to absorb the momentum created by his powerful toss.

Suddenly, as often happens in situations like this, everything went into slow motion. The life ring arced slowly and gracefully up, up, and up high into the sky. And then, assisted by the wind, it sailed straight toward Jack. Despite the gravity of the situation, Blake could not help but smile. Never, not if he had made that toss a thousand times, could his aim have been more perfect.

First, the ring splashed into the water five feet beyond Jack. And then, a second or so later, the line fluttered down from the sky and landed squarely across the top of Jack's head. Jack instinctively reached up, grabbed the line, and pulled the ring to him...he then slipped his head and right arm through the ring...and held on as tightly as he could.

And with that, as suddenly as it had begun, the slow motion effect ended and everything returned to normal speed. With a powerful two-armed shove, Blake pushed his body away from the railing, grabbed the line with both hands, and started pulling. By doing so, he was not simply retrieving the line; he was also pulling the ring...and Jack...toward safety.

Moments earlier, when Ava realized the rogue wave had washed Jack overboard, she had been overcome with panic...her panic had yielded to hysteria...her hysteria had yielded to shock...and her shock had yielded to paralysis. Ever since that moment she had simply sat there, paralyzed, unable to move a muscle, while watching Blake toss the cushions and life ring toward Jack. And, like Blake, she had been mesmerized by the ring's graceful—and incredibly accurate—arc across the sky.

However, the instant Blake grasped the line and started pulling Jack toward safety, a second burst of adrenaline surged through Ava's bloodstream. As if a spell had been broken, she immediately sprang to her feet, sprinted across the *Mary Beth*'s wildly gyrating deck, stood shoulder-to-shoulder beside Blake, and, with perfectly-timed movements, reached out, grabbed the line, and meshed her hands with his hands. And then, as skillfully as if she and Blake had practiced the procedure a thousand times, they pulled the line, the ring—and the totally exhausted body of Jack

Smith—to the stern of the *Mary Beth*.

The instant Jack reached the boat, Blake dropped the line, leaned over the rail, and used both hands to grab one of Jack's wrists. A second later—again, as if she and Blake had practiced the procedure a thousand times—Ava also dropped the line, leaned over the rail, extended both of her arms, and grabbed Jack's other wrist. Continuing to work as a team, she and Blake pulled Jack up the transom, over the rail, and into the *Mary Beth*'s cockpit.

For a moment, Ava's chest heaved as she gasped for breath and stared down at Jack. She then dropped to her knees, dove forward, and threw her arms around Jack's neck.

Unlike Ava, Blake had not experienced a second burst of adrenaline. So now, instead of being filled with renewed energy as she had been, he was totally exhausted. He took two steps back, spread his feet wide apart, and braced himself as best he could on wobbly, unsteady legs. And then, while his body swayed backwards and forwards in harmony with the ocean's swells, he watched helplessly as Jack found enough energy to lift his arms, wrap them around Ava's shoulders, and embrace her. While Blake continued watching, Jack kissed Ava—kissed her *repeatedly*—first planting a kiss on her forehead, followed by a kiss on one of her cheeks, and, finally, multiple kisses on her neck. Only after expressing his love and affection for Ava did Jack look up at Blake, give him a grateful nod, and mouth two words.

"Thank you."

Time stood still as Blake stared down at Jack and Ava, and Jack and Ava continued embracing each other, two lovers either oblivious to, or not caring about, Blake's presence. Jack finally whispered something to Ava...Ava whispered something to Jack in reply...and Ava reciprocated the many kisses Jack had given her by kissing him lightly, once on each cheek, and once squarely—and oh, so tenderly—in the middle of his forehead. Ava finally gave Jack one final hug, pushed herself to her knees, and, with the last of her adrenaline-induced strength, helped Jack crawl to the forward end of the port-side bench.

Jack stared at the rail a moment, as if he considered it to be a highly-desired, but very distant—and unattainable—goal. Nonetheless, encouraged and assisted by Ava, he gathered up his energy, extended his left arm, and grasped the rail. And finally, again with Ava's encouragement and assistance, he pulled himself onto the bench.

Ava remained on her hands and knees until Jack finished seating himself on the bench and wrapping his arms around the rail. She then extended her right arm, grasped the rail, pulled herself up, and sat down on the bench beside Jack. After wrapping her arms around the rail, she looked at Jack and gazed deeply, lovingly—and, Blake noticed, adoringly—into his eyes.

Only when both Jack and Ava were safely and securely seated on the port-side bench did Blake turn his back to them, step through the companionway hatch, and descend the ladder into the flooded cabin. At first, he just stood there, alarmed by how much deeper the water had become during his absence. He then shuffled his feet around in the waist-deep water, located the bucket, leaned over, retrieved the bucket, and resumed bailing.

Prior to the rogue wave, water inside the cabin had reached the middle of Blake's thigh. It now lapped at his belt line. During his absence, the *Mary Beth* had settled an additional eight inches into the sea.

The *Mary Beth* was sinking.

And she was sinking fast.

Blake lifted the bucket chest high and placed it on the companionway's raised threshold—or coaming, as it is referred to in nautical terms. He then tipped the bucket over and watched two gallons of seawater pour out of the bucket and onto the cockpit deck. Moments later, as he had done hundreds, and perhaps thousands, of times during the night—he was too tired to estimate the actual number—he again lowered the bucket, waited for it to fill with water, and repeated the process again.

And again.

And again.

And again.

In the early hours of the *Mary Beth*'s ordeal, during those moments she had first begun to leak, each bucket of water poured from her cabin had added minutes to her life...those minutes had added up to hours...and those hours had gotten both the *Mary Beth* and her passengers through the long and stormy night.

In those early hours, the gaps in the seams of the *Mary Beth*'s hull had been fewer and smaller than they were now. For the first half of the night, Blake and Jack had almost kept up with the inflow of water. However, as the night progressed, those gaps had grown, both in number and size. As a result, seawater now flowed into the *Mary Beth* at a much higher rate than Blake and Jack could bail it out. However, as Blake continually reminded himself, each lift of the bucket removed two gallons of water from the cabin and returned it to the sea. But Blake also reminded himself that each lift no longer added minutes to the *Mary Beth*'s life.

It added but seconds.

Blake softened that sobering realization by telling himself, if not for his and Jack's efforts, the *Mary Beth* would have lost her fight against the sea and sunk to the bottom of the ocean many hours ago. But still, despite the possession of such positive knowledge, Blake-the-accountant remained, as always, Blake-the-realist. He could not allow himself to gloat over his and Jack's past success...because he knew the *Mary Beth*'s leaks, which had been relatively minor during the storm's early hours, were now raging torrents. There was no way possible for his and Jack's meager efforts to keep up with the inflow of water.

Despite being aware of the ultimate outcome, Blake prodded himself onward by reminding himself each bucket of water mattered. While the realist part of his genetic makeup told him his and Jack's efforts would be futile in the long run, the cold, calculating, accountant part of his makeup told him each second the *Mary Beth* remained afloat equated to, not only another second of life, but another second of hope for her passengers. Time and time again he waited for the bucket to fill...lifted the bucket chest high...poured its contents out of the cabin...and watched the water flow across the cockpit deck, through the scuppers, and back into the sea.

Blake was now totally exhausted. He needed to rest. He *had* to rest. So, he paused a moment...closed his eyes...took a deep breath...and exhaled that breath through pursed lips and puffed cheeks.

And then, Blake chastised himself.

What do you think you're doing?

You don't have time to rest!

Every...bucket...counts.

Blake knew, regardless of how tired he was, he had to continue bailing water. Regardless of how distraught he was, he had to think positive thoughts. It required a major effort, but he forced himself, time and time again, to fill the bucket, lift the bucket, and pour the bucket's contents out of the cabin and onto the cockpit deck. He constantly reminded himself, even though the situation appeared hopeless in the long run, each lift of the bucket meant the *Mary Beth* would remain afloat an additional second or two.

Who knows? When added together, all those extra seconds might mean the difference between life and death...for Jack...for Ava...and for me.

So, Blake again lowered the bucket...

And, again, he waited for the bucket to fill.

Giving up...

Is not...

An option.

Blake-the-sailor swore he would fight until the bitter end.

Every...

Bucket...

Counts.

But Blake-the-realist knew the ultimate outcome.

The Mary Beth...

Will sink.

And Blake-the-sailor knew the *Mary Beth* would sink within the next hour.

Blake was not the only one that knew the *Mary Beth* had entered her final hour. Jack and Ava knew it, too. Consigned to their fate, they remained seated on the cockpit's port-side bench, clinging tightly to each other with one arm, and tightly to the rail with the other. They watched with resignation as, time and time again, Blake lowered the bucket...waited for the bucket to fill...lifted the bucket chest high...balanced the bucket on the companionway coaming...and tilted the bucket onto its side.

Each time Blake tilted the bucket, he, along with Jack and Ava, watched two gallons of water pour out of the cabin, flow across the cockpit deck, drain through the scuppers, and return to the sea from which they had come.

And, each time Blake waited for the bucket to empty, he stole a quick glance at Jack and Ava to make certain they were okay.

Those frequent glances, which were noted by Jack and Ava, confirmed something they had accepted as fact many hours earlier: No matter how intensely Blake focused on the task at hand, his primary concern—indeed, at times his *only* concern—was the safety of his passengers.

Dip…lift…pour.

Dip…lift…pour.

Dip…lift…pour.

Countless dozens of times Blake dipped the bucket, waited for it to fill, lifted the bucket chest-high, sat it on the companionway coaming, tilted the bucket onto its side, and glanced at Jack and Ava while waiting for the bucket's contents to empty onto the cockpit deck.

On most occasions, Blake gave Jack and Ava little more than a quick glance—no more than one or two seconds, just long enough to confirm they remained safe.

However, on one occasion, as Blake studied Jack and Ava with a long, lingering gaze, a final, stabbing pain pierced his heart.

Because Ava no longer sat with one arm wrapped around Jack and the other arm wrapped around the rail. She now sat with *both* arms wrapped around Jack's waist and, as Blake noted, her head buried deeply—*and lovingly*—in Jack's chest.

Long hours of battling the storm had drained Blake's physical energy. And now, with the final and complete realization that Ava had been, was now, and forever would be totally devoted to Jack, the last ounce of his *emotional* energy drained from his body.

CHAPTER 27

Blake stared at Jack and Ava a moment longer. And then, devoid of all energy, he allowed the empty bucket to slide off the coaming, fall to his side, and fill with water. As soon as the bucket was full he tried to lift it, just as he had done countless times before. His first attempt failed, so he stiffened his back, spread his feet wide apart, and made a second attempt to lift it. He failed with that effort, as well.

Blake stared at the heavily-constructed galvanized bucket, accepted the fact he no longer possessed enough strength to lift it when filled with sixteen pounds of seawater, and tilted it so half of its contents—eight precious pounds...*a full gallon*...of water—flowed back into the cabin. He then repositioned his legs...straightened his back...bunched the muscles in his shoulders...and made another attempt. Finally, with a back he swore would snap in two at any moment, and with shoulders burning so badly he swore they had already burst into flames, he managed to lift the bucket chest high, just high enough to pour its eight pounds of water—*a single gallon* —onto the cockpit deck.

Even though Blake was exhausted and in extreme pain, his accountant's mind churned through the numbers. Eight pounds of water—which he swore weighed eight tons—gave the *Mary Beth* but a few extra seconds of life. Just how many seconds? Ten? Always the realist, Blake knew it was more like five seconds...and maybe as little as one or two. He figured, even if it *was* as long as five or ten seconds, as tired as he was it would take twice that long to lower the bucket, fill it half full, and lift it high enough to pour its contents—*a mere gallon of water*—out of the cabin, onto the cockpit deck, through the scuppers, and back into the sea.

The bottom line?

The *Mary Beth* was taking on water...

At a faster rate...

Than Blake could bail it out.

In other words...

The *Mary Beth* was sinking.

And she was sinking faster than ever before.

Jack, of course, had no way of reading Blake's thoughts—but he had no problem reading Blake's twisted grimace. Aware of Blake's pain and exhaustion, Jack considered trading places so Blake could have a few moments of much-needed rest. The issue became a moot point when Blake stopped bailing water, lifted his head, stared directly into Jack's eyes, and gave him three weary *come here* waves of his left hand. Jack knew Blake was pleading with him, not with words, but with an exhausted and defeated expression, to come take his place.

Jack was not a sailor, but he knew the most basic and over-riding facts: His and Blake's combined efforts to keep the *Mary Beth* afloat had been gallant, and to some degree successful, during the early stages of their plight; however, any further effort to save the *Mary Beth* would be a waste of what little energy they still possessed. So, during the time it took Blake's mind to calculate how much longer the *Mary Beth* could remain afloat, Jack's mind simply accepted the basic facts—*the same facts*—Blake had accepted long ago.

The *Mary Beth* was sinking.

And she was sinking fast.

But Jack also reasoned, as Blake had reasoned moments earlier, as long as the *Mary Beth* remained afloat, her passengers *also* remained afloat. And, as long as the *Mary Beth*'s passengers remained afloat, there remained a chance, slim though that chance may be, they might be rescued.

Jack gave Blake a reluctant nod of his head. He then kissed Ava on the forehead, peeled her arms from around his waist, rose to his feet, placed Ava's hands on the rail, and waited until she wrapped her arms around it. Not until certain Ava had secured herself to the Mary Beth did Jack turn away from her and take a step toward the companionway hatch.

And then...

As if Jack's feet had suddenly become glued to the deck...

He just stood there...

Leaned his head back...

And stared straight up.

This intrigued Blake. What could be so interesting as to capture Jack's full attention? A quick glance at Ava revealed she had also tilted her head back, and, like Jack, was staring straight up into the emptiest and blackest sky one could imagine.

What could Jack and Ava be looking at?

Blake leaned his torso out of the cabin, twisted his neck, and contorted his body until he, too, was looking straight up. There was nothing to be seen. Nothing but featureless, coal-black sky. So, Blake again looked at Jack and Ava, who were *still* staring into the featureless, coal-black sky.

Blake finally realized neither Jack nor Ava had actually *seen* anything. They had *heard* something. And now, he heard it, too. Not a sound born of the storm—neither wind, nor rain, nor wave—but a completely different sound. An unnatural, man-made, throbbing sound. At first, Blake thought it to be his imagination, but the fact Jack and Ava also heard it gave him hope, a hope unlike any he had experienced since their ordeal had begun.

The source of the sound was far off in the distance.

So Blake willed it to get closer.

And, within seconds, his heart beat faster and faster.

Because the sound *was* getting closer.

It rose and fell with the wind.

Grew louder.

Then softer.

Then louder again.

It finally grew so loud its volume no longer rose and fell.

It had become a steady, throbbing sound that beat against Blake's chest.

First Blake, then Jack, and finally Ava recognized the sound to be the rapid, unmistakable, whop-whop-whop of a helicopter's main rotor. Their hearts beat with renewed hope as the helicopter drew closer.

Closer.

Ever closer.

Soon, in addition to the whop-whop-whop sound of the main rotor, the *Mary Beth*'s passengers heard the unmistakable, high-pitched whine of a pair of powerful jet turbines. The whine grew louder and louder until it all but drowned out the whop-whop-whop of the rotor...and it *did* drown out the hiss of falling rain, the roar of waves, and the whistle of wind.

All three of the *Mary Beth*'s passengers stood spell-bound as a Coast Guard helicopter—its distinctive orange-and-white paint scheme standing out in bold contrast against the backdrop of the black clouds above it and the angry, white-capped waves behind it —flew directly towards them on its homeward leg after rescuing the husband and wife crew from a disabled sailboat. The helicopter came so close that Blake, along with Jack and Ava, clearly saw the pilot and co-pilot's faces as they flew directly over the *Mary Beth* at an altitude of no more than one hundred feet. However, to the disappointment of all three, the helicopter continued its straight-as-an-arrow course, never deviating to the right nor to the left, without showing any signs of slowing down.

Blake climbed the ladder, joined Jack and Ava on the cockpit deck, and stared forward, straight across the roof of the cabin, never taking his eyes off the retreating helicopter. For a moment, he held his breath, believing the pilot and co-pilot had been so intent on monitoring their instruments—so intent upon maintaining control of their helicopter—they had failed to see the *Mary Beth*.

After all, Blake reasoned, *if one of them had seen us, the pilot would have immediately slowed down and set a new course that would take him, his helicopter, and his crew back to the Mary Beth.*

But the pilot had *not* slowed down. Nor had he deviated from his course. Blake, expecting the helicopter to vanish into the mist and rain, exhaled the breath he had not been aware he was holding.

And then, Blake held his breath again.

Had his eyes deceived him?

No! Blake's eyes had *not* deceived him. Either the pilot or one of his crewmen *had* seen the *Mary Beth*, because the pilot was reducing his airspeed and coaxing the helicopter into an ever-tightening, right-hand turn. While keeping his eyes on the helicopter, Blake watched with renewed hope as the pilot continued slowing down—and continued tightening his turn. Finally, after completing a one-hundred-and-eighty degree turn, the pilot set off on a new course. A course that would take his helicopter straight to the *Mary Beth*.

The helicopter again flew directly overhead...and, again, flew a course that took it beyond, the *Mary Beth*. This time, however, the pilot flew but a short distance past the sinking boat before making another tight, one-hundred-and-eighty-degree, right-hand turn. Blake continued staring, this time with renewed hope, as the pilot coaxed his helicopter into hover mode directly above the *Mary Beth*.

Thanks to Blake's make-shift sea anchor, the *Mary Beth*'s bow pointed directly into the wind, which made it an easy task for the pilot to align his helicopter with the *Mary Beth*'s deck and hold it more-or-less stationary directly above the *Mary Beth*'s open cockpit. Once again, Blake, Jack, and Ava stared straight up. But, this time, they were not staring at an empty, coal-black sky; they were staring at the gleaming, orange-and-white belly of a Coast Guard Helicopter.

The helicopter's twin turbines screamed louder than ever, so loudly they drowned out all the other sounds...even the whop-whop-whop of the main rotor.

Blake, fully aware of how lucky he and his passengers were, inhaled deeply. He then heaved an explosive sigh of relief, closed his eyes, and mumbled a quick...but very sincere...prayer of thanks. If the helicopter's flight path had been as little as one hundred yards to either side, there would have been no chance for the pilot, or any member of his crew, to see the *Mary Beth*.

Blake stared at the pilot, who, until the last minute or so, had been struggling to keep his aircraft airborne and on a course that would take his helicopter—along with himself, his crew, and his rescued passengers—to a safe landing at his home base. In weather like this, just keeping the helicopter right-side-up...and above the towering wave tops...had been a difficult-enough task.

But now, the pilot found himself tackling a task many times more difficult: holding the helicopter as motionless as possible directly above the *Mary Beth* while fighting gusty, gale-force winds and some of the roughest turbulence in which he had ever flown. Updrafts and downdrafts, compounded by the incessant rising and falling of the *Mary Beth*'s deck, presented both the pilot and his crew a challenge as great as any they had ever faced.

The hoist operator, who sat a few feet behind the pilot in the helicopter's open doorway, stared straight down at the *Mary Beth*'s passengers. Blake could not see the hoist controls, but he knew the operator had either toggled a switch or pressed a button, because a small, wire-mesh basket had begun its descent toward the *Mary Beth.* The eyes of Blake, Jack, and Ava darted back and forth between the operator and the basket until a second crewman appeared in the doorway. For a few seconds, the second crewman simply stared down at the *Mary Beth*'s passengers. And then, using his right hand, he lifted an electronic bullhorn to his mouth, squeezed the trigger-like button built into its pistol grip, and shouted instructions.

"One at a time. I repeat: *One...at...a time*. We have room for all three of you."

Blake had recently done some reading about the Coast Guard and knew, on a typical mission, their rescue helicopters carried a crew of four: two pilots, a flight mechanic, and a rescue swimmer. He had already assumed the man operating the hoist was the flight mechanic...which meant the other man, the man with the bullhorn, was the rescue swimmer.

Blake watched the swimmer lift his left hand to the side of his head and press one of his headphones more snugly against his ear. And then, when Blake saw the swimmer's lips move, he assumed...quite correctly...the swimmer had asked the pilot to repeat his command. The pilot apparently did so and, after listening a moment, the swimmer lifted the bullhorn to his mouth and spoke again to those aboard the *Mary Beth*. As before, he spoke slowly and distinctly.

"Cap says we're low on fuel, so let's not waste any time."

Jack and Blake worked as a team to stabilize the basket as best they could while waiting for Ava to sit down inside it. Even after the flight mechanic reversed the hoist and lifted the basket off the deck, they continued to stabilize the basket, both men gripping the rim with both hands, until it cleared the cabin's roof. Only then did they release the basket and stand there, staring straight up, as the basket rose, with agonizing slowness, toward the helicopter's open doorway.

In a display of well-practiced teamwork, the flight mechanic and the rescue swimmer—both of whom Blake assumed were securely attached to the interior of the helicopter by safety harnesses—leaned outside the open doorway, grasped the basket, and pulled it, along with its treasured cargo, inside. After what seemed an eternity—though Jack and Blake knew it could only have been a matter of seconds—the empty basket swung out of the open doorway and began its second descent toward the *Mary Beth.*

Jack and Blake reached for the basket but only managed to touch it with their fingertips, neither man able to get a grip on it before a gust of wind accelerated it past them. Blake managed to grab the basket on its second pass, then Jack got a hand on it, and, finally, the two of them wrestled it over the gunwale and held it steady while the flight mechanic lowered it the remaining five feet to the deck.

Blake immediately motioned for Jack to climb in, but Jack

shook his head and jabbed the index finger of his right hand toward Blake. Blake correctly interpreted Jack's gesture as an indication it was he, and not Jack, who should be the next person rescued. The two men argued a moment, again using gestures instead of words. Only if they had screamed as loudly as they could would either man have been able to make himself heard over the combined sounds of the whistling wind, the roaring waves, the whop-whop-whop of the helicopter's main rotor, and the incredibly loud whine of the twin turbines.

Blake finally settled the argument—in *his* mind, at least—the moment he noticed an approaching rain squall, the blackest squall he had ever seen. In a single, sweeping glance he surveyed Jack's body from head to toe. Only three soft targets availed themselves: Jack's face; the tiny portion of Jack's abdomen not covered by his life jacket; and Jack's exposed groin. Blake immediately ruled out the face and groin. And then, aware he had but seconds to act, he balled the fingers of his right hand into a tight fist, summoned all of his energy, and punched Jack midway between his navel and his sternum.

Blake stared at Jack in surprised satisfaction. He had never been in a fight—had never had a reason to hit anyone—so he had never thrown a punch. Not even a practice punch. As a result, the punch he threw was not all that powerful.

But it was right on target.

Jack, caught completely off guard, had not braced himself for Blake's punch. He gave Blake a surprised stare. And then, when the punch took full effect, he dropped to his knees, doubled over in agony, and tried in vain to make his diaphragm—and his lungs— start working again. Meanwhile, aware Jack's paralysis would last but a few seconds, Blake slapped the palms of both hands onto

Jack's shoulders and shoved him backwards.

Jack toppled into the basket.

Blake looked up at the flight mechanic, stretched out both arms, and punched holes in the air with his upturned thumbs. However, before the hoist operator could react, Jack had recovered somewhat from Blake's punch and was trying to sit up. Blake instinctively raised his right arm as high as it would go, balled his fingers into a tight fist, and, with all the power he could muster, slammed it down with the same motion he would have used to swing a heavy hammer.

For the second time—and again with perfect aim—Blake drove his fist squarely into Jack's solar plexus. As unprepared for Blake's second punch as he had been the first—and, again, momentarily paralyzed—Jack collapsed into the basket.

Blake doubted he would get a third chance, so he immediately turned his attention away from Jack, looked up at the helicopter, and jabbed both thumbs into the air. But this time, the flight mechanic, who had failed to respond quickly enough to Blake's earlier "up" signal, had toggled the hoist's switch and begun lifting the basket the instant Blake drove his fist into Jack's solar plexus. Blake, quickly realized his second thumbs-up had been unnecessary. He lowered his arms, grabbed the rim of the basket with both hands, and kept it stable until the hoist operator lifted it above his head.

Only when the basket rose so high it began lifting Blake off the deck did he loosen his grip and allow the weight of his body to pull his fingers away from the rim. He then looked up...*straight* up...and studied the faces of those staring down at him. First, he studied the flight mechanic, whose attention remained focused upon the basket. He then studied the rescue swimmer, who appeared to have no interest whatsoever in the basket or its contents. Blake wondered why until he realized the swimmer was no longer concerned with Jack, because he now thought only of Blake...the one person yet to be rescued.

Ava's face appeared between the flight mechanic and the rescue swimmer. Blake looked deeply into her eyes...allowed his eyes to linger on hers a moment...and gave her a dramatic nod of his head. Finally, with a second and even-more dramatic nod, he rolled his eyes downward toward Jack.

Blake's message to Ava was very clear.

Jack is all yours.

Blake fought the urge to look at Ava again. He wanted to gaze into her eyes as long as possible. However, fully aware of the urgency of the situation, he returned his attention to the crew members and gave them another frantic hand signal. This time, however, instead of jabbing the air vertically with a double thumbs-up as he had done before, he jabbed the air *horizontally*, using the index fingers of both hands in an effort to direct the crew's attention toward the rapidly approaching rain squall. Neither the flight mechanic nor the rescue swimmer looked in the direction Blake was pointing.

Don't you two get it?

With an exaggerated grimace, Blake repeated his hand signal time and time again, each time jabbing the air more frantically than the time before. But now, instead of pointing only with his index fingers, he used the full length of both arms in a desperate effort to get his message across. The flight mechanic, his attention focused upon the basket, continued ignoring Blake's signal. But the rescue swimmer, after staring at Blake perhaps a second or two longer, turned his head in the direction Blake was pointing. And then, as if he had seen nothing out of the ordinary, the swimmer calmly looked down at Blake again.

"Dammit!" shouted Blake. *"Dammitdammitdammit!"*

The swimmer, of course, couldn't hear Blake's words, so Blake *again* punched the air with both arms and the forefingers of both hands, each stroke longer, and each stroke more exaggerated, than the stroke before.

Blake found it easy to forgive the flight mechanic. After all, it had been the flight mechanic's duty to remain focused upon his immediate task—which, of course, was to lift the Texan-laden basket from the sinking *Mary Beth* to the safety of the helicopter.

But Blake found it impossible to forgive the rescue swimmer.

All of this happened in two or three blinks of an eye...which was about how long it took the rescue swimmer's subconscious mind to process the subliminal message his eyes had sent to it. As if jolted by an electrical shock, he popped his eyes wide open, snapped his head in the direction Blake was pointing, and gave the squall a second look.

A *longer* look.

A more *intense* look.

The swimmer studied the squall a couple of seconds, then spoke into the helicopter's intercom to inform the pilot of the impending danger. And the pilot, who had more experience than all the other members of his crew put together—and, as pilot-in-command, had been more in tune with the weather than any of the other crew members—immediately heeded the swimmer's alert, looked in the direction indicated, and recognized the impenetrable wall of black rain for what it was. A second or so later he began a maneuver that would take his helicopter, himself, his crew—and his rescued passengers—away from the rapidly-approaching torrential downpour.

Blake repeatedly shifted his eyes back and forth between the helicopter and the basket dangling beneath it. Of two things he was absolutely certain. First, the pilot and co-pilot were intensely focused upon navigating their helicopter away from the storm...exactly as they should be doing. And, second, the flight mechanic was equally focused upon lifting the basket, along with its contents, to the open doorway...exactly as he should be doing.

But Blake could not understand why the fourth crew member —the rescue swimmer—was doing absolutely nothing.

He was simply sitting there.

Staring at Blake.

This angered Blake. It angered Blake a lot. But only for a few seconds, because he quickly realized there was absolutely nothing the swimmer could do but lift the bullhorn to his mouth, squeeze the trigger, and shout a new set of instructions.

Which is exactly what he did.

"Stay with your boat. I repeat: *Stay...with...your...boat*. We'll return after this squall passes."

Blake, now completely sapped of all energy—both physical and emotional—sagged to his knees. He knew the rescue swimmer had meant for his words to sound encouraging. And, perhaps, to an inexperienced sailor, the rescue swimmer's words *would* have sounded encouraging. But Blake was not an inexperienced sailor. He was just the opposite. His father had introduced him to the sea long before he was born...while still in his mother's womb.

Blake knew, even before the swimmer finished shouting his instructions, he would never see him, nor the helicopter, ever again. Even if the helicopter had sufficient fuel to linger—and Blake knew it did not—it would take a miracle for the pilot and his crew to find the *Mary Beth* in the midst of a storm. *Any* storm. *Especially* a storm as severe as this storm. In weather such as this it would be virtually impossible for a pilot to return to the exact same spot, in the middle of a featureless ocean, using nothing but dead reckoning. Only if the pilot had been wise enough...and quick enough...to set a waypoint on his GPS would he be able to return to the exact same spot.

But Blake reasoned, even if the pilot *did* return to the exact same spot, it would do him no good...because the *Mary Beth* would no longer be there. The wind, the waves, and the current would have moved her, forcing the pilot to spend more time, and burn more of his rapidly-dwindling fuel supply, while searching for her. By the time the pilot *did* find the *Mary Beth*—assuming he and his crew were lucky enough to do so—insufficient fuel would remain in the helicopter's tanks to allow him to linger long enough for his crew to lower the basket, rescue Blake, and make it back to base.

And then, a glimmer of hope flickered in Blake's heart. *Certainly* the helicopter was equipped with radar. As soon as the squall passed, the pilot would simply locate the *Mary Beth* on his radar and fly straight to her. Not a second of time, nor a drop of fuel, would be wasted while looking for her.

But then,, as quickly as it had come, Blake's new-found optimism yielded to pessimism. He had already reasoned the pilot was burning into his fuel reserve, and he now reasoned only the most foolish of pilots would waste his or her fuel reserve to attempt to return to the *Mary Beth* and lift Blake off her deck. He had also ruled out the GPS scenario, because GPS would return the pilot to the precise spot where the *Mary Beth* had *previously* been, *not* to where she was now. And, finally, he ruled out the radar scenario, because the helicopter was equipped with *weather* radar, not *ground* radar. Blake had no doubt the helicopter's radar was optimized for airborne objects, and would be virtually useless in helping the pilot detect a swamped boat that spent ninety-five percent of its time concealed in the deep troughs that lay between thirty, forty, and the occasional fifty foot white-capped waves.

Blake imagined himself into the pilot's seat and considered the pilot's options. Would he cut his losses and return to base with all but one sailor saved? Or would he risk the near certainty of running out of fuel, ditching his helicopter into a storm-tossed sea, and losing everyone on board because he had been stupid enough to linger too long in a foolhardy attempt to rescue one more hapless sailor?

Blake already knew the answer to that question.

He would never see the helicopter again.

He was alone.

Well, almost alone.

He still had the *Mary Beth* to keep him company.

But only for a short time.

Because the *Mary Beth* was sinking.

She was sinking fast.

And, when she sank, it would just be him...

Blake Turner...

Alone...

Truly alone...

In every sense of the word...

In the middle of an angry and unforgiving sea.

For the first time in his life, Blake understood...*truly* understood...the full and harsh meaning of the word "alone." The helicopter would soon be gone—in fact, it had already left—and the *Mary Beth* was only minutes away from sinking beneath the waves.

Both helpless and hopeless, Blake remained on his knees in the center of the *Mary Beth*'s cockpit while staring at the retreating helicopter. The flight mechanic, the rescue swimmer, and Ava...all three securely strapped inside the helicopter—along with Jack, whose basket continued to swing to and fro beneath the helicopter—stared down at Blake. All four were helpless to do anything but watch the *Mary Beth* grow smaller and smaller as the pilot maneuvered his aircraft farther and farther away from the oncoming downpour. They watched with mind-numbing finality as the black squall enveloped the *Mary Beth.*

And she vanished from sight.

Never to be seen again.

CHAPTER 28

Blake could no longer see the helicopter, but he could hear the shrill whine of its twin turbines and the rapid, rhythmic, whop-whop-whop of its main rotor. In his heart, he hoped the pilot would turn around, seek out a hole in the squall line, fly through it, and return to pick him up. In his mind, however, Blake knew better.

And so did the pilot.

Once again, the whine of the helicopter's turbines, and the rhythmic whop-whop-whop of its main rotor, rose and fell with the wind. The sounds grew fainter with each oscillation.

Fainter...

Fainter...

Ever fainter.

Until...

The sounds of the helicopter were gone.

Once again, Blake heard nothing but the hiss of falling rain, the howl of wind, and the roar of waves. Despite the bleakness of his situation, he whispered a quick, unselfish prayer that the pilot, along with his helicopter, his crew, and his passengers—especially Ava—would make it to safety.

Blake took a final, lingering look at the area of the black sky into which the helicopter had disappeared. He listened a few extra moments, hoping to hear the whop-whop-whop of its main rotor, while knowing he would hear those sounds if—and only if—the pilot turned his aircraft around and returned to pick him up.

And reason told Blake that would never happen.

Nonetheless, he continued listening for five full minutes. And then, after deciding the sounds of the storm were the only sounds he could hear—and the only sounds he *would* hear—he turned his full attention to the *Mary Beth*, which now sat so low in the sea that water flowed *into* her scuppers rather than *out*. Instead of sitting high and dry and draining water overboard as they had been designed to do, the scuppers now sat below the waterline, an open invitation for the sea to rush in and hasten the *Mary Beth*'s demise.

Blake realized the time for wishful thinking had come and gone. The helicopter had come and gone. And the *Mary Beth* had but seconds to live. Perhaps a minute. Two at the most. He watched with resignation as seawater rose above the coaming, poured through the hatch, spilled down the companionway ladder, and flowed into the cabin.

In the end, the *Mary Beth,* proved herself to be the proud girl Blake had always known her to be. Even in her moment of death, she remained on an even keel. Blake rose from his knees and watched with stoicism as she sank lower and lower into the water. For a brief moment, he considered wading to the side of the cockpit and climbing over the rail, but quickly realized there would be no need to do so. Instead of abandoning the *Mary Beth*, he simply remained standing in the center of her cockpit and floated away as her deck sank from under his feet.

Blake, now suspended on the surface by his life jacket, watched with deep sadness as the roof of the *Mary Beth*'s cabin disappeared beneath the sea. Only her short mast, the lantern, and the lantern's feeble orange flame—still burning in defiance of the storm—remained visible. Seconds later, first the lantern, and then the tip of the short mast from which it hung, surrendered to the forces of nature and slipped beneath the waves.

The unforgiving sea had claimed another victim.

And the squall passed as quickly as it had come.

As if Mother Nature had completed the task she had set out to do, the wind died down, the sea became calm, the clouds parted, and a surprisingly hot sun shone down upon Blake Turner, who repeatedly scanned the horizon...and saw nothing.

No boats.

No ships.

Nothing.

Blake had no choice but to accept the fateful hand he had been dealt. He had watched the *Mary Beth* die, and assumed it would be but a matter of time until he also died. How much time? Always...*always*...the analytical accountant, he began tallying the numbers.

It had been twenty-four hours since he last ate any food, and almost as long since he drank any water. His research into all things nautical had taught him a man can live up to three weeks without food...but only three days without water.

One of those days had already come and gone.

Blake had read several accounts in which people had written elaborate descriptions of their survival in situations similar to the one in which he now found himself. Some of those survivors had suffered alone. Others had miraculously endured their ordeal while witnessing their comrades' final hallucination-filled moments. Blake frowned. If the sharks did not get him—and he felt certain they would—dehydration, along with the insanity that comes with it, definitely would.

And yet, Blake could not help smiling. Because he would soon join the *Mary Beth* in her watery grave. And he would do so content with the knowledge he had saved his beloved Ava.

And her beloved Jack.

ANCHOR
PART THREE
CHAPTER 29

Less than five minutes of fuel remained in the helicopter's tanks when it landed at a Coast Guard station near New York City. Jack and Ava, along with the husband-and-wife crew of the disabled sailboat, were given warm, dry clothing, provided something to eat and drink, and subjected to brief—but mandatory—medical exams. When all that had been done, a Coast Guardsman debriefed the husband-and-wife sailboat crew about their ordeal in one room while, in a different room, another Coast Guardsman quizzed Jack and Ava about the sequence of events that led up to—and included—the disappearance of Blake Turner and the *Mary Beth*.

Finally, after all the appropriate procedures had been completed, and all the required paperwork had been filled out, one Coast Guardsman transported the sailboat crew to their home in Boston, while another Coast Guardsman transported Jack and Ava to their apartment in New York City. Jack and Ava went straight to bed, got a few hours of much-needed rest, returned to the theater, and, without missing a single show, resumed their roles in *Hamburg*. Day after day, week after week, and month after month they maintained their grueling routine of seven shows a week without a single break.

Until...

Late on a Saturday afternoon...

Jack set into motion an event that would forever change both his and Ava's lives.

Saturday morning had begun like any other Saturday morning. And, for a while, it seemed Saturday afternoon would proceed as any other Saturday afternoon. Precisely at two o'clock, as they had done for months on end, Ava, followed four minutes and twenty seconds later by Jack, stepped onto the stage to perform their roles in *Hamburg.* And then, two and a half hours later, at four thirty in the afternoon, Jack and Ava *continued* doing as they had done for months on end by returning to the stage for the first of their obligatory curtain calls before returning to the men's and women's dressing rooms. Jack, who always finished removing his costume and makeup long before Ava did, walked down the hallway and waited patiently outside the women's dressing room until Ava emerged.

As always, Jack hooked the crook of his arm into the crook of Ava's arm and led her down the hallway to the theater's back door.

As always, Jack paused only as long as it took to turn on his theatrical smile.

As always, Jack opened the door, stepped outside, waved to the crowd, and led Ava down the steps.

As always, Jack shielded Ava from her throng of screaming fans as they waded through the crowd.

And...

As always...

Jack opened the back door of a taxi, turned to face the crowd, and smiled one more time while waiting for Ava to climb inside.

And then...

Not as always...

Jack abruptly dispensed with protocol and did something he had never done. Instead of giving the crowd a final grin, a final wave, and crawling into the cab behind Ava, he stepped aside and allowed Zane to crawl inside. By the time Ava realized it was Zane, and not Jack, who was sitting in the cab beside her, Jack had already climbed into the back seat of a different taxi.

"Go, man, go! Step on the gas! Go! Step on it! *Now*, man. *Now*!"

With surprising calmness, the driver responded to Jack's urgent demands and powered the taxi away from the curb even as Jack was in the process of pulling his long legs inside. Jack finally managed to fold one leg between himself and the back of the front seat, pulled in his other leg, and slammed the door.

Despite the fact Ava knew it was too late—Jack's taxi had pulled away from the curb and was already speeding away—she leaned across Zane's lap and yelled for Jack to stop. Jack, of course, never heard Ava's words. Even if he had, he would have ignored them.

Meanwhile, the taxi driver calmly merged with the traffic, looked into his rear-view mirror, and made eye contact with Jack.

"Where to, Mac? Just where is it you're wanting to go in such an all-fired hurry? Hey! Aren't you Jack Smith, the actor in...?"

"Yes. That would be me."

"Where's your lady? My wife and I have been to your play twice. She reads all the tabloids, and, at one time or another, pictures of you two have been on the cover of every one of them. You make a cute couple, by the way."

Jack ignored the driver's flattery, gave him an address, and stressed to him that time was of the utmost importance. As an afterthought, Jack told the driver he would give him the biggest tip anyone had ever given him—but only if he kept the gas pedal pushed as close to the floor as he dared. Sensing Jack was not in a talkative mood, the driver wisely discontinued his efforts to strike up a conversation and, instead, concentrated on his driving.

Upon arriving at his destination, Jack opened his door and began unfolding his legs from the taxi before the driver finished braking to a stop. And then, as soon as the taxi came to rest, Jack poured his lanky frame out of the backseat and ordered the driver to wait for him. A few seconds later, as he was striding away from the taxi, Jack looked over his shoulder and reminded the driver to keep his meter running.

Jack walked briskly down a long pier that jutted out from the bank and into the Hudson River twenty miles upstream of New York City. Midway down the pier, he slowed his pace and reverently approached the slip where, several months earlier, he had jumped and landed with a heavy, boat-jarring thud—with no reverence whatsoever—onto the cockpit deck of Blake Turner's antique thirty-five foot *Mary Beth*. The *Mary Beth* no longer sat there...which did not surprise Jack, as he had not expected her to be there. Instead, a sleek, modern, forty-five foot cabin cruiser occupied the slip the *Mary Beth* had previously called home.

For a full minute Jack just stood there, admiring what appeared to be a brand-new boat. He studied the boat from stem to stern, then closed his eyes, took a deep breath, and allowed his vivid, theater-trained imagination to take him back through time...back to the day he had stood in this exact same spot...back to the moment he had leapt aboard the *Mary Beth*.

And then, for what seemed the ten thousandth time, Jack's mind raced through the tumultuous events of the fateful voyage that sent the *Mary Beth* to the depths of Davy Jones' locker—the same events, and the same voyage, that removed Blake Turner from his and Ava's lives.

Jack pulled his mind back to the present, opened his eyes, and took a long look at the highly-polished fiberglass cabin cruiser that floated beside the dock. In stark contrast to the *Mary Beth*'s tumultuous twenty-four hours on a storm-tossed sea, this boat sat perfectly still on the calm, late-afternoon waters of the Hudson River.

Jack again panned his eyes to the tip of the pulpit that extended several feet beyond the boat's bow. He then slowly moved his eyes along the smooth lines of her cabin. And last, but not least, he admired the graceful curves of her cockpit and stern. Rather than leaping into the cockpit, as he had done on the day of the *Mary Beth*'s fateful voyage, he gently eased himself down from the dock, stepped gingerly onto the boat's gunwale, and quietly lowered himself to the deck.

And then...

Jack just stood there...

Hesitant to proceed any farther.

He took a deep breath to gather his courage...held the breath a few seconds...forcefully expelled the breath through pursed lips and puffed cheeks...squared his shoulders...and used the knuckles of his right fist to rap sharply, three times, on the cabin door.

And then...

Jack just stood there...

Waiting for a response from someone inside the boat.

Several seconds passed. Having failed to get a response, Jack took another deep breath, raised his fist, and swung it forward. Just when his knuckles were about to connect with the polished panel, the door swung wide open.

And then...

Jack just stood there...

Only, this time, Jack was not standing alone. Nor was he staring at a closed door. He was staring directly into the surprisingly-calm face of the boat's owner. And, Jack noticed, the owner never flinched—not a single muscle—despite the fact his knuckles were poised in the air mere inches from the tip of the man's nose.

The boat's owner simply stared at Jack.

And Jack just stood there...

Staring back at the boat's owner.

For the first time in his life, the verbose Jack Smith had no idea as to what he should say, how he should say it, or what he should do. Instead, the boat's owner, a quiet and reserved man, took it upon himself to break the long silence.

"Hello, Jack. Another five minutes and you would have missed me. How did you know I would be here?"

Jack uncurled the fingers of his right fist, raised his left arm, and placed the palms of both hands on the man's shoulders.

"This is one nice rig you've got, Blakey Boy. Mind if I come in?"

Jack had asked a rhetorical question, as he had no intention of giving Blake even the slightest chance to offer an answer. In fact, even before he finished speaking, Jack began pushing Blake backwards, almost knocking him off his feet as he did so. Jack then followed Blake into the cabin.

"I, um, I don't, uh, I don't guess so..." stammered Blake while trying to avoid losing his balance while being pushed backwards. And then, after chuckling softly, Blake added, "...considering the fact you're already inside."

Jack spoke rapidly, stringing together totally unrelated thoughts while bouncing back and forth between a serious, all-business tone and a casual, conversational tone.

"I'm kind of in a hurry, Blake, so I'm only asking for two minutes of your time. Man! This boat is nice. *Really* nice. Zane said he saw you at the play the other night. I told him he was mistaken, because you drowned in that storm. But, over the next two or three days, Zane kept *insisting* it was you. How much did a boat like this set you back? I tried to call your company this morning, to find out if you still work there. But, of course, it being Saturday, I only got an answering service. The operator gave me your company's normal work hours and asked if I would like to leave a message. I told her thanks, but no thanks...leaving a message was *not* what I wanted to do. Man! The carpet in our apartment is nowhere *near* as nice as this carpet. So! I hung up the phone. And then, I remembered you said something about working with a guy named Fred Johnson. Don't ask me how I remembered Freddie Boy's name. Actually, I did *not* remember Freddie's name. Not *all* of it, anyway. I only remembered the 'Fred' part. Ava came up with the 'Johnson' part. I swear, Blake. Nothing—*not one thing*—in our apartment is *half* as nice as the stuff you've got in your boat. You know how many Fred Johnsons live in New York City? It took me all morning to track ol' Freddie Boy down. And when I finally did? Surprise, surprise! It took a little coaxing, but he slipped up and admitted you did *not* drown in that storm. He also said you still work with him at.... Oh, what was the name of that place? Waxler? Werxler? Something like that. Anyway, I tried and tried, but I couldn't get Freddie Boy to tell me where you lived. He kept saying he had been sworn to secrecy...or some such nonsense."

Throughout his monologue, Jack's eyes kept moving constantly, taking in every detail of the spacious cabin—spacious, at least, when compared to the much smaller cabin aboard the *Mary Beth*—and admiring the cabin's nautically-themed appointments. Jack finally stopped talking, not long enough to allow Blake to say anything, but long enough to let out a low whistle.

"I've gotta hand it to you, Blake. This is one classy rig."

Blake glanced at the shiny brass clock, identical to the one that went down with the Mary Beth. He then cleared his throat.

"I'd love to stay here and chat about old times, Jack, but I'm kind of in a hurry. Besides, I really need to..."

As if to ignore Blake's comment, Jack rudely interrupted and picked up his narrative right where he left off.

"Yes Sir, it took a lot of coaxing to squeeze some information out of that Freddie guy. Like I said, he finally admitted to me that, yes, you *are* alive, but, no, you no longer live in an apartment. That's when I got impatient and told Little Freddie I needed to know where you had moved to. I told him, 'I need to know today...right now...*this...very...minute*!' I guess that made ol' Freddie Boy a bit nervous, because he repeated the 'secrecy' nonsense and said he had promised he wouldn't tell anybody anything about you...*especially* about where you lived. You know something, Blake? That struck me as rather odd. Why would someone like you have something to hide? And, of even more importance, just what could that something be? I told Little Freddie I had a special interest in you...that my reasons were none of his business...and I simply *had* to know where I could find you. And then, when I *again* told Freddie I needed to know—and I needed to know *right now, at this very moment*..."

Jack paused, but only as long as it took to catch his breath.

"Well, I must have pushed Freddie's buttons one time too many...perhaps a little too hard...and, who knows? I may have pushed the wrong button. Because, all of a sudden, he became really suspicious of me, and *wham*! Out of the blue, while I was in the middle of a sentence, he hung up the phone. I tried to call him back, but he never answered. I called him three more times from my phone, but he *still* didn't answer. I finally decided he had caller ID and knew it was me, so I called him from other peoples' phones. Of course, that didn't do any good, either. I guess he suspected *all* those calls were from me, because I never got him to answer again. I considered tracking ol' Freddie Boy down so I could talk face-to-face with him...however, when I got to thinking about the fact Zane swore up and down he had seen you alive....well, *that*, combined with the fact this Freddie guy had all but *confirmed* you were alive by reacting so strangely...and so *strongly*...to all my questions...."

Jack paused again. And, again, he paused only as long as it took to take a couple of quick, short breaths. He then continued his monologue.

"After stepping back and piecing everything together, I convinced myself you were, indeed, still alive. Of course, I had no idea *where* you were still alive, so I decided to follow my gut feeling. You *do* know what my gut feeling was, don't you? No, no, and no-no-no! Don't bother to guess, because I'm gonna *tell* you what my gut feeling was. I said to myself, 'If I was a guy that loved boats as much as that Blake Turner does...and, if I lost the only boat I ever owned...by golly, I'd go out, buy myself another boat, and live on the blamed thing.' So I came out here to check out my hunch. And guess what? You *did* buy another boat. And you *are* living on it."

Jack paused again. And, this time, Blake decided to pounce on the opportunity to say something. He opened his mouth, but only managed to speak one word before Jack resumed talking.

"Jack..."

"You know what, Blake? I've always wondered what it would

be like to live on a boat. But we're not talking about *me*. We're talking about *you.* So, once again, Blake, I asked myself, 'What kind of boat would Blakey Boy buy? *Especially* if he wanted to live on it?' And then I asked myself, 'And where would Blakey Boy keep his boat?' Once again, Blake, I followed my gut feeling, and *Voila!* Here we are, standing in the cabin of your Home Sweet Home, tied up to the same dock, and in the same spot, you kept the *Mary Beth*."

Jack paused again, but, this time, it wasn't to take a breath. It was to lock his eyes upon Blake's eyes...and to stare into the depths of Blake's soul.

"But *really* Blake? Where have you been the past three months? After all that happened during that storm—not to mention whatever hell you went through *after* that storm—how could you *possibly* want to own another boat...let alone *live* on one?"

Suddenly, as suddenly as he had become animated, Jack became motionless. He stood as still—and as silent—as the proverbial post. Meanwhile, he stared deeply into Blake's eyes, waiting for an explanation. Blake stared back. And, finally, after several long seconds, and after giving Jack a nervous smile, he broke the awkward silence.

"I'm not rushing you to leave, Jack, but a few minutes ago you claimed you were in a hurry and asked for two minutes of my time. I'm confident those two minutes have long since come and gone."

"Yeah, yeah, yeah. No argument there, Blakey Boy. So I'll ask for *another* two minutes of your time. But *only* two. So start talking."

"Jack, it will take a lot more than two minutes to answer all of your questions. In fact, it will take more than two minutes to answer just *one* of them."

"Two minutes, Blake. *Two...minutes.* Unless I miss my guess, you're in as much of a hurry as I am, so I suggest you start talking."

"Well, Jack, for starters, I bobbed up and down in the Atlantic Ocean for three days. I came close to dying...and *would* have died had the bright orange of my life jacket not caught the eye of George Moranis, owner and skipper of the *Lady Jean*, an out-bound fishing boat. George picked me up, immediately realized what bad shape I was in, and, without a moment of hesitation, ordered his crew to turn his boat around and set a course to the nearest port. I told George no, he should belay that order. I was certain, if given a little time, I would be all right. I then told George I couldn't bear to be the cause of an aborted fishing trip. 'And besides,' I told him, 'I'm in no hurry to get back to shore. I have a lot of thinking to do.' I stressed to George that I was willing to remain on his boat for the duration of his trip—provided, of course, my presence didn't inconvenience him or his crew. He gave me some water, got me out of my wet clothes, and wrapped some warm blankets around me. Half an hour later, he reevaluated my condition, decided I wasn't so far gone that I would die on him, and used his satellite phone to call my boss. George explained the situation, assured my boss I would be okay, and told him I had expressed the desire to use sick leave until I recovered from three days in the water. After that, I would use vacation. My boss told George he trusted me and whatever I wanted to do was okay with him."

With that, Blake became silent. And Jack—who had shown no emotion whatsoever during Blake's speech—simply tilted his head forward, raised his eyebrows, and rotated his wrists until his open palms faced upward...an unmistakable signal he wanted to hear more.

"Okay, Jack. I've answered your first question, which was: What happened to me, both during...and after...the storm. So let's move on to the second question: Why did I buy a new boat?"

Blake rolled both his head and his eyes from one side of the cabin to the other. And then, with an outward sweep of both hands, he indicated he was referring to everything, both inside the boat—and outside.

"I suppose my near-fatal ordeal at sea, followed by two weeks of working as an extra hand on a fishing boat with no pay beyond a warm bunk and hot food—which, by the way, was my suggestion..."

Blake paused a couple of seconds.

"Sorry. I jumped ahead of myself. George and his crew insisted they pay me for the work I did, but I wouldn't let them. They said I had done a good job for them, and demanded I accept a percentage of the profit. I told them saving my life had been ample payment for what little service I had provided in return. But, I digress.

"I suppose my ordeal at sea would have been enough to last most people a lifetime. But not me. I found the experience to be quite an adventure. In fact, I found it downright exhilarating. So, instead of driving me *away* from the sea, it whetted my appetite for *more* of the sea. So much more that, upon returning to port, even before I reached my apartment, I began shopping for a boat to replace the *Mary Beth*. I got an unbelievable 'must-sell deal' on this one, the *Hudson Queen*."

"Like I said, Blake, the *Queen*'s a nice rig."

Jack punctuated his comment with puckered lips and several nods of approval.

"Thank you, Jack. The *Queen* may not be brand new, but she's a lot newer, and a lot more comfortable—not to mention a lot safer —than the *Mary Beth* ever hoped to be. She has two engines instead of one, so the chance of getting stalled at sea due to lack of power is virtually nil. In addition to that, the *Queen* is powered by diesel engines, which are more efficient, and far more dependable, than the *Mary Beth*'s ancient, used-up gas burner. At reduced throttle, they give the *Queen* twice the range, on the same amount of fuel, with a top speed ten knots faster than that of the *Mary Beth*."

Jack glanced at the brass clock, realized how late it was, and grimaced.

"Blake, it's time we address the *real* purpose of my visit. Why have you not come to see Ava?"

"I *have* come to see Ava. I went to see *Hamburg* the night I returned to New York, and I've attended at least two shows a week ever since. I usually go on Tuesdays and Fridays. As you know, the theater is dark on Monday, so I go on Tuesday to break up my week, and I go on Friday in order to leave the remainder of my weekend free—which, as you might guess, allows me more time to enjoy the *Queen.*"

Jack stared at Blake a moment, as if trying to process everything Blake had just told him. He then dropped the dry monotone he had used while asking his questions and spoke in a voice filled with emotion.

"I'm not talking about the *show*, Blake. I'm talking about *Ava.* Why have you not let Ava know you're still alive? Do you not realize...has it not occurred to you...that all this time...she thought...*we* thought...you were dead?"

"Of *course* I realize that, Jack. I realized it from the start. And I thought it would be best—not just for me, but for *all* of us—if I left it that way."

"How can you even *think* such a thing, Blake? Let alone *say* it? Why—after all we went through during that storm—*why* would you not want Ava to know you survived? I can understand you not wanting *me* to know you survived, but why on earth would you not want *Ava* to know?"

"Let's dispense with whatever game you're playing, Jack. It's time...it's long *past* time...we stop lying to each other."

Blake looked deeply into Jack's eyes, spoke very slowly, and chose his words very carefully.

"Jack...when that storm overtook us...when I saw how Ava reacted when she realized you had been washed overboard...and when I saw how she held on to you after we pulled you back onto the boat...well, that's when it became obvious to me...once and for all, and whether I liked it or not...you were deeply in love with Ava, and Ava was deeply in love with you. That was a defining moment for me. I made a vow, right then and right there, I would never come between you two again."

With that off his chest, Blake found it easy to discuss his failed relationship with Ava. He smiled a comfortable smile, followed the smile with a soft chuckle, and continued.

"You know something, Jack? Now that I look back on it, I don't know what made me think I could come between you and Ava in the first place. That's why, when I realized there was barely enough time for the crew of that helicopter to lift just one of us off the *Mary Beth*, there was never an issue—not in *my* mind, at least—as to which of us it should be. "

Jack creased his brow and narrowed his eyes. Other than that, his expression never changed. He just stood there—and stared at Blake—for several long seconds. Finally, he raised his right hand, pointed his index finger straight up, and opened his mouth...as if about to say something of great importance. However, as if he suddenly had second thoughts, he retracted his finger, dropped his hand to his side, and glanced at the brass clock. This time, when he realized just how late he really was, he abruptly changed the subject.

"Have you read the latest reviews about Ava?"

Jack resumed speaking before Blake could respond.

"The critics say her recent performances have been nowhere near as good as they used to be. Oh, you know what I mean. Before the 'accident,' as Zach refers to it." And then, in a decidedly bitter tone, Jack added, "In fact, most of those worthless scoundrels say Ava is all but washed up."

"Yes, I *have* read the reviews, Jack, and I feel for both of you. All of this was my fault. *All* of it. If I had checked the weather before leaving the dock, or monitored radio traffic like I usually do, I would not have taken the *Mary Beth* out to sea. And, if I had not taken the *Mary Beth* out to sea, none of this would have happened. Ava would still be at the top of her form, the *Mary Beth* would still be going strong, and..."

Jack interrupted Blake mid-sentence.

"Blake! While we were in the middle of that storm I tried to tell you something, but it's obvious you were not listening. So, I'm going to say it one more time—and, *this* time, I want you to listen, and I want you to listen...*very*...carefully."

Jack placed his hands on Blake's shoulders, just as he had done on the *Mary Beth,* and turned Blake's body until they stood squarely face-to-face.

"*Look* at me, Blake. Look me eye-to eye. I want to make absolutely certain you hear what I'm about to say. Do I have your undivided attention?"

"Yes, Jack, I'm listening."

"Blake, don't...be...so...*hard*...on...yourself. It's *my* fault we went out to sea. And it's *my* fault you were off your game. So, at the risk of being repetitive..."

Jack paused a moment for emphasis.

"Don't..be...so...*hard*...on...yourself.*"

Jack gave Blake a moment to absorb what he had said. And then, he spoke in a much lighter tone.

"What say we put all that behind us? I think it's time we move on to something else. Did you read Zach Nelson's latest column? Did you read what *he* said about Ava?"

"Yes, Jack, I did."

Jack paused again, not for emphasis, but to reflect on Zach's latest column...which allowed Blake time to reflect on it, as well. Zach believed Ava had been crippled, both physically and emotionally, during her ordeal at sea. To support his theory, Zach claimed Ava's performances had grown weaker and weaker with each showing of *Hamburg*. He claimed she no longer possessed the qualities that, in the past, had endeared her to her fans. Zach ended his column by saying Ava Bechtel had sunk into the depths of despair, and her career was all but over.

When Jack spoke again, his expression was serious, and his tone grave.

"Do you agree with Zach?"

"On some points, yes. I agree something inside Ava...that *something* that made her such a great performer...has died. But I don't believe, not for a New York minute, her career is over."

"Something inside Ava *did* die, Blake. That something was *you*."

CHAPTER 30

Blake's eyes glazed over as he stared blankly and uncomprehendingly at Jack.

"Me? I don't understand, Jack. Even a blind person can see the special chemistry that binds you and Ava."

Blake's mind flashed through the hundreds of times he had watched Jack and Ava walk hand-in-hand—and sometimes arm-in-arm—from one taxi to the theater before each show began, and from the theater to another taxi after each show ended. And, for what seemed the ten thousandth time, he relived the moment he stood on wobbly legs staring down at Jack and Ava as they clung to each other while lying on the *Mary Beth*'s deck. And, finally, Blake stared at the image forever imprinted upon his mind—the image of Ava's head buried deeply in Jack's chest, and her arms wrapped tightly around Jack's waist during their last moments together aboard the *Mary Beth*.

It took an effort, but Blake finally managed to refocus his eyes, pull himself back to the present, and look at Jack—who was clearly waiting for Blake to provide more information. Blake correctly assumed Jack wanted to hear a more thorough explanation as to why he had behaved the way he had behaved near the end of their cruise.

"Jack, I had hoped, by meeting Ava on the *Mary Beth*, far away from New York City, she and I could have some time alone. You know what I mean. Time without you. Time without Zane. Time without anyone showing up to interfere. You can't imagine my anger when I discovered Ava had invited you to come along. And later, when I saw how she reacted the moment she realized you had been washed overboard...and when I saw her cling to you after we pulled you back on board.... Well, like I said Jack, that was a defining moment for me...the moment I accepted the fact, once and for all, that Ava belongs to you, and I had been a total fool to think she could ever belong to me."

Blake paused a moment, hoping Jack would rescue him from making a full and awkward confession. But Jack remained motionless. Expressionless. Silent. Attentive. And, something totally against his character, extremely patient. He stared at Blake for several more seconds, then raised his eyebrows, cocked his head slightly downward and to one side, and turned his palms upward—once again giving Blake the unmistakable hint he wanted to hear more. Blake recognized the hint for what it was and continued.

"I knew, the instant I saw that squall bearing down upon us, the Coast Guard helicopter had virtually no time to remain on station. I figured it had one minute...two at most...barely enough time to lift just one of us off the *Mary Beth.* No chance whatsoever to offload *both* of us. Again, Jack, I know I'm beating a dead horse, but, by then, something had become perfectly clear to me. Ava was meant to be with you. *Not me.* That's why I made certain *you* were the one who got into the basket...*you* were the one who got lifted off my boat...and *you* were the one who got hoisted up to the helicopter."

Jack again glanced at the brass clock, noted the time, and stole a quick glance at his watch to make sure the clock was not just running, but was also showing the correct time. When he confirmed the clock, indeed, was both running *and* showing the correct time, a serious look of concern appeared on his face. He opened his mouth to speak again—not to comment on Blake's confession, but to abruptly change the subject.

"Blake, when I got here you said you were about to go somewhere. At the risk of being nosy, just where is it you were going?"

"To the theater. As I told you earlier, I usually go on Tuesday and Friday nights. I was unable to go last night—I had a midnight deadline on one of my accounts—so I thought I would go tonight."

"Got a good ticket?"

"Center seat, fourth row."

"Best seat in the house! Need a lift? No! Don't answer that! Doesn't matter whether you need a lift or not, you're riding with me. We'll continue this conversation in my taxi. I asked the driver to wait. And, after the play is over, I'll make sure you get delivered, safe and sound, back to your boat. Oh, one more thing; you won't be needing those drug-store glasses, bushy eyebrows, fake beard, brown wig, and whatever else you were about to put on."

Jack had been staring at the various items Blake had arranged on a small table next to the sofa. He raked everything off the table and into the trash basket that sat beside it.

"You won't need to wear a disguise, Blake. Not tonight, nor any other night, ever again."

Without offering an explanation or waiting for a response, Jack opened the door and pushed Blake out of the *Queen*'s cabin. Jack followed Blake through the door, pulled the door almost shut, and looked at Blake.

"Got your ticket? Got the key to your boat?"

Blake patted his pants pocket, and then patted his shirt pocket.

"Yes, I have both, but..."

Without waiting for Blake to finish his sentence, Jack pulled the door until he heard the latch click...attempted to open the door to confirm it was locked...and spoke in an upbeat tone.

"Tonight, Blakey Boy, you're gonna ride to the play with me. And we don't have a moment to lose! So, let's get moving. I'll explain everything on the way."

Jack led Blake to the waiting taxi, opened the back door, and motioned for Blake to climb inside. Jack then motioned for Blake to slide across the seat, waited while he did so, and crawled in behind him. Finally, just as he had done when leaving the theater, Jack told the driver to step on the gas long before he completed the process of pulling his long, lanky legs inside. By the time he got his legs folded in front of him, and his feet planted on the floor, the taxi was up to speed and roaring through the parking lot. Only then did Jack close the door, buckle his seat belt, and turn to face Blake...who was still wrestling with the buckle on his own seat belt.

"You know something, Blake? Now would be a good time for me to give you a big apology. Actually, I owe you *two* apologies. The first one is for the fact I jumped to conclusions about you. I had you figured all wrong. I sincerely—but mistakenly—assumed you were like all the other sicko fans who stalk Ava. Most of them just want to get her autograph, and some want her to pose with them for a photograph. I don't suppose anything is wrong with a person wanting to do either of those things, but way too many people want to *touch* her...to put their *hands* on her. Some have snipped off...and some have even yanked out...clumps of her hair. Some have torn pieces off her clothing. And a few have actually tried...but, fortunately, failed...to go farther than that."

Jack paused a moment, as if to withdraw into his own thoughts. He then snapped his head around and looked directly at Blake.

"How 'bout you, Blake? I'm sure you've gotten Ava's

autograph and some photos of you and her, but have you ever snipped off a lock of her hair, or a piece of her clothing? Even more important: Have you ever touched Ava in an uninvited or inappropriate manner?"

Blake stared at Jack as if the man had gone crazy. Of *course* he had Ava's autograph, and of *course* he had some photographs...mostly just of Ava, but he also had a few 'selfies' in which they had posed together. However, it had never occurred to Blake to snip off a lock of Ava's hair or a scrap of her clothing. And never—*never, ever*—had he touched her in an inappropriate manner.

Blake smiled...

His smile grew wider...

And then...

His smile grew even wider.

Finally, beaming from ear to ear, he looked up at Jack and shook his head.

"No, Jack. I have never taken advantage of Ava. Not in any way, shape, form, or fashion."

Jack beamed a comfortable smile, and calmly shook his head.

"I didn't think so."

Jack paused a moment, took a deep breath to prepare himself for what he was about to say next, and exhaled his breath in a loud whoosh.

"Like I said, Blake. I owe you *another* apology. An even *bigger* apology. An apology for the fact I always refused to listen to Ava whenever she tried to talk to me about her relationship with you. Oh, believe me, Ava *tried* to talk about you—she tried time and time again—but I either shouted her down or turned a deaf ear."

Jack lowered his voice and became dead serious.

"I hate you lost the *Mary Beth*, Blake. And I hate you spent three days floating around in the Atlantic Ocean. However, if it makes you feel any better, something good came from it. It forced me to listen to what Ava had to say. Not what she had to say about *me*...not what she had to say about *her*...and not what she had to say about me *and* her—but what she had to say about *you* and her. Especially what she had to say about *you.* Believe it or not, you were the main topic of our conversation while we were out there on your boat. We started talking about you the moment that storm hit us...we talked about you *during* that storm...and we have talked about nothing *but* you since the Coast Guard lifted us off your boat. Being stranded out there in the middle of the Atlantic Ocean—and the running conversation I've had with Ava ever since—have made three things perfectly clear to me."

"Oh? What would they be?"

"You were Ava's rock. Her anchor. Her calm port in a violent storm."

"I'm not following you, Jack."

"Blake, it's no secret that Ava loves to perform in front of a live audience. She loves to hear laughter, cheers, and applause more than anything in the world...especially when the laughter, cheers, and applause are directed at her during or after one of her performances. However, when that final curtain call has ended, Ava wants nothing more than to go to her dressing room, close the door, and hide from all the glamor and the glitter."

Jack paused a moment, but only long enough to catch his breath.

"From the day Ava left Germany and flew to the United States —more specifically, from the moment she stepped off that plane here in New York City—Zane and I have done all within our power to shield her from the mob that gropes at her, pulls her hair, and tears at her clothing."

Jack again lowered his voice. And, for the first time, he spoke in a surprisingly humble and apologetic tone.

"That's why I followed Ava to your boat, Blake. Whatever else you do, don't blame her for my being there. I know you think she invited me to tag along, but nothing could be farther from the truth."

Jack chuckled softly.

"Believe it or not, Blake, Ava was more surprised than you when I jumped off the dock and landed on the deck of your boat. She thought she had planned the trip without anyone but the two of you knowing about it. But she was wrong. Remember the night Ava called you? The night you dictated instructions to her as to when and where you should meet? Well, as it so happened, Christine— Christine, by the way, is Zane's sister, and Ava's roommate.

"Christine entered the den of our apartment while Ava was on the phone with you. Ava immediately hung up the phone and told Christine it had been a wrong number. At the time, Christine didn't think much about it. However, that scene kept gnawing away at the back of her mind long after she went to bed, and it finally occurred to her the phone had never rung...which meant there had never been a wrong number. *There never could have been a wrong number...because no one ever called*. For the next hour, over and over, Christine reviewed that scene in her mind. She finally came to the conclusion Ava had never *received* a call from anyone, because Ava had *made* a call, and hung up the phone the moment Christine entered the room."

Jack paused a moment, mainly to catch his breath, but also to compose what he would say next.

"Eventually, Christine remembered an additional tidbit of information: Ava had hung up the phone with one hand while slipping her other hand into the pocket of her housecoat. So, taking care not to awaken Ava, Christine got out of bed and searched through the pockets of Ava's housecoat. As expected, she found the small sheet of paper onto which Ava had written the date, the time, and the place the two of you were to meet. Christine copied all the information onto another sheet of paper, returned the original note to the pocket of Ava's housecoat, and, early the next morning, gave the copy to me."

Jack again paused, mostly to collect his thoughts, but also to take another deep breath and release a long, heavy sigh. He then spoke with a tone of finality.

"No, Blake, Ava never asked me to tag along with her, nor did I do the stereotypical Hollywood cops-and-robbers thing by hailing a taxi and telling its driver to follow Ava's taxi. Fact is, I left our apartment early that morning—*very* early—and arrived at the marina two and a half hours before Ava did. She thought she had gotten out of bed and slipped out of the apartment long before I woke up. In reality, *I* got out of bed and slipped out of the apartment long before *she* woke up. As a result, I was already there, at the marina, lying in wait when she arrived."

Jack's mind carried him to a previous moment in time. When he next spoke, his voice sounded dreamy and distant.

"You know something, Blake? Looking back on everything, and knowing what I know now—I mean, now that I know you were not...and never had been...a threat to Ava—I'm rather ashamed of myself. I'm ashamed I went to such great lengths to keep you two apart."

Jack spent a few more seconds reviewing the past, then

refocused his eyes and pulled his mind back to the present.

"*However*, Blake, in my own defense, at the time I did those things I assumed you were a perverted, sex-hungry stalker with a diabolical scheme in store for Ava—and I was determined, regardless of what I had to do, to prevent you from hurting her."

Jack paused again, took another deep breath, exhaled yet another sigh, and looked into Blake's eyes.

"Blake, let's go back to the day you took us out on the *Mary Beth.* As I've already mentioned, even before you began preparing your boat, long before you pulled away from the dock, Ava began telling me about you, about her, and about the relationship *between* you and her. Of course, as you already know, I refused to listen to a single word she had to say. To be more accurate, I refused to listen to Ava until the weather turned bad. From that moment on, I have listened to every syllable that comes out of Ava's mouth."

Jack rubbed his hands on his thighs, turned his palms upright, and studied them...as if he had tried to clean them of some unseen grime.

"That storm changed everything, Blake. For one thing, it forced me to listen to what Ava had to say about you. And later...after the storm grew worse...after I observed you for a while...and after I got to know you better...I realized you wanted to be near Ava, not because she was the most beautiful woman on the planet—and she *is*, you know—and not because she was the hottest star on Broadway—and yes, she is that, too—but simply because she was Ava."

Jack suddenly drove the heel of his right fist into the palm of his left hand, which created a loud *smack* sound that startled the taxi driver...who, of course, had been eavesdropping on Jack and

Blake's conversation. The driver flinched, swerved to the left, and came within an inch of hitting an on-coming vehicle. A moment later, as soon as the driver regained control of his taxi, his eyes met Jack's eyes in the rear-view mirror.

Jack gave the driver a sheepish grin.

"Sorry, Bud. I promise I won't do *that* again."

Jack punctuated his apology by giving the driver a shrug of his shoulders and a twisted, penitent smile. With his apology made...and, he hoped, accepted...Jack turned to face Blake. He then picked up where he left off.

"I was blinded by my zeal to protect Ava. If I had been willing to listen to her...not just weeks, but *months* before we took that cruise on your boat...if I had been willing to hear what she had to say about you a long, long time ago...none of this would have happened. Again, Blake, you should not blame yourself for what happened out there. Absolutely none of it was your fault. *None* of it. If you don't understand anything else, you *have* to understand that. *None of what happened out there...absolutely none of it...was your fault.* If I had not interfered...if I had put a little trust in Ava...if I had kept my nose out of her business...you would still have the *Mary Beth*, Ava's star would still be shining brightly, and...."

Jack glanced at his watch, scanned the slow-moving traffic, pursed his lips, and wrinkled his brow. He then pulled his mind back inside the taxi...and back into his narrative.

"After we had been on your boat for a while...after I realized you were not the sicko stalker I thought you were...."

Jack again glanced at his watch and, this time, the unmistakable look of alarm and panic shone in his eyes.

"Forgive me, Blake. The time...actually, the *lack* of time...has me a little stressed out right now. On top of that, I'm not very good at making apologies. Perhaps...."

Jack paused a moment, deep in thought.

"Perhaps it would help if I take a few steps back, take a deep breath, and start over."

Blake waited patiently while Jack did exactly that.

"The things Ava told me, combined with your actions during that storm, convinced me you were an all-right guy. You had opportunities....two *perfect* opportunities...to get rid of me—and you passed up both of them. It would have been easy for you to miss me when you threw that life ring—especially with conditions the way they were—but you nailed me with a perfectly-aimed toss. And later, when I offered you the opportunity to climb into the basket, fully aware it would be *you* and not *me* left behind, you made certain *I* was the one who got into the basket, knowing full well *you* would be the one left behind."

Blake had been silent as long as he could stand it.

"Jack, as I've already explained to you, it became perfectly clear to me that Ava belonged with *you...not me.*"

"Tell me something, Blake. Were you in love with Ava? No...no, no, no! Don't bother to answer that question. Of *course* you were in love with Ava. You loved Ava so much you were willing to die for her. What I *really* want to know is this: Do you *still* love Ava?"

Blake opened his mouth to speak, but Jack cut him off by giving him a big smile and a firm pat on the knee.

"No need to answer that question, either, Blake. I may be the biggest fool that ever lived, but I am *not* an idiot. Even *I* am smart enough to realize you don't come to see *Hamburg* twice a week simply because you like the show. *Nobody* likes *any* show that much. And I *know* you haven't been coming to see me."

"But Jack, it's so obvious a blind man can see it. Ava is in love with *you*. She panicked the moment she realized you had been washed overboard. And she threw her arms around you the instant we pulled you back onto the boat. Except on the occasions Ava met me in private, I have never—*never, ever*—seen one of you without the other. You and Ava are always together. You're either holding hands, walking arm in arm, or..."

"Yes, Blake, I have to agree with you. You are one hundred percent correct. Ava *is* in love with me...Ava has *always* loved me...I have *always* loved Ava...and we'll *continue* to love each other—long after the two of you get married."

Blake's eyes narrowed and his brow wrinkled in confusion.

"Whoa, Jack. You just lost me. I mean...*this* time...you *totally* lost me."

Jack grinned, gave Blake another pat on the knee, and then laughed.

CHAPTER 31

"Ava is my *sister*, Blake."

"Your *sister?* But that...that...that's *impossible*."

Blake twisted his body until he looked squarely into Jack's face.

"Texas Jack and Ava Berlin? Brother and sister? No way on earth! You two can't *possibly* be related. I've never known two people who are more *un*alike. You share no similarities. None whatsoever."

Jack smiled. And then, without a hint of his brash, Texas persona, he spoke to Blake in a warm, sentimental, brotherly voice.

"My father, Henry Smith, worked as a laborer in the Texas oil fields. Dad died when I was ten years old. A year or so after his death, Mom fell in love with an engineer named Bernhardt Bechtel —from Germany, of course. Mom and Bernie got married...Mom got pregnant...the three of us moved to Germany...and the rest is history. I'll leave it to Ava to fill you in with all the details."

Before Blake could comment, Jack opened the door, poured his lanky frame out of the taxi, and urged Blake to do the same. Jack then asked the driver how much he owed him and handed him several large bills. Finally, as an afterthought, Jack handed the man a couple more bills, told him to keep the change, spun away from the taxi, and broke into a run.

The driver's eyes opened wide in surprise. And then, when he realized how big a tip Jack had given him, a huge grin spread across his face. The driver yelled out a grateful, "Hey! Thanks, Buddy!" but had no way of knowing whether or not Jack heard him, because, by the time the driver looked up, Jack had already disappeared into the crowd and was yelling over his shoulder.

"You'll have to run fast, Blake, if you hope to keep up with me."

Blake, captivated by the driver's reaction, had allowed Jack to get a head start. He gave the driver a smile, spun away from the taxi, and sped off in hot pursuit, his short legs pumping double-time in an effort to match Jack's long, lanky stride.

"We gotta run fast, Blake. Thanks to our late start...and this traffic jam...we don't have a moment to lose."

Blake continued sprinting until he caught up with Jack. And then, after slowing to a fast trot, he followed Jack down another block, around the corner, up the steps, and through the theater's back door. Blake had hoped, once they got inside, Jack would slow to a walk, but Jack never broke stride as he continued jogging down a long, dimly lit hallway.

Not until he reached the end of the hallway did Jack stop running. He took a few seconds to compose himself, flung open a door, and entered a huge room in which actors, actresses, and stage hands were making last minute preparations for the musical. Ava, who, for the last several minutes had been pacing nervously back and forth across the room, stopped walking the moment she heard someone shout:

"There he is!"

"Jack!" exclaimed Ava. And then, speaking in German—the first time Blake had heard Ava speak in her native tongue—she sternly demanded, "Wo bist du gewesen? Und warum bist du so spat?"

Blake spoke no German, so he had no way of knowing Ava had asked, "Where have you been? And why are you so late?" But it quickly occurred to him that Jack, who had lived more than twenty years of his life in Germany, understood every word of Ava's questions.

But Jack did not answer Ava's questions. At least, he didn't answer with words. He simply gave her a sweet smile, lifted his eyebrows, and nodded twice—the first time using only his head, and the second time using an exaggerated roll of his head, and an even-more exaggerated roll of his eyes—in Blake's direction. Ava, still flustered by Jack's late arrival, pursed her lips in anger and stared at him an extra moment before looking in the direction he had nodded.

The instant Ava saw Blake she became as silent, as motionless —and twice as cold—as a block of granite. She continued staring at Blake—and Blake continued staring at her—until the stage manager burst into the room and closed the door behind him.

"Show time, two minutes!"

A second or two later, the stage manager saw Jack.

"Ah, Jack. I see you made it. You had us worried. I sent George down to wardrobe to change out of his regular costume and get suited up for your role. He argued with me, but finally agreed to do it, despite the fact Zane insisted you were merely running an errand and would be here in time."

At that precise moment, George, Jack's understudy—and who, indeed, had gone to wardrobe and changed costumes so he could fill the lead role—strode into the room. He stopped walking the instant he realized Jack had arrived.

"Aw, Man. Now I gotta go change again."

Ava and Blake, oblivious to George, Jack, the stage manager, and everyone else in the room, continued staring at each other. Neither said a word, and neither moved a muscle except to take shallow and nervous breaths. Finally, in an effort to end the stalemate, Jack stepped behind Blake, placed his hands on Blake's shoulders, and nudged him towards Ava.

"The clock is ticking, Blake. I'm gonna leave you two love birds while I go down to wardrobe and climb into my costume. As we in the world of entertainment say, 'The show *must* go on.'"

Blake and Ava continued staring at each other until the stage manager glanced at his watch.

"Ninety seconds!"

Zane spun around to face the stage manager.

"Stop looking at your damned watch, Al. Why don't you do something more useful, like running out there and telling Randal to wait five minutes before starting the overture?"

"I can't do that!"

"Just *do* it!" demanded Zane. "And do it *now*!"

"Okay, okay, I'll do it. But...if I get fired...."

"Just *do* it!"

Zane's angry scowl, the tone of his voice—and the fact he had begun striding across the room toward Al—told the stage manager he had *better* do it, or Zane would resort to violence.

Al left the room while muttering something under his breath. Blake stared a moment at the door through which Al had exited, then glanced at Zane, who had turned away from the spot where Al had been standing and was now staring straight at him. Zane gave Blake a smile, followed by a deep nod of his head, and an emphatic roll of his eyes, toward Ava—a not-so-subtle hint to Blake that he had but seconds to act and should take advantage of every one of those seconds.

Blake took a deep breath to steady his nerves. He then took Ava's hands into his hands and looked deeply into her eyes. While exhaling, Blake gave Ava's hands a gentle squeeze...but he could think of nothing to say. He simply stood there, gazing into Ava's cold eyes, and cradling her limp hands in his.

Ava finally broke the silence.

"Blake...all this time...I thought...*we* thought...you were dead. Why have you not come to see me? At least...at least explain why you never sent word to us that you survived that storm...that you are still alive."

"Ava, I thought you were in love with Jack. Not until a few minutes ago...when Jack explained to me...when Jack told me that he and you..."

Ava's eyes suddenly lit up.

"How *stupid* of me. I am such a dummkopf."

Ava squeezed Blake's hands, gave him an exasperated smile, and began speaking in half sentences.

"I can't believe...all this time...I thought...I just *assumed*...you knew Jack was my brother."

A collective gasp could be heard from most of the actors, actresses, and stage hands gathered in the room. Ava glanced around at the surprised faces.

"I thought *everyone* knew."

"No!" exclaimed one of the actresses. "You and Jack were so close—I mean, you *live* together, for crying out loud. We just assumed you were lovers."

The overture began. Either Al had failed to reach the orchestra pit in time, or Randal had denied his request.

"Hurry, Ava," someone shouted. "You have less than one minute to get on stage."

Blake and Ava gazed deeply into each others' eyes, each communicating to the other an unfulfilled longing. They gazed at each other several long seconds, and then spoke in unison.

"Will I...?"

Blake gave Ava a warm smile.

"Ladies first."

"Will I see you after the play?"

Blake's smile grew wider and warmer.

"Same question I was about to ask you."

Ava gave Blake's hands another quick squeeze, then abruptly withdrew her hands from his, wrapped her arms around his neck, and pulled his face down to hers. She then gave him a short kiss, little more than a quick peck on the lips. Finally, after gazing into Blake's eyes a moment...those beautiful, sky-blue eyes...she pulled his face down to hers a second time and gave him another kiss—this one filled with intense passion, and lasting much longer than the first.

And then...

Ava abruptly pushed away from Blake...

Spun on her heels...

And ran out the door.

ANCHOR

EPILOGUE

During that night's curtain calls—all *six* curtain calls—the crowd gave Ava the longest and loudest ovations she had ever received. And the next morning, Zachary Nelson, whose column was printed beneath a half-page, full-color photograph of Ava's vibrant, beaming face, poured out his praise for her most recent performance. Zach claimed it to be the best performance he had ever seen by anyone, and declared it nullified all the negative articles he had written about Ava during the past several weeks. Zach went on to assure his readers that Ava's powerful and emotional performance guaranteed *Hamburg* would be a sell-out hit on Broadway for many years to come...and proof that Ava Bechtel had earned her place among the stars.

What Zachary Nelson did not say, and what Zachary Nelson did not know, was the fact Ava Bechtel had produced the most powerful performance of her life—not for him, not for the other critics attending the show, and not for the sold-out crowd—but for the man sitting in the center seat on the fourth row.

Made in the USA
Columbia, SC
16 July 2020